A BRIDE BY MORNING

THE PRIVATE ARRANGEMENTS SERIES

His Scandalous Lessons
Tempting the Scoundrel
A Bride by Morning
A Touch Wicked

A BRIDE BY MORNING

Private Arrangements
#3

Katrina Kendrick

An Aria Book

First published in the UK in 2023 by Head of Zeus,
part of Bloomsbury Publishing Plc

9 7 5 3 1 2 4 6 8

A catalogue record for this book is available from the British Library.

ISBN (PB): 9781837931736
ISBN (E): 9781837931729

Cover design: HoZ / Meg Shepherd & Jessie Price

Typeset by Siliconchips Services Ltd UK

MIX
Paper | Supporting
responsible forestry
FSC® C171272

Printed and bound in Great Britain by
CPI Group (UK) Ltd, Croydon CR0 4YY

Head of Zeus
First Floor East
5–8 Hardwick Street
London EC1R 4RG

WWW.HEADOFZEUS.COM

With many thanks to my husband, fans of this series, and all the friends I pester through text messages.

PROLOGUE

SURREY, 1863

Don't cry. Don't cry. Miss Lydia Cecil had repeated the same thought for days now.

Sometime that morning, Lydia wrangled a modicum of control over her emotions. Her maid had dressed her in a festive, lemon-coloured frock, but it did little to lighten Lydia's sombre mood. Black might have been a more appropriate hue, but it felt like too much of a dramatic statement. After all, no one had actually died.

But saying goodbye to someone she loved seemed like a death in its own right.

Gabriel St Clair waited in her aunt's drawing room. He leaned against the window frame, tapping his gloves against his trousers. On any other day, Lydia would have caught her breath at the sight of him. He cut an impressive figure, even at the tender age of nineteen, with a perfectly tailored suit accentuating his athletic build, the result of hours spent at his swimming club. Gabriel's dark auburn locks glinted in the morning light, but the severity etched on his face suggested that the weather was as ill-suited to his mood as it was to hers.

All at once, Lydia's eyes stung again. But she blinked back her tears and joined him in the drawing room.

"Gabriel," she said.

He turned from the window. His green eyes swept over her before settling on her bright, lemon-hued dress. His smile appeared more like a reflex than genuine amusement. "Off for a picnic, are we? A farewell party in my honour?"

Lydia let out a shaky breath, shutting the door behind her. It might have been more proper to leave it ajar, but she craved these last moments with him in privacy.

"Don't tease me," she said. "Not when you've come to say goodbye."

That little smile faded, replaced by a remorseful, beseeching look. "I'll only be gone a few years. Then I'll come back—"

"Unless you're given a post in another country," she interjected, closing the gap between them. "Isn't that the nature of diplomatic service? You go where they tell you to?"

Lydia gazed out the window at the rolling hills of Surrey, where she and Gabriel had grown up as neighbours. Since she had come to live with Lady Derby after her parents' sudden death ten years prior, Gabriel had been her only friend. Lydia adored her aunt and the other village matriarchs, but children her age were not exactly thick on the ground. But Lady Derby had mentioned that the second son of her nearest neighbour, the Earl of Montgomery, was a mere two years Lydia's senior – and so she and Gabriel became fast friends.

She had endured Gabriel's absence while he was away at Eton. And then again when he'd gone up to Oxford. They continued their childhood camaraderie solely through letters until he returned, and then it was as if he had never left. But now...

It's only a few years. Only a few years. Why did those words sound so absolute? In her friendless world, only a few years resembled an eternity.

"I suppose so," Gabriel admitted. "But I need time away from England if I want an ambassadorship. This is better than a grand tour, don't you think?"

"The grand tour has a finite end," Lydia countered. Her gaze remained on the hills; if she looked at him now, she really would start crying.

"When credit has run out." Gabriel tapped his gloves against his trousers again. "I'm trying not to be a son who shows up on his father's doorstep every few months with his hand outstretched."

She understood second sons did not have the same security as an heir. While some were fortunate to have generous fathers and older siblings, others had to make their own way. Gabriel had always longed to travel, to see the world and establish himself. She had admired that about him and sat by the little pond near Meadowcroft, making daisy chains while Gabriel described places he yearned to visit. Lydia had tried to conceal her blush of desire when he spoke to her in French, German, Italian, Russian, Spanish, and Portuguese. So many languages that she couldn't understand, but she had concentrated on the smooth baritone of his voice, basking in its warmth like sunlight.

But now he was leaving again.

Lydia swallowed back every protest, unwilling to ruin this for him. How could she be so selfish? In the end, she said, "Then promise me you'll write," she said. "You were a terrible correspondent at Oxford, and I want to know all about Vienna or wherever else you end up. Promise me you'll tell me everything."

Gabriel's lips curved up in the same charming smile she'd adored since she was six. "I promise," he said, his hand reaching out to caress her cheek. Lydia went entirely still. He had touched her many times over the years, but with never more than a platonic pat on the shoulder. However, something about how he stroked a thumb across her face now was different. "Delay it for me, Lydia."

Delay it? The words caught in her throat. They had never discussed their future, but it was glaringly apparent that she had loved him for years. But did he mean...

"Why?" she asked.

Lydia wanted to keep his answer in her memories. A motivation to wait. A reason to let her heart have hope.

"Because for weeks now, I've imagined some pompous duke asking for your hand, and when I return, I'd like to court you properly before I marry you," he said, his voice light. Then, before Lydia could respond, his gaze flicked to the mantelpiece clock, and he straightened up. His hand fell away from her cheek. "Time for me to go. Promise me you'll wait for me?"

"I'll wait for you," she pledged. Her heart swelled with anticipation. He wanted to marry her. "I promise."

Two years later, when Lydia should have made her debut

in society, she kept her pledge. She stalled her first season by one year.

And then by two.

And then again by three.

By the time Lydia was two-and-twenty, her Aunt Frances had begun delicately pointing out that Gabriel had ceased answering her letters nearly two years before. Lady Derby's sympathetic manner tried to conceal her pity, but her aunt clearly believed Gabriel had moved on, forgotten Lydia, and taken a post in another country with no intention of returning to court her.

But Lydia had made him a vow; she would not break it.

Seven years after he left, Gabriel St Clair returned to England after the tragic death of his father and elder brother in a rail accident. The new Earl of Montgomery had been forced to retire from the diplomatic service and take his father's seat in the House of Lords.

When Lydia appeared on his doorstep to offer her condolences, Gabriel's butler turned her away.

And the first time Lydia saw him after all those years, Gabriel pretended he didn't even know her.

1

LONDON

Ten years later

Gabriel St Clair despised attending balls for a multitude of reasons.

First, the jaunty tune played by the modest orchestra perforated his eardrums. Then, the oppressive heat of the ballroom, as hundreds of attendees congregated and danced. Third, the small talk with the simpering debutantes and their overbearing mothers, all to maintain the façade of London's most charming gentleman.

But all were trivial inconveniences compared to the one thing that irked him the most: smiling. Damn, but Gabriel loathed smiling.

Maintaining that cordial expression minute after minute and hour after hour took work. It took unwavering diligence and perseverance, despite the pounding headache throbbing in his temples.

He'd held out for the better part of two hours. But he couldn't help but wonder if his pleasant façade had cracked at the edges and revealed a maniacal grimace beneath.

However, if it had, the lady he danced with would have gone running in the other direction. Instead, Miss Howard looked up at him with flushed cheeks and starry eyes, convinced she was in the company of a perfect gentleman. Society matrons called him the catch of the season.

Poor, poor Miss Howard. Poor, poor society matrons.

They were all his wretched dupes.

"—enjoy holidaying in Brighton," Miss Howard was saying as Gabriel twirled her around the ballroom in a graceful waltz. "But for my next excursion, I long to explore Scotland. Have you ever visited Scotland?"

"I have," he replied, determined not to let his voice betray his mounting headache. He couldn't afford for his mask to slip. "Enchanting views, if you don't mind the rugged conditions."

Christ, what he wouldn't give to be in that remote corner of the country, relaxing on the secluded property he'd purchased away from the clamour of London. He would let the rain and cold seep into his bones. Bask in the glacial winds of the Highlands.

He was, after all, a creature of ice now.

Miss Howard wrinkled her nose. "Rugged? In what way?"

Gabriel returned his attention to her. "Turbulent roads outside the lowlands," he replied. "Inclement weather that causes long delays."

To him, these qualities in Scotland were ideal; they preserved its isolation. He didn't have to pretend for anyone there, certainly not for adoring debutantes.

"Oh. Perhaps not Scotland, then." She brightened. "But you were in the diplomatic service? Where would you recommend?"

Gabriel felt his blood run cold. It only lasted a moment; Miss Howard didn't appear to notice the slight hesitation. His recovery was swift enough. Gabriel ought to have grown used to queries about his past employment – it wasn't often that a peer of the realm did anything as common as work, even if he hadn't inherited the title unexpectedly. But every time someone asked, his mask almost slipped.

It was only through years of practise that Gabriel regained his composure and put on a smile for Miss Howard, smoothly spinning her round to make up for his earlier lapse.

"I'm afraid the places I travelled to weren't half as enchanting as Brighton," Gabriel replied, trying to keep his tone light and easy; his performance was withering at the edges. Then, as the music faded, he bowed over Miss Howard's hand. "Nor was the company anywhere near as delightful."

Miss Howard blushed and giggled. He guided her back to the observant matron who had watched them dance with a joy suggesting she dreamed of wedding bells. Gabriel would have to disappoint her. He thanked Miss Howard for the pleasure of her company, grinned at her mother, and left them.

There. Gabriel had completed his three dances for the evening, and in another hour, he could leave. This ritual was as regular as clockwork, a dance of obligation he performed for the sake of his reputation.

Gabriel nodded a greeting to a few other guests as he strolled over to where Mattias Wentworth conversed with their hostess, Lady Coningsby. When Wentworth noticed Gabriel's approach, he quickly excused himself.

Gabriel and Wentworth went to a corner of the ballroom where no one would overhear them.

"She give you anything?" Gabriel asked quietly, leaning against a marble column.

One hour. He needed to hold on for just one more hour. Then he could go home and avoid invitations to every ball, garden party, and fête for the next sennight. Then he could lose himself in a woman's embrace, let his body take over until he was numb enough to perform his duties as the Earl of Montgomery once more.

Until he could forget the weight of his secrets pressing down on him, forget the past that still haunted him.

Wentworth greeted an acquaintance with a quick wave before turning back to Gabriel. "Not a damn thing of consequence. She's either entirely ignorant of her husband's activities or the best actress who ever lived. I suggested the possibility of investing in Lord Coningsby's shipping business, and she monopolised the entire conversation by talking about silk. I was ready to tear my own ears off before you arrived."

Gabriel tapped his finger restlessly against a nearby column. "I told you, if Coningsby is selling secrets to Russia, he's hardly going to confide in his wife. She's a waste of time."

Wentworth looked annoyed. "What has you so bloody sour?"

Not what.

Who.

Gabriel's eyes scanned the room, searching for the most isolated corner of the ballroom. And there she was, as he had feared. Lydia Cecil. She sat with her hands folded neatly in her lap, watching the dancers with detached interest, as if she were a spectator at a play. Gabriel would have considered not attending if he had known she would be here. Lydia was a part of the past he wanted to leave behind.

Despite himself, Gabriel's gaze lingered on her. Her soft pink dress complemented her pale complexion, which was now delicately flushed from the warmth of the ballroom. A single curl of dark hair had escaped her carefully arranged coiffure and rested on her collarbone. It tempted Gabriel like a beckoning finger.

In his absence, Lydia's youthful gaucherie had taken on a new, almost glacial demeanour. From his vantage point, she appeared as remote and sharp-edged as Arctic ice floating in the Atlantic, and just as unapproachable.

At seven-and-twenty, Lydia was considered firmly on the shelf, but her Aunt Frances, Lady Derby, brought her to gatherings as a companion. A flame of remorse burned in Gabriel's chest. After all, he was responsible for her current predicament.

Promise you'll wait for me.

I'll wait for you. I promise.

Lydia's head rose, and their eyes locked. His guilt blazed hotter. You're a curse of a girl, he wanted to tell her, squashing that weakness in his heart like a pest. The bane of my bloody existence.

Lydia was a constant reminder of what he could have been if he had stayed in that room ten years ago.

Wait for me.

As if she heard his thoughts, her lips tightened, and she looked away. Their moment was over.

Good. Let Lydia think Gabriel hated her. It was better that way.

The din of the ballroom filtered back into Gabriel's senses. "I have a headache," he finally said to Wentworth.

Wentworth snorted. "You've grown soft in your retirement."

"But I'm not truly retired, am I? You keep calling on me for favours." Gabriel noticed Lord Coningsby enter the ballroom. "There's Coningsby. Distract him while I search the house."

As Wentworth went off to engage their host in conversation, Gabriel slipped out of the ballroom and made his way to Lord Coningsby's study. For once, he was grateful to fall back into his old habits. He had to leave Lydia behind; she belonged in glittering ballrooms, surrounded by pleasant chatter.

He belonged in the shadows, because the world had shattered the boy she once loved. And Gabriel wasn't sure he could ever put the pieces back together again.

ᴄᴍ 2 ᴍᴄ

B alls had always made Miss Lydia Cecil uneasy.
    While conversing in a drawing room came more easily to her these days, she found it nearly impossible to talk amid the din of the ballroom. The cacophony of conversation against the background of screeching orchestra violins was an assault on her senses. If a gentleman took it upon himself to request a dance from Lydia, he would soon discover that words eluded her. Her answers were too curt to be polite.

No wonder she's an old maid, she'd heard a peer mutter to his friend when he thought she couldn't hear. *A woman that frigid would be dull in bed, besides.*

After that, Lydia stopped accepting dance requests. Instead, she retreated to her small corner of the room, answering politely when Aunt Frances included her in conversations with other society matrons. Lydia tried not to notice how the older women regarded her with a maternal sort of pity.

Such a sweet girl, the matrons said. *A shame she'll never marry.*

Lady Derby was an expert at navigating conversations away from Lydia's lack of marriage prospects. After all, the matrons were oblivious to the fact that the cause of her unfortunate circumstance was a man they all considered a catch. Eventually, they all accepted that Miss Lydia Cecil was destined to remain her aunt's devoted companion, and she became invisible. She was no longer invited to take tea with debutantes, and men no longer asked her to dance. Lydia was, in essence, an extension of Lady Derby.

Rather like a servant, a duchess had once laughed.

It was just as well, Lydia supposed. She enjoyed the company of her aunt and the other matrons. Her little corner of the ballroom was a sanctuary away from the courtship rituals, where she watched couples dance and admired their graceful movements.

She overheard a few dialogues, carefully parsing their words in her mind like a puzzle. Once it was clear that Gabriel would not return to make her his bride, she had intended to commit these conversations to memory and deploy them herself. But as a debutante of advanced age, the required social graces had always eluded her. She could practically feel the eyes of the *ton* scrutinising her every move and action, eager to pounce upon the slightest misstep. Why else would a lady of her pedigree wait so long to seek a suitable match? What, they asked, was wrong with her?

Now, at seven-and-twenty, she had become the cold, dull Lydia Cecil they believed her to be.

Entirely by accident.

One matron said something to Lydia, and she forced a

smile in reply, struggling to think over the raucous clamour of the ballroom. Aunt Frances looked at her with kind sympathy. Lady Derby had suggested she stay home for the night, but Lydia refused to admit defeat and succumb to a life of seclusion, which felt like an admission that something was wrong with her.

An admission that *he* was correct when he decided she was not good enough for him, after all.

As if her thoughts summoned *him*, there he was. Standing across the ballroom with a man she recognised as The Hon. Mattias Wentworth, second son of the Earl of Stafford.

Their eyes met.

Lydia felt every molecule in her body go still. The crowd's din faded to a dull hum, and her vision narrowed to a pinpoint. Against her will, she was struck by memories of sunny picnics, of dancing in the garden, and of listening to him speak a dozen languages she couldn't understand.

But Gabriel St Clair had transformed from the boy she knew in childhood. His striking features had only become more handsome with time, and his infectious smile was notorious for making women blush at every ball he attended. His body had also changed, with broadened shoulders and a waistcoat that hugged the flat planes of his belly. Even the cut of his trousers could not entirely conceal the musculature of his thighs. But despite his good looks, something was unsettling about him. Something almost reptilian lurking behind those pale green eyes.

It was disorienting to see such indifference in a face she had once adored.

Wait for me.

He gave her an almost mocking flash of his teeth, as if he

read her thoughts. No, that stranger near the terrace doors wasn't the Gabriel she knew. She didn't know this man.

She didn't like this man.

She sharply looked away, trying to concentrate on the polite chatter of society matrons. The ballroom noise inundated her senses again.

Mrs Fitzroy asked Lydia something she hardly heard. Lydia responded with a polite smile that she hoped passed as an answer. She couldn't help stealing a glance in Gabriel's direction.

He was gone.

His absence did little to ease the sudden ache in Lydia's chest – grief had dug its claws into her years ago.

"Aunt," she said. The matrons quieted. "Will you please excuse me? I need a moment in the ladies' powder room."

Aunt Frances frowned. "Is everything all right, dear?"

"I'm feeling a bit overheated," Lydia explained apologetically. The other matrons cooed in sympathy, fanning themselves to emphasise their agreement. "I'll only be gone for a moment. Would you like me to fetch you anything while I'm away?"

"No, my love," Lady Derby reassured her, giving Lydia's hand a gentle pat. "Take all the time you need."

With a grateful nod to her aunt and the other women, Lydia made her way to the ballroom's double doors. People smiled at her as she passed, but Lydia didn't react. She didn't have it in her to pretend, to put on a show. They could all think what they wanted about her being an ice queen, but she knew the truth.

Gabriel, after all, had been her architect.

The hallway outside offered little respite from the noise

and the chaos. Lydia's breaths grew shallow, her heart racing. She needed a quiet place to collect herself, to steady her thoughts. She rushed down the hall, her hand grasping at the handle of a random room, and found herself in Lord Coningsby's study. The mahogany desk gleamed in the light filtering from the hallway, and the air was redolent with the aroma of cigar smoke and brandy.

Lydia closed the door behind her and staggered over to the plush leather divan in the centre of the room. She slid behind it where no one would find her and pressed her forehead to her knees.

"Keep calm," she whispered. "Calm. Calm. Calm."

She breathed the word out in a steady chant. She had done this so many times since Gabriel had stopped answering her letters. Since he had returned to England and treated her like a nuisance, a vexing little girl who was too infatuated with him for her own good.

Memories of Gabriel assaulted her.

Lydia stood at the door of Gabriel's London townhouse, hoping to be granted entry before anyone saw a lady on the doorstep of a bachelor's residence. She swallowed back her apprehension as she rang the bell.

Lydia had heard of Gabriel's return months ago, shortly after the tragic deaths of his father and brother. She was eager to see him, to demand answers for why he had stopped writing back. But she didn't want to intrude while he was still grieving. So she wrote a note with the only words she could think of:

Dear Gabriel,

I'm so sorry for your loss. Should you have need of

a friend in London, I am presently two streets away in Berkeley Square.

Ever your friend,

Miss Lydia Cecil

He never replied, nor did he visit her. Lydia grew concerned, missing her childhood companion more and more with each passing day. So there she was, standing on his doorstep, risking what was left of her reputation.

The butler opened the door and appeared surprised by the presence of a lady, let alone one before breakfast. Lydia straightened her shoulders in determination. "Good morning. Will you please inform Lord Montgomery that Miss Lydia Cecil is here to see him?"

The butler's lips tensed slightly. "I'm afraid his lordship is not receiving visitors."

Lydia understood. Gabriel was still in mourning, and it was early in the morning. She scolded herself for her impatience. But surely, he would make an exception for her, or at least let the butler know when would be a better time to return?

Lydia tried her best to sound composed as she spoke to the butler. "Could you please inform him? He doesn't need to see me, but could you tell him about my visit and ask for a response? If he's awake, that is."

She knew he would be. Gabriel rose at dawn, just like she did.

Despite her best efforts, the butler must have sensed the urgency in her voice. He sighed and said, "Very well. Come inside and wait, please."

Lydia waited in the foyer until the butler returned. The

solemn look on his face felt like a hand squeezing her heart.
"His lordship asked that I inform you," he said delicately.
"He asked that I inform you he is not accepting visitors."

"Of course," Lydia murmured. "Then I'll choose a better
time. Not so early—"

The butler twitched. "He added that if you return to this
address again, you will be refused entry."

Lydia's entire foundation was crumbling. "I – oh." Tears
stung her eyes. "Did he say anything else?" Please tell me he
said something else. He must have.

"No, miss," the butler added apologetically, "I'm afraid I
have to ask you to leave, miss."

And then he shut the door in her face.

Lydia's body shuddered as she squeezed her eyes shut.
Three years had passed since the initial sting of Gabriel's
rejection, and his behaviour only grew more aloof. She
tried to approach him at gatherings, and he disregarded
her. He turned his back and acted as though she were a
stranger.

Then there was the Duchess of Hastings' house party one
year ago. Lydia was determined to get answers from him.

The guests assembled on the west lawn for a game of
croquet. Caroline had persuaded Gabriel to join before he
realised that Lydia, too, would be playing. When he saw her,
his winning smile almost faltered. Lydia had seen him at
balls and fêtes since his return and recognised the artifice of
that smile. It was beautiful enough to hide the hollowness
behind it.

As she stepped forward, his jaw tightened. When he
struck the ball with his mallet, it veered off course and
landed in a bramble bush.

"Bad luck, old chap," the Marquess of Granby said with a chuckle.

"All players must stand beside their balls until their next turn," Caroline added apologetically. Gabriel's ball had gone far from their party.

As Gabriel flashed a grin at one of the other debutantes, Lydia saw her opportunity.

As soon as it was her turn, she aimed her mallet. Years of frustration and hurt aided precision, and her ball smacked right into Gabriel's, sending it rolling under the bramble thicket.

Gabriel's gaze turned to ice.

And now they would have only each other for company until their next turn.

As Lydia approached, Gabriel tensed. But he masked it with a polite nod, his voice dripping with honey. "Miss Cecil," he said, drawing out the syllables like a practised liar.

It was apparent that he intended to say nothing else. Instead, he calmly watched the others play.

"That's all you have to say to me?" Lydia gritted her teeth, keeping her voice low so the others couldn't hear her misery. She longed to scream at him, to make him feel even a fraction of the pain she had endured.

Seven years of waiting for him with no word, all because he had asked.

Seven. Years.

But by the time she realised what a fool she had been, her marriage prospects had withered away like the desolate tundra. And, like that same tundra, she had earned a reputation for aloofness.

All because of him.

His reply was as cold as a frozen wasteland. "I don't see what else I could add," he replied, watching the others – no doubt eager to take his turn and escape her company, never to speak to her again.

Lydia's body trembled as if shards of glass had invaded her bloodstream. She knew, deep down, that her anger would only push him further away. He was like a boat set adrift, and she could only watch helplessly as the storm tore him away from her. Like trying to hold on to smoke.

"Look at me," she said softly. There it was, the tightening of his hand on the mallet. Knuckles turning white. The first fissure in his shield. "Look at me, Gabriel."

When he did, it was like a bolt of lightning struck her. The Gabriel she knew was gone, replaced by an empty shell of a man. He looked at her with an emotionless gaze, and a chill slid over her. Who was this man? What had he done with Gabriel? It was as if he had died, and this stranger was merely wearing his skin.

"Montgomery," he corrected in a voice she didn't recognise.

"You've always been Gabriel to me."

"And now I'm Gabriel to no one," he replied, his tone weary. "Miss Cecil, we knew each other a lifetime ago. We were just children."

"We were not children when you made me promise to wait for you," Lydia said, her voice rising angrily. She didn't care who heard her now. She waved her mallet in the air, punctuating each word. "We were not children when you wrote me letters telling me to keep waiting. Letters I kept even when you stopped writing."

His façade crumbled before her eyes. The easy smile he

had for others shattered like glass against the rocks. His boat was adrift, abandoned and in ruins, and the splinters cut Lydia to the bone. "Listen to me, you curse of a girl," he spat, his voice as cold as the winter storm. "The letters stopped for a reason. It should be abundantly clear that I feel nothing for you. I'm not going to marry you."

Lydia's breath seized up in her lungs, and she felt as though she were drowning. "Then I want all my letters back," she whispered. She wanted to erase every word she had ever written to him. All those years of her life she'd wasted. So many hours and years she had cried over him.

Gabriel straightened, nodding at the others shouting that it was his turn. "I have no letters to return to you," he said coldly. "I threw them out with the rubbish."

Then he reached into the brambles and retrieved his ball, knocking it across the lawn with a hard swing of his mallet. He walked away from her without a backwards glance.

Lydia's hands clenched in her gown as she shuddered violently. She had tried to forget his words, to heal the mess he had made in her heart. But try as she might, that wound remained open and festering, her most vital organ callously discarded. And she had nothing left to give to another man.

But she still had herself. She still had Aunt Frances.

She gathered herself behind the divan in the quiet study that was not hers. Moments like these were all she had to mend herself, one breath at a time.

Lydia's breathing slowed as she tried to calm herself, but the sound of the study door opening and closing shattered her peace. Heavy footsteps made their way across the carpet, heading straight towards the divan.

Lydia froze, every thought in her head gone in an instant.

What would she do if Lord Coningsby found her there? What would she do if—

But it wasn't Lord Coningsby who went to the desk.

It was Gabriel St Clair.

A bitter laugh rose in her throat. Of course it would be him. The very moment she had gathered herself enough to return to the ballroom, he appeared. But what was he doing in Lord Coningsby's study? Was he searching for a quiet space, just like she was?

Her hopes were dashed as she saw him begin to search through the earl's papers. Lydia stayed perfectly still, tilting her head to get a better view. He hadn't spotted her yet, despite the divan being in full view of the desk. It was a moment of reprieve, allowing her to observe him unguarded as he thumbed through the papers with delicate precision.

Gabriel's expression was one of intense, unwavering concentration as he pored over the papers. His forehead was pinched in a frown as he pushed aside documents and stacked them with meticulous care. It was a marked contrast to his carefree demeanour in the ballroom.

Was he *looking* for something?

He opened a drawer and ran his fingers along the underside of the wood, then gave it a deliberate nudge. With a soft click, a false bottom popped open, and Gabriel pulled out a few papers. He slid a small book and pencil out of his jacket pocket and jotted something down.

When he finished, he replaced the documents with the utmost care, sliding the false drawer back into place until everything appeared undisturbed. Then Gabriel straightened and turned to leave.

And spotted her.

∾ 3 ∾

Gabriel's renowned talents in espionage abandoned him entirely.

He struggled to process Lydia's unexpected appearance in Lord Coningsby's study. Her lovely face often filled his mind when his concentration drifted from his missions – imagining what she would think of him if she ever discovered the truth about his life abroad.

But this was different, even for Gabriel. It was exceedingly rare that his mind called her forth when he focused on gathering information.

No, Gabriel only ever pictured Lydia Cecil when he assassinated someone.

It seemed strange that her image should appear in Coningsby's study, so long after he'd last killed a man for Queen and country. But there must have been a purpose – the confidential documents inside were related to a man Gabriel believed he'd taken out. His final assassination before returning to England.

Boris Medvedev. The leader of the Syndicate, an international crime ring that Gabriel had spent years infiltrating. Three years ago, Gabriel had shoved a blade through Medvedev's skull, but evidently failed to kill him.

And Lydia was there in that study, a subtle reminder of the life Gabriel had sacrificed before becoming Her Majesty's best spy.

But – no. The vision of Lydia in his mind had always been disapproving; like a solitary member of a Greek chorus, she catalogued his every sin.

The Lydia sitting behind the divan in Lord Coningsby's study observed him with bewilderment. And that meant she was a very *real* woman who had just witnessed Gabriel rifle through his host's desk and uncover a hidden compartment filled with correspondence between Coningsby and Russian criminals.

Gabriel's training was the only thing keeping him calm as he smiled at Lydia with an amusement he absolutely did not feel.

"Miss Lydia Cecil," he said smoothly, returning his small notebook and pencil to the inner pocket of his jacket.

Her eye caught the movement, with a look that was all too perceptive. This was why he stayed the hell away from her. One moment, he thought he had circumstances under control, and the next, his thoughts were a litany of profanity.

She was too clever for her own good.

Lydia's attention returned to his face. "Montgomery."

Gabriel's smile tightened imperceptibly as he recalled his words at the Duchess of Hastings' house party: *Now I'm Gabriel to no one.*

You wouldn't want me as I am now, Gabriel thought to Lydia. *That boy you knew doesn't even exist anymore. You would hate the man I've become.*

Gabriel leaned against the desk. "Do you intend to keep sitting there, or shall I offer you my hand?"

Lydia sniffed. "No. I don't want your help."

Gabriel's expression remained cordial while he absorbed every aspect of her features. Pale freckles that had faded as she reached adulthood, a full lower lip begging to be nipped between kisses. God, but he'd imagined teasing that lower lip for years.

All images of kissing her fled when he noticed the slight mottling of her skin. Had she been crying?

Gabriel wondered if he had caused it or someone else. He almost hoped it was another man whom he could threaten. Gabriel snapped bones with brutal efficiency, after all. He had an aptitude for violence. But mending a woman's heart was not a talent he possessed.

He only knew how to break things.

"Very well," he said, with the politeness he'd mastered. "Then I'll leave you alone. Good evening, Miss Cecil."

But when he reached the door, Lydia's voice rang out behind him: "Do you make a habit of peeking through your host's personal documents, or am I witnessing a new hobby of yours?"

Gabriel paused, his hand clenching on the doorknob. He schooled his features into a pleasant mask before facing her – and nearly lost his composure. She had risen to her feet like a Valkyrie, a war goddess. She would not have been out of place on a battlefield wearing gleaming armour and carrying a blood-soaked sword. Miss Lydia Cecil's eyes were weapons; that was the only way to describe how they pierced his every performance like a damned blade.

"You shouldn't throw about wild accusations, Miss Cecil," he said reproachfully. He needed to leave that room before he did something idiotic, like kiss her. "Coningsby is occupied with his guests and asked that I review the details of a business transaction we plan to discuss."

Lydia edged around the divan, her movements almost languid now. Gabriel couldn't help but stare. Where the hell had she learned to walk like that? If she were the Valkyrie, she would be grinning at him victoriously across a field of bodies. This was a creature designed to tempt a damaged man like him.

"Strange," she murmured, trailing her fingertip across the upholstery of the divan. Gabriel found himself riveted by the movement, by the thought of her soft hands hidden beneath those silk gloves. He wished they'd touched him everywhere back in Surrey. Now he only had memories of longing. "To discuss business in the middle of a ball when an appointment would have suited better. Are you lying to me, *Montgomery*?"

Gabriel dropped his hand from the doorknob as surprise flared through him. Perhaps Wentworth was right: maybe he was going soft, losing his skill. That irritated him. If Medvedev were still alive, Gabriel would need every talent he possessed. "I wasn't aware you were an expert in trade, Miss Cecil," he said impatiently. "If you're so eager to participate in investments, you ought to say so. I'll let Coningsby know."

"I'm not an expert in trade, no," she said, coming closer. Like a tide licking at his boots, her movements were slow and inexorable. And he, for some ludicrous, incomprehensible reason, was rooted to the floor. "I am, however, very well acquainted with liars."

She was current, dragging him into dark water, confusing his every thought. He'd believed himself so skilled before, so utterly confident in his ability to charm. He ought to have recalled that Lydia Cecil did not excel at social niceties; her reputation for iciness was, in truth, a unique brand of honesty to which his peers neglected to give the respect it deserved. Gabriel had missed it during his years away.

Now she wielded that candour like a pistol. But Gabriel had learned that lies were his weapon. They were evenly matched: her honesty and his falsehoods. "Is it that you're very well acquainted with liars," he said, gentling his voice, "or that you have a particular interest in hating me, specifically?"

For a moment, she looked stricken, and an echoing ache stirred in Gabriel's chest: that guilt he'd tried to bury deep as a grave. Over the years, killing had taken so many emotions out of him; he'd need to fight or seek pleasure to feel alive again. But guilt? That was his one constant. Lydia was Gabriel's burden – a curse of a girl, the responsibility of what he did to her infecting him like rot.

Lydia's eyes met his, and that piercing stare threatened his calm. She had irises the dark gold of vintage whisky, like the dim flicker of flames in the darkness.

"I don't hate you," she said. And then she stepped closer and surprised Gabriel by setting the palm of her hand on his chest. She repeated in a whisper, "I don't hate you."

A spark flared inside him at the mere touch of her hand. He marvelled at the gentle pressure, how it created hairline fractures in the solid wall of ice in his bloodstream. When he came home to England, the memories of his missions had taken up violent residence in his mind. And the only thing he did to forget – to melt the ice, to feel something, *anything* – was to either seek out a fight or find a woman willing to let him use her in the way of an animal seeking release. He'd finish, and the barricades of ice would freeze over again, stronger than ever.

And all Lydia had done was lay one hand on him, and every part of him went motionless. Gabriel had a wild urge to tear off her glove. Press her warmth to his face. Breathe in the scent of her. Let her fracture more of the glacier taking up so much space that there was no room left inside him for a soul.

But then her hand moved. Before Gabriel could guess her intention, her fingers slipped inside his coat, grasped his little notebook, and plucked it out. She held it up. "And if I look in this book, what will I find?"

Gabriel's jaw clenched. "I don't recall you being this brazen."

"I don't recall you being such a cad, so we're both disappointed." Lydia opened the cover.

"*Lydia*," he said in a warning tone.

She raised her eyebrows in surprise. "So I'm *Lydia* now, am I?"

"Better I call you by your name than all the other words in my mind," he muttered. He extended his hand. "Give it back."

"No." Then she flipped the pages and read. Her brow creased in puzzlement as she skimmed a few sentences and snapped theo book shut. She leaned forward and pressed the item into his hand. As her fingers brushed against his, she raised her dark eyes. "I wouldn't have thought business notes for a casual discussion would need to be written in code. But as you said, I'm not an expert in trade. Only in lies." She released the book and reached past him for the doorknob. "And yours have occupied my mind for years."

She left the study.

And the wall of ice within Gabriel's body began to crack.

4

Lydia's visit to Caroline Stafford, Duchess of Hastings, was a reprieve from the turmoil of the previous evening. She'd spent the entire day turning what happened in Lord Coningsby's study over in her mind.

Lady Derby had remarked on Lydia's distraction at breakfast and peppered her with questions. Lydia replied that she was unwell, an excuse as effective as using whisky to douse a fire. Lady Derby fretted over Lydia's temperature and pale skin, suggesting they summon a doctor. Lydia managed to escape the house by insisting that she had an unavoidable appointment.

On the way to Caroline's, Lydia puzzled over the symbols she'd seen in Gabriel's book. His cramped handwriting was challenging enough to read, but without a cipher, she couldn't understand what she had seen at all. Was Lord Coningsby involved, somehow, in Gabriel's work for the diplomatic service? And if so, then why had Gabriel covertly gone through his belongings?

So many questions rattled around in Lydia's thoughts. Worse: Gabriel's proximity in that study had dislodged far too many of the memories and feelings she had sought to bury. All those nights spent crying into her pillow came back and slammed into her with the intensity of a tidal wave. The grief and longing had not dulled with time; they pricked at her like a thousand tiny thorns.

There was a certain stupidity in feelings; they were not ruled by logic. If they had been, Lydia wouldn't have permitted Gabriel to occupy another moment of her day.

She would never allow herself to miss him.

"You're quiet this afternoon," Caroline said, jarring Lydia from her reverie. "Is something the matter?"

Lydia shook her head, feeling the need to explain herself, no matter how feeble the excuse. "I'm just out of sorts, that's all."

Caroline clicked her tongue and poured another round of tea. "Don't you dare try to evade my question."

"I'm not," Lydia insisted.

"You're doing that thing with your face again," Caroline said, pointing an accusing finger. "The one where you resemble a puppy about to be dunked in a tub."

Lydia grimaced at the comparison. "And you get insufferably smug when you're correct."

Caroline's lips curved into a self-satisfied grin. "I'm *always* correct. Now tell me. My house has been dreadfully dull lately, and I need a good scandal to liven things up."

A twinge of guilt pricked Lydia when she realised she found Caroline's home so tranquil because it had only one occupant. Besides the staff, the duchess lived alone, having been separated from the Duke of Hastings for eight long years.

"I can't tell if you're concerned or threatening me," Lydia said, taking her teacup and saucer from Caroline.

"Oh, it's both. And I'll hold the cake hostage until you tell me everything."

"Imagine what people would say if I told them you had a cruel streak."

"No one would ever believe you." Caroline grinned and gracefully smoothed down her day dress. "Now, tell me what's really wrong and I'll reconsider the cake."

Lydia stared out the window of the sitting room, her gaze falling on the rooftop of Gabriel's residence. Strange, how he could be so close and yet so far away. His house at the opposite end of the square might as well have been in Kabul.

Lydia released a slow breath. "What do you know about Lord Montgomery's time in the diplomatic service?" she asked.

Caroline seemed surprised by the question. She set down her teacup and considered thoughtfully. "Very little, I'm afraid. Even though we're cousins, we weren't particularly close before he left, and he's remained stubbornly silent since his retirement." She cleared her throat delicately. "But weren't you... friends in childhood? Of a sort?"

While Lydia had told Caroline of her previous friendship with Gabriel, the duchess didn't know how close they really had been. Lydia kept that to herself, and Lady Derby, likewise, never divulged the extent of her niece's relationship with the new Lord Montgomery. It would have harmed Lydia's reputation, implied she was ruined. She did not have the social standing to weather such gossip when all of society so adored Gabriel.

"We were more than friends," Lydia revealed quietly. "Or I thought we were."

Caroline's features softened. "Oh, Lydia."

Lydia blinked back the sting of tears, willing them away. She wouldn't let them fall; she'd already wasted too many hours crying over him. "He asked me to wait for his return," she continued, her voice flat now. "So he could court me. But then he left, and..." Became unrecognisable. Became the sort of man who sifted through someone else's documents and wrote notes in code.

Lydia's mind kept repeating a word, a single syllable that reframed the years he spent abroad. That word left Lydia feeling as unbalanced as if she were standing on the edge of a precipice. She rejected it every time, but the word refused to be dislodged from her thoughts.

She dismissed the notion again, firmly making her mind blank once more.

"I see," Caroline said gently.

Lydia's hands tightened around her teacup. Yes, Lydia imagined the duchess did see. They had become friends after Lady Derby decided to give a monthly stipend to one of Caroline's charities; Lydia had recognised a yearning in the duchess that matched her own. A mirrored grief for someone not dead but lost just the same. Everyone knew the Duke and Duchess of Hastings maintained a cordial relationship – neither said a bad word about the other in public, and their situation was hardly more unusual than that of many aristocratic marriages.

But Lydia knew there was more to it than that. She knew

Caroline loved her husband and that what had happened between them remained as painful a memory as the words Gabriel had spoken before he left her.

Wait for me.

Lydia straightened her shoulders and stared down at her tea. "I know that Lord Montgomery went first to Vienna to work in the embassy there. Then he later went to Paris and Zürich. After that, his superiors asked him to depart for Kabul." She pressed her lips together. "In Kabul, he stopped responding to my letters, and I don't know where he went after that."

Caroline winced sympathetically. "He was abroad for seven years." She sighed. "Priorities change."

"I suppose they do." Lydia shrugged. "Perhaps that's why he returned and acted as if I was a stranger. I was no longer a priority."

"That's not what I meant." The duchess clasped her hands pensively. "Have you considered the possibility that you're not the stranger?" Caroline paused. "He is."

Lydia imagined Gabriel the previous night at Lord Coningsby's ball before their confrontation in the study. He had been dancing with Miss Alice Howard, his dashing smile drawing Lydia's attention. She had come to memorise that carefree smile, and how it set everyone around him at ease.

But he did not hold that smile for Lydia. It faded as quickly as a snuffed candle flame leaving the unrecognisable man beneath. Lydia wondered if he resented her for it – that she alone could take one look at him and declare him a fraud.

The single-syllable word rolled around in her mind again like a rock caught against a current, the sharp edges sanding down, changing form. An answer to the questions she sought.

"You're thinking something else now," Caroline said with interest.

Lydia set down her tea. "A puzzle I'm interested in solving."

Caroline's smile returned. "I adore puzzles, especially when they have to do with foolish men. Tell me."

Lydia hesitated, but then reached into her reticule for the small sheet of paper. Upon arriving home, she'd quickly noted down the symbols she had seen in Gabriel's book and then spent the better part of a sleepless night attempting to decode what he'd written.

She unfolded the sheet and slid it across the table. "There. I've been trying to solve that all morning."

With a bemused expression, Caroline skimmed the note. "A cryptogram?" Her eyes met Lydia's briefly. "And this is… to do with Monty?"

"It might be."

"You're being mysterious. The only thing I love more than a puzzle is a mystery." She considered the symbols again. "This isn't common knowledge, but Julian and I used to send notes in code before we were married." She gave a wistful smile. "He was the first model for my paintings. It would have been a scandal if we'd been caught."

Lydia was one of the few people who knew the Duchess of Hastings was also the famed nude painter Henry Morgan, whose work hung prominently in galleries and aristocratic homes across the country. It would create an uproar if it ever came to light.

"Can you solve it?" Lydia asked.

Caroline studied the code with a frown. "I'll try."

Determined now, Caroline rose from her chair and retrieved ink, pen, and paper from the letter-writing desk in the corner of the room. She resettled in her seat. "Twenty-two symbols. Was M—" She cleared her throat. "The person who wrote this, that is. Were they pressed for time?"

"Yes." Lydia leaned forward. "Is that relevant?"

Caroline tapped her pen in consideration. "Of course. It reduces the likelihood of code complexity. But a crib would speed this along." At Lydia's questioning look, she explained, "A word or phrase that we know for certain is in this message. For example, many messages begin with *I*, but this one starts with a longer word."

"A name?" Lydia's heart slammed against her chest. "Coningsby."

Caroline went still. Then she cleared her throat and said, "Now I'm even *more* interested." Dutifully, she copied the translation onto her paper, solving eight distinct symbols. "Now I can deduce that this word" – she tapped the note – "is 'days.' I assume a written number precedes it, and 'three' has the distinction of being the only one with the same letter twice in succession. Give me a moment."

Lydia watched while Caroline quickly used *Coningsby* as the crib to solve the rest of the cryptogram. "You are *brilliant*," she breathed.

"I know," Caroline said with a distracted smile. Then she frowned over one final word. "This is another name, I think. Unless the person Coningsby intends to meet really *is* named *Bear*? I assume he isn't meeting an *actual* bear."

Lydia scrutinised the note Caroline had managed to translate swiftly: *Coningsby will meet Bear three days hence, after midnight at the Docklands.*

Bear. Lydia puzzled over the name as she mentally reassessed what she knew of Gabriel's background. Her mind finally accepted the single-syllable word that had haunted her for hours and admitted its truth.

Spy.

∽ 5 ∽

G abriel watched Wentworth pace his study.

"What the devil do you mean, you were seen?" Wentworth snarled.

The spymaster's whisky sat entirely abandoned on the mahogany desk as Wentworth once again walked round the room. Gabriel had hardly ever witnessed his superior this agitated; he usually sat calmly behind the desk while they conferred at his modest townhouse near Fleet Street.

Gabriel could hardly blame Wentworth, certainly not when his own composure was so threadbare. How long had it been since he'd felt so unsteady? Years. Not since Kabul. Gabriel had foolishly believed he was no longer capable of experiencing emotions that threatened his focus – but put Lydia in a room with him, and his control evaporated in minutes.

Now, instead of concerning himself with the knowledge that Medvedev was still alive, he'd spent the entire day picturing Lydia. Lydia in Coningsby's study, rising to her feet like a Valkyrie. Lydia and an expression in her eyes that flared hotter than molten steel. Lydia, pressing her hand to his chest – and he, wishing there were no clothes to separate their skin.

Lydia bloody Cecil, his beautiful curse of a girl.

"She won't say anything," Gabriel said, sipping his whisky with an indifference he did not feel. It wouldn't do to reveal to Wentworth just how erratic his thoughts were. Lydia had come back into his life with a force that shattered his equilibrium.

For a spy, that was dangerous.

Hell, it was downright lethal for a man with as many enemies as Gabriel.

Wentworth, who had finally recalled the snifter of whisky sitting on his desk, choked on the beverage. "A woman?" He set his glass down with a sharp rap. "Don't tell me you brought a woman into Coningsby's study with you. If that's true, I will put my hands around your damned throat and squeeze the life out of you."

Gabriel leaned back in his chair, irritated now. Ruffling Wentworth's usually stoic demeanour had a certain appeal, and Gabriel would be the first to admit that he indulged in many vices – gambling, drink, whoring – in an attempt to spark some life inside his dead heart. But they never came at the expense of his work.

"In all the years you've known me," he said in annoyance, "have I ever once compromised even the most trivial reconnaissance mission?"

Wentworth gave him a long, thoughtful look. Gabriel might have squirmed apprehensively had he not been long accustomed to such scrutiny. Wentworth, after all, was such an accomplished spymaster that his position in the Home Office didn't formally exist. Instead, his post at the Metropolitan Police served as a cover for more covert government work.

"No," he finally said. "But even the lowest file clerk at the offices has heard tales of your carousing."

Frost and iron cascaded through Gabriel's veins as they locked stares. He'd always known Wentworth was aware of his predilections for drink and loose women since he'd returned from Moscow three years past. "My nocturnal activities are my own concern," he said, icicles dripping from every word. "She was in Coningsby's study when I arrived."

Wentworth straightened, irritation flickering across his features. "And you didn't notice a whole damn woman in the room with you? Their ballgowns aren't exactly inconspicuous, Monty. You made the error of an incompetent amateur." Then, before Gabriel could tell him to go to hell, Wentworth circled his desk and plucked his pen from the holder to jot a note. "What's her name?"

"Miss Lydia Cecil," Gabriel said reluctantly.

Wentworth's head jerked up. "Isn't that the woman who used to send letters to the Home Office? Hundreds, if I recall." His eyes narrowed. "What have you been telling her?"

Gabriel's jaw tightened. "Nothing. If she knew I was in Moscow, she wouldn't have needed your offices to forward her messages to me, would she?"

The spymaster still seemed wary, but returned his attention to the note on his desk. "I'll instruct my agents to look into Miss Cecil. Even spinsters have secrets. We'll hold the information against her if she gets any foolish notions about spreading gossip."

"No." A red brume came down across Gabriel's vision. Images of violence congealed in his mind at the thought of the idiots at the Home Office gathering intelligence against Lydia for the purposes of blackmail.

Wentworth didn't look up. "Don't provoke me further, Monty. I haven't punched you in the face only because you're no longer officially working for the government. But now I'm cleaning up two of your messes. Leaving Boris Medvedev alive was careless, and now I have the Russian leader of the Syndicate on my patch. If the existence of this woman compromises us—"

Gabriel rose to his feet. "I said Miss Cecil won't be a problem. I write my notes in code."

Wentworth paused in exasperation. "And all this woman has to do is mention that she saw you rifling through Coningsby's personal papers. If Medvedev catches word of it and investigates you, he might notice you bear an uncanny resemblance to the Alexei Borislov Zhelyabov who infiltrated the Syndicate and failed to assassinate him. And that's *if* he doesn't know about you already. I think the knife you stuck in his face might have given him an incentive to investigate you."

Hearing the alias he had used during his operation in Moscow did little to improve Gabriel's temper. The Syndicate, after all, was responsible for the man he had become. In Kabul, Medvedev's agents murdered his superior, and Gabriel took on the unpleasant twin roles of spy and assassin. A killer instructed by his country to give a name to every bullet and every blade.

He stopped writing to Lydia after that. He'd thought long and hard about the man he'd become and thought: *She's not for you. She'll never be for you.*

You will break this girl.

"Let me deal with Miss Cecil," Gabriel said.

Wentworth's pen paused over the note. "Don't make me clean up her corpse, Monty."

The very idea of hurting Lydia sent a stab of wrath through Gabriel. He marvelled at it. This anger was so different from the coldness that had occupied his heart for years. Only for her. Somehow, seeing Lydia in that study had invigorated him. She had pushed past the desiccated husk in his chest he'd called a heart. That she'd left him so discomfited was only natural; his body, after all, had long since grown used to the ice beneath his skin. The thing he'd thought so permanent was fragile, after all. She'd left him unbalanced.

"I said I'd deal with her," he said sharply. "I didn't say I'd kill her. We were friends in childhood."

Surprise flared in Wentworth's features. "You had friends?"

Gabriel gave him a stern look. "I understand that you know me as something of a bastard, but I wasn't always like this. She and I grew up together in Surrey. Why do you think she sent all those letters to your offices?" *And if I weren't an idiot, I would have married her that day ten years ago.*

But now... he was not built for marriage. He had hardened himself a long time ago; the exterior was a façade. Inside, he was a beast – an animal.

A wolf.

Wentworth sighed and set down his pen. "Fine," he said.

"I believe I heard her aunt planned to attend Lady Brome's annual ball in two days. Dance with Miss Cecil, purport to be her friend again if you must. Whatever you need to do to persuade her that what she saw in Coningsby's study was nothing out of the ordinary."

Gabriel's gaze sharpened. "That's the night Coningsby wrote in his diary."

The other man gave Gabriel an impatient look. "Indeed. You clean one mess, and my men and I will visit the Docklands and take care of the other. Don't mess this up, Monty."

Gabriel watched Lydia from across the ballroom.

She took up so little space, yet he was aware of her with every part of his body. He knew he'd find her in the corner of the ballroom with Lady Derby. And there she was, observing the dancing couples with an emotion he did not comprehend. Though she had kindled his long-dormant feelings, they came to him like a forgotten language: entirely familiar and yet indecipherable. It worried Gabriel that she could leave him so unfocused when he ought to have been concentrating on Medvedev.

And yet... he couldn't bring himself to think of his nemesis.

Gabriel studied every aspect of Lydia, from the soft curls in her hair to her skin's glow in the candlelight. Who was this woman now? How had she transformed into that warrior goddess in Coningsby's study? His childhood friend had been the very essence of delicate and kind. What had happened to her in the years since? Gabriel had been so determined to avoid Lydia that he hadn't bothered to consider how she, too, might be fundamentally altered.

She was a cryptograph he couldn't crack. It vexed Gabriel. He was used to decoding things: messages, people, movements. Understanding motivations. Why not hers? Why couldn't he decrypt her?

"Lord Montgomery."

The matron and debutante who now approached him smiled, and every part of Gabriel congealed to ice even as he returned their greeting with a friendly nod. The matron relaxed. He had, after all, perfected this role. Gabriel understood that people were generally willing to trust a handsome gentleman who did and said all the right things.

They'd never know that he was a wolf who smiled only to show his teeth.

"Lady Archer, is it?" he said, gently taking the older lady's hand and squeezing her fingers. "And Lady Cressida. A pleasure."

His grin stretched over the bones of his face – he visualised it as a grotesque sneer that did little to hide the predator that had taken up residence within his bones. But the effect, he knew, was entirely his imagination; mother and daughter blushed at his attentions. Lady Cressida meekly lowered her lashes in the way of a practised debutante.

Gabriel thought once more of Lydia and the steel in her eyes. She would lower them for no one. Their gaze would meet like two swords clashing.

"I hope you'll pardon my impertinence at approaching without a formal introduction," Lady Archer said. "I've been living near Alnwick until Cressida was ready to enter society, but I was a good friend of your mother's. God rest her soul."

Gabriel's cordial expression remained in place. Though he hadn't known his mother – she'd died in childbirth – he'd heard only kind things about her.

"I'm always pleased to meet someone who knew and loved my mother," he replied smoothly. Like most of the sentiments he expressed in society, this was a lie. Any compliments about his mother, father, and brother only served to remind him that he was a stranger in his family. They would all be revolted by the man he'd become.

Lady Archer spoke again, but a movement in Gabriel's periphery drew his attention. The matron before him took no notice of the imperceptible shift, the way his body moved ever so slightly toward Lydia as if he were a weathervane pivoting with a new direction of the wind.

Lydia excused herself from her aunt and hastened across the ballroom. The back of her pale pink dress swayed in a frothy concoction of lace and silk as she hurried towards the terrace with the speed of prey darting through the forest.

I'm a hunter, sweetheart, he thought to himself. *Wherever you go, I'll find you.*

He thought he felt her eyes rest on him the moment before she slipped through the open terrace doors and out of the ballroom.

"—isn't that lovely?" Lady Archer was asking.

Blinking, Gabriel turned his attention back to the matron, who was clearly counting on him to ask her daughter to dance. He had, after all, not claimed any dances yet that evening. His habitual three had become a familiar pattern to the mothers in that ballroom.

46

Lady Archer was about to be sorely disappointed.

Gabriel spoke for a few minutes and then murmured, "I beg your forgiveness, but I'm afraid I must depart for the evening. Good night, Lady Archer. Lady Cressida."

The night was brisk as he stepped out onto the terrace. A few other couples conversed near the open doors, taking advantage of the darkness to stand closer than convention commonly allowed.

But Lydia was nowhere to be found.

Gabriel descended the terrace steps into the garden, traversing the pathways as he considered the girl he'd once known: her apprehension over social interaction, nerves that often rendered her inarticulate. Lydia would be likely to seek a private recess in the gardens for solitude. Use it to gather herself.

After a few minutes of quiet searching, he found her. Gabriel paused as he took in the sight. Lydia was seated on the edge of the fountain, a discarded shawl and gloves nearby. God, but she was beautiful. The glow of the full moon and the garden torches lovingly caressed the delicate bones of her face, bathing her in pale light as she dropped a bare fingertip into the fountain water. Lydia traced circles across the surface as if she were stroking a lover's bare skin.

He watched that motion with a fevered sort of focus, noting the fragile bones of her hand, the graceful arch of her wrist. The soft splash of water somehow penetrated the din in his mind that hungered to feel something. And she accomplished in one small movement what he'd destructively sought for years.

You will break her, his head reminded him.

Gabriel was jolted by the memory and fought to compose himself. Then he stepped out of the shadows. "Miss Cecil."

Lydia jerked her hand out of the water with a startled gasp. "Oh," she said, with an almost displeased look. "You."

Was she meeting a man in the garden? Gabriel had been so focused on what he recalled of her social unease that he hadn't considered that possibility.

The mere thought of another man touching her set something deep within him on edge, something fierce and wild and wrathful. "Were you expecting someone?"

Her lips tightened as she reached for her discarded gloves. "If I was?"

He'd demand to know why the fool was meeting her in darkened gardens instead of marrying her. He'd made that mistake once and regretted it ever since.

"Tell me." He wanted to know the idiot by name.

"And now you demand answers. Such strange behaviour for a man who sought to avoid me since returning to England three years ago." At his silence, Lydia made a soft noise and tapped her gloves against her dress. "If you must know, I came to be alone."

Relief alleviated the tension in his shoulders. Gabriel didn't like it. "You shouldn't be out in the dark."

Her laugh was brittle. "You ought to reconsider your concerns, Lord Montgomery," Lydia said. "I might think you care."

I do, he wanted to say. *I care far too much*.

That old consideration for her welfare had him edging closer. "Come. I'll escort you safely back to the ballroom."

"No." Lydia's gaze met his. "Why did you follow me? Somehow, I don't think it was to scold me for my solitude."

Gabriel straightened as he recalled Wentworth's words. *Clean up your mess.*

He didn't have time to worry about Lydia's reputation. Not with Medvedev in London. Wentworth's men might even have him in custody by now, and if they did, Gabriel wanted to be there. The Russian could implicate the rest of the Syndicate, which had only grown in the three years since Gabriel left Moscow. Even London had its own faction of the crime ring.

"I'd appreciate it if you didn't mention what you saw in Coningsby's study to anyone," he said briskly. "Even better, forget you saw me in there, and I'll do the same for you."

Lydia was silent as she studied him. Her eyes were more penetrating than Wentworth's; such acuity in a mere look was a skill, after all. She might have made an excellent operative, keen observer that she was.

Lydia inclined her head silently.

Good. That done, Gabriel pivoted to leave the gardens, but her voice rang out behind him. "But only if you tell me who Bear is."

He froze, then slowly turned to face her. The look on Lydia's face was as triumphant as that of a battlefield goddess, his Valkyrie with her flaming sword. The very sight of her threatened his balance. How had the girl he left behind so many years ago become this woman with a voice like fine whisky and a smile like a knife's edge? Who *was* she?

"You solved my cryptogram," he said stiffly.

"I did." Lydia smiled and leaned back. "So, who is Bear?"

Gabriel drew closer. Lydia's smile faded as he kneeled and set his hands against the stonework on either side of her. She had yet to learn her lesson. She could not treat him like the boy from Surrey.

"Listen to me," he said, in a voice as hard as steel. "Forget that message. Forget you ever saw that name. Do both, and you can go back to your aunt's charming little townhouse in Mayfair and sleep soundly tonight. But do not play games with me when you don't even know the rules."

Gabriel ought to have recalled that while he was no longer the boy from Surrey, she was not the girl he knew, either.

Her gaze matched his as she leaned forward within the cage of his arms, offering a silent challenge. "Tell me the rules, then," she said. "I'm a quick learner."

He was close enough to feel her heat. Close enough that they breathed the same air. Gabriel's eyes dropped to her lips as desire shot through him like an arrow.

"You curse of a girl," he whispered the moment before his lips met hers.

6

Lydia went still as Gabriel's lips touched hers.

But it was not the slow kiss of a man striving to seduce her. Instead, it was a punishment, a reprimand for her earlier question. Gabriel leaned over her, pushing her back against the bench as he plundered her mouth like a conquering force. His tongue swept against hers and rendered her breathless.

But Gabriel ought to have remembered that Lydia would not be intimidated by anyone, certainly not by him. She was not a little girl to be shown a lesson. She might not comprehend his rules, but she could devise her own.

Lydia bit Gabriel's lower lip hard.

When he jerked back, she gave him no quarter. She seized his lapel and tugged him close. Gabriel stiffened with surprise as she returned his kiss with one of her own. She was a battalion meeting his enemy siege. Their lips met like duelling swords, every touch becoming a battleground.

But then the kiss changed.

A frenzied desire caught hold of them both. Lydia sensed the shift in Gabriel's body, in the pulse that thrummed beneath her fingers. He growled low in his throat. Their kiss was no longer a punishment, no longer a game. It was the air they needed to breathe. It was ten years of repressed frustration and anger, grief, and yearning.

Lydia showed Gabriel everything he could have had for a decade if only he had been honest with her. She showed him what she'd thought about in the darkness even after he rejected her. That kiss represented every night she had agonised over his abandonment. It was 322 unanswered letters. It was every look she'd sent him from remote, desolate corners of ballrooms, wishing he would acknowledge her existence.

Notice me.

Remember me.

Remember us.

Gabriel tore away from her, panting. "What are you doing to me?" he whispered.

Their breath mingled, mouths inches apart. Lydia caught her lower lip between her teeth, hoping that was answer enough.

Then a shadow shifted in Lydia's periphery.

Metal glinted in the moonlight.

And three men stepped out of the shadows holding weapons at the ready.

Gabriel moved faster than Lydia could blink. He shoved her to the ground just as the men attacked. The sickening crunch of fists striking flesh jarred her into action, and Lydia rolled over to see Gabriel engaging with all three attackers in a violent dance. Fear flared through Lydia, but then she noticed Gabriel's expression: a grim acceptance as he circled the other men.

"Pyotr. Dimitri. Mikhail." His smile was cold as he said something in Russian.

Lydia froze. He *knew* these men?

The man named Pyotr replied in terse Russian and called Gabriel by a name that Lydia didn't recognise: Alexei Borislov. Lydia's gaze settled on Gabriel. She studied his severe features, this man she had loved as a child but who had become a stranger to her.

Spy, her thoughts whispered. Here was more confirmation of that word, the dark precipice of his past beckoning her closer to the edge.

The other men lunged, and Gabriel pivoted. Lydia couldn't help but appreciate his body in motion, so beautiful and deadly. How could she have foolishly forgotten how he could move with the sleek dexterity of a predator? Even in his evening finery, he fought as swiftly as a jungle cat. The agility with which he handled the three men was extraordinary.

Lydia was so shocked that she hadn't fled away from the danger.

The hesitation cost her.

One of the men spun away from Gabriel and seized Lydia by the arm. The attacker hauled her up against him and put his blade to her throat. "She's a pretty thing." This time, the man spoke in accented English – for Lydia's benefit, she gathered. Gabriel paused, his lips flattening. "Yours, *zver*?"

Gabriel carefully watched the other two assailants even as he spoke to the man who held Lydia captive. "Let her go, Mikhail. She has nothing to do with this."

"No?" Lydia held her breath as Mikhail sniffed the line of her neck. "Then you won't mind me having her. I've never fucked an English noblewoman."

Gabriel snapped something in Russian, and Mikhail pressed the blade deeper into Lydia's skin. With the slightest pressure, he could slit her throat. "In English. I don't like listening to a liar in my mother tongue, *zver*. Or perhaps I should call you by your real name, *Lord Montgomery*."

Gabriel stiffened. "Let her go," he repeated. His voice was as sharp as broken glass.

"Not yet." Mikhail's breath was hot on Lydia's skin. "I think the boss might want a look at her. Or maybe I'll just slit her throat right here as punishment for your betrayal, *zver*. You seem to care about this one."

Gabriel's eyes flickered to Lydia.

Then he struck as fast as a cobra. He grasped a blade concealed within his coat and flung it.

Right into Mikhail's eye.

Lydia gasped as Mikhail's sudden heft nearly tipped her backward. She frantically wrestled with the hand still holding a blade, forcing it away from her exposed throat. The dead weight of the corpse made her knees buckle, and she struggled to get out from beneath it. As she struggled to get out from beneath the body, she heard the revolting crunch of fists and flesh as Gabriel fought the other men.

With a soft grunt, Lydia rolled the corpse off her. She scrambled away to witness Gabriel shove a second small blade into the second man's gut. Lydia pressed a hand to her mouth as her vision swam. She dimly registered the third assailant making the wise choice to escape, his boots pounding down the garden path away from the fountain.

Gabriel hesitated. His head swung around as he took in one corpse, then the other. And then...

Her.

Their eyes met.

Gabriel went still, and Lydia became aware of the blood splattered across her face and bodice. Of the stains that tarnished her delicate silk dress. Gabriel was in marginally better shape – his black evening jacket likely hid stains worse than hers – but the blood on his knuckles was prominent even in the low light of the garden torches.

And he still held that dripping knife. How many weapons had he kept hidden beneath all that finery?

There was nothing of the boy she knew in his face. Nothing at all. She hardly recognised this stranger whose body seemed created for brutality. He wasn't any different from the blade in his hand, forged for the same terrible purpose.

Gabriel approached Lydia slowly, kneeling beside her. But when he reached for her, she couldn't help but flinch. His fingers curled into the palm of his hand. "Are you hurt?" he asked curtly.

She shook her head, dazed. Unable to speak. All she could do was stare mutely as the last ten years rearranged themselves in her mind, as she finally tumbled from the edge of the dark precipice. *Spy*, she'd thought. But then her attention snagged again on the knife in his grip, and she almost laughed at her stupidity. His position, after all, would not officially exist, would it?

Assassin.

Gabriel set the blade aside. "Lydia." His voice was quiet. It almost sounded like the man she knew, some hint of a plea in the three syllables of her name.

"Don't apologise to me." Her words were collected, calmer than she truly felt. She couldn't have an apology from him. Not now. Not tonight. Not when all her memories of him lay at the bottom of an abyss like a heap of broken glass.

Gabriel gave a nod, concentrating on her blood-splattered skin. With a soft noise, he turned to the fountain and plunged his hands in the water to clean them off. Then he withdrew a handkerchief from his pocket and soaked it. He reached for Lydia once more, his movements deliberate, as if waiting for her to retreat again. When she didn't, he began wiping the blood from her face.

"You're sure he didn't hurt you?" he asked.

"I don't—" Lydia cleared her throat. "I don't think so."

He wordlessly resumed his ministrations, his touch gentle. Even his expression had softened, as if he understood the questions that troubled her. The thoughts that threatened her already tattered composure. If she looked just past his shoulder, she'd see one of the dead men—

"Keep your eyes on me," he ordered, his voice quiet.

But that did little to help. This man could be tender one moment and a killer the next. The hand that scrubbed her so carefully could wield a blade with brutal efficiency. He had stabbed a man as easily as he was now cleaning the proof of his violence from her skin.

What happened to you? Lydia wanted to ask him. *What happened to the boy I knew after every letter I sent went unanswered?*

His face hardened imperceptibly, as if he heard her. *Don't ask*, his expression said. *Do not ask me those things. You will not like the explanation I give you.* Those answers were as forbidden to her as his heart.

Lydia swallowed back her questions. She was silent as he moved his handkerchief to her neck and gently rubbed the skin there. She hoped he couldn't feel her pulse through the cloth, but perhaps it didn't matter. Her chest rose and fell in agitation. She couldn't get her breath to settle. Every moment she spent in the garden close to the men he killed only made things worse. Her very foundations were crumbling.

"You'll have to use your shawl to cover the blood on your dress," he said.

With trembling hands, she managed to don her gloves and arrange the shawl around her shoulders, clutching the delicate fabric across the front of her dress. "What about... the men?"

She couldn't say, *the corpses.*

Her voice was rough; she could barely breathe in. How was he so calm? He had killed two men, and it hardly fazed him.

"Let me worry about them," he said shortly.

Lydia pressed her lips together as Gabriel helped her stand. If he killed with such skill, he likely often dealt with bodies. That awareness sent a stabbing pain through Lydia. She had stood up to him earlier, so confident in her suspicions. And in mere minutes, he'd forced her to re-evaluate everything.

Including if she'd ever truly known him at all.

"You could have killed me," she whispered. "When he had the blade to my throat." Would he have cared? Would he have missed her?

His jaw tightened. "I've never missed a target with a knife."

A shudder went through her at the casual way he said

it, at the implication that he did this often. "And if I hadn't been quicker after you threw it?" Her words were brisk. Fear had made her reckless. "If I hadn't thought to push his hand away when your weapon hit its mark?"

His features constricted. "Come." He said the word so sharply that Lydia had to stop herself from flinching. She swayed as he tugged her down the garden path, but Gabriel's firm hold kept her upright. He did not bother to answer. "At the terrace, we'll part," he said, his voice terse. "Go to your aunt. Tell her you're unwell and must be escorted home. When you're in the carriage, don't be alarmed if you think you're being followed. I'll ask my man to keep watch over your house tonight."

At the terrace stairs, Lydia turned to Gabriel. "What about you?"

Nothing of the charming scoundrel remained in his features now. All along, she'd known it was a performance, but there in the garden was the first time for years she'd seen his face exhibit such honesty. In truth, he possessed a severe countenance, his austere features shadowed in the gloom. She was beginning to understand that he operated more in the dark than in the light.

Pain prickled across her skin at the thought. She missed his genuine smile.

"I have someone I need to speak to." Then, to her surprise, Gabriel reached for her. He brushed a soft thumb across her cheekbone, the touch as light as moth wings. "I'm sorry," he said softly. But he did not say what he apologised for – if it was the blade to her throat, the men he'd killed, or if it was everything. Then he dropped his hand. "I'll call on you in a few days. Now in you go."

On trembling legs, Lydia climbed the terrace stairs and entered the ballroom. She held her breath and kept her head down as she passed through the crowds of assembled aristocrats to where her aunt stood with the other matrons. She had no way of knowing if Gabriel had managed to clean all the blood off her face, or if her hair still held its coiffure after the attack. For once, Lydia was relieved that spinsterhood offered a certain invisibility. She could slip through the ballroom and leave early without stares or gossip.

Please don't let Aunt Frances notice anything out of the ordinary, Lydia prayed.

But Lady Derby's brows snapped together as soon as she saw her niece. "Lydia, darling, are you all right?"

Lydia swallowed her panic. Surely, if Gabriel hadn't cleaned all the blood off, someone would have remarked on it.

"You do look quite pale," Mrs Fitzroy said.

"I'm a bit lightheaded," Lydia replied truthfully. "With your permission, Aunt, I'd like to depart early."

The other matrons made sympathetic noises while Lady Derby frowned anxiously. "See?" she said, regarding Lydia sternly. "I told you I ought to have called on the doctor yesterday. She's been ill since the Coningsby ball," she explained to the others.

More sympathetic noises.

Lydia fanned her face with a hand. "It's only the heat. I don't require a doctor."

"Mm." Lady Derby didn't seem convinced. "Here, take my arm and I'll accompany you to the carriage. You seem unsteady."

It wasn't until they got home and Lady Derby bustled Lydia up to her bedchamber that she let herself breathe. She leaned against the door for support and dropped the shawl from her shoulders. Across the room, she caught sight of her reflection in the gilded mirror.

She would have to throw out the dress before the maids saw it. Those bloodstains had no plausible explanation.

7

Once Gabriel had covered Mikhail and Pyotr's bodies with the overgrown foliage in the Bromes' garden, he dispatched a flurry of missives to Wentworth's agents asking for a clean-up. The men would wait for the ball to end, the house to settle, and then quietly load the corpses for disposal before morning. Gabriel compensated the five men well for the unexpected responsibility.

After completing that foul business and changing his clothes, Gabriel paid Wentworth a late visit. The butler was used to men with certain credentials coming and going at odd hours; he'd been paid to ask no questions.

Wentworth was composing messages at his desk when Gabriel strode in. "Tell me your men have Medvedev in custody," Gabriel said without preamble.

The spymaster tossed his pen down and ran a frustrated hand through his hair. "He never showed."

Gabriel's hands curled into fists. "What happened?"

Wentworth reached into his cabinet for two snifters and a

decanter, pouring two fingers into each glass. He passed one to Gabriel. "My men intercepted Coningsby, who waited for over an hour by the docks. So either someone warned Medvedev, or he suspected the meeting was compromised."

Gabriel savoured the burn of spirits on his tongue. "I'll say one thing for him, he's a cautious bastard. He wouldn't be alive if he weren't."

"Coningsby's agreed to inform on the Syndicate as long as his involvement stays out of the broadsheets," Wentworth said, sitting back in his chair. "But I'm not confident he'll give us anything now Medvedev has confirmed you're alive, in London, and not named Alexei Borislov Zhelyabov."

Gabriel leaned against the window frame and looked out over the road. Though he had taken an extended detour on his journey to Wentworth's, he wondered if one of Medvedev's men had still managed to follow him. If they were watching the house from the dark London street. "You think that's why he brought my old associates to England? Someone gave him information as to my true identity?"

Wentworth considered that. "It's possible that Medvedev wanted to hunt you down. It's also possible that he'll use the opportunity to connect with London members of the Syndicate. I've already advised Her Majesty that our best agents are standing by to accompany her to an undisclosed location and we're supplying additional security around Parliament. The Syndicate's numbers in London remain limited, but it may not stay that way with Medvedev here." The other man studied Gabriel. "One of my men came for a debrief before your arrival. I heard your evening with Miss Cecil went poorly."

Gabriel suppressed a wince by downing his glass of

whisky. A vision of Lydia flashed into his mind: the pink rosebud dress flared around her on the ground, splattered with blood. The look on her face... it was as if her entire world had shattered.

You always knew you were destined to break her, he thought to himself. *At least now she knows who and what you are.*

"Do you require the particulars," he asked, keeping his voice admirably calm, "or have your agents made a practice of gossiping about my life now?"

Wentworth made an amused noise. "Don't consider yourself unique – the Home Office is worse than a room filled with society matrons," he said. "Especially when they have bodies to dispose of and a gentlewoman to guard." He put up a hand when Gabriel opened his mouth to speak. "Don't tell me – let me guess. Miss Cecil witnessed you kill two men tonight."

More images flashed. Lydia's breath had been so uneven that it shook her entire body. Blood had marked her pale face with angry slashes of red.

Lydia had sought refuge in the seclusion of the Bromes' beautiful garden and walked away tainted by Gabriel's brutal actions. She witnessed the brutality from which he had striven for so long to shield her. But he ought to have understood that Miss Lydia Cecil would discover his true past one way or another. She had a talent for clawing at the soil beneath which he'd buried his secrets.

Lydia challenged him like no one else. Even her kiss had been a duel – she'd matched him touch for touch.

Gabriel's heart had flared to life, wakened by the taste of her, the sensation of her lips on his. It was as if he'd been in purgatory, a ghost of flesh and blood. He wandered through the world but was dead in every way that mattered.

And now, fate had intervened. Mikhail's knife had roused another emotion he'd long thought cleansed from his mind: fear.

His only options had been to expose himself as a spy or lose her. Better she comprehended the man he truly was than live out her days believing him still to be the boy she knew.

"They attacked while I was with Miss Cecil in the garden," Gabriel explained. "Two unnamed criminals can be hidden, a gentlewoman with her throat slit in the middle of a ball might attract some attention. So I chose her life over my cover." *I'd choose it again.*

Wentworth's hand curled into a fist on his desk. "Understood," he said with a sharp nod. His expression was shuttered, but not before Gabriel noticed the way memories flickered across the spymaster's face.

Wentworth had hidden his true profession from his own wife. Then, five years earlier, he'd arrived home to find her murdered by a still-unidentified assailant. He imagined that if Mattias Wentworth could relive the day of the attack, he'd choose his wife over his clandestine occupation.

Gabriel pretended he hadn't noticed Wentworth's reaction. "Dimitri will be with Medvedev by now," he said, referring to the third assailant. He'd tried searching for the other man after seeing Lydia to safety, but the crush of carriages, servants, and guests outside the Bromes' home made it easy for the man to escape. "He'll undoubtedly have Miss Cecil identified and tracked within a day. Believe me, he'll seek any opportunity to use her to punish me."

Wentworth leaned back with a sigh. "Yes, I recall the Syndicate's laws from your dispatches."

Even Gabriel's brothers in the Syndicate had understood they couldn't completely trust each other. They established a criminal code that guarded against vulnerabilities: families, lovers, children, wives – all of them were potential weaknesses. Joining the Syndicate meant leaving behind everyone except the brotherhood.

"I'll pay your men for their time if they remain stationed outside Miss Cecil's home until we catch Medvedev," Gabriel said.

"Mm." Wentworth tapped his fingers against his desk. "I'll permit them, but they can't enter Lady Derby's residence, and they'll have precious little opportunity to familiarise themselves with the property and staff. Pay a servant enough, and they'll supply information to anyone who asks, including Medvedev."

Gabriel stared out of the window again, his mind working. It did not escape his notice that the talents he'd often used in the business of death now had to be employed to keep someone alive. But Lydia had always been the exception to his every rule. She was the voice of his conscience – or whatever fragments remained of it.

Even her kiss had been a rebuke. A shrewd reminder that for all his efforts to push her away, she'd always be in his head. In his every thought.

He'd never forget that she kissed like a conqueror.

"Her aunt has a house in Surrey," Gabriel said. "The property is near Meadowcroft, and I know it well from my youth. If Miss Cecil is out of London, Medvedev will be forced to devise a new strategy. That will give us more time to find him."

Wentworth looked doubtful. "And how do you plan to have Miss Cecil convince Lady Derby to leave London in the middle of the season? Even for a beloved niece, that's asking a great deal."

"Perhaps an illness—"

Wentworth shook his head. "Miss Cecil isn't an agent, and you can't have her lie to Lady Derby for the length of time it takes to find Medvedev."

"She'll do it if it means surviving." Gabriel's voice was almost sharp now. His composure was crumbling. Anger superseded everything – anger and fear.

He was afraid for Lydia.

Astonishment crossed Wentworth's face, which was all the proof Gabriel required.

Wentworth let out a breath. "Even if Miss Cecil were willing, your proposal would put Lady Derby at risk. Unless you mean to reveal yourself to Miss Cecil's aunt while you're at it." At Gabriel's look, he said, "I thought not. Then you know there's only one other way to ensure Miss Cecil withdraws to Surrey without her aunt."

"No."

Wentworth raised his hands in a gesture of supplication. "If you have another idea, let me hear it. I'm impatient to know your alternative."

Gabriel gazed sightlessly out at the gas lamps across the square as his thoughts whirled. His wolf paced through his mind, impatient to smash through the already-fracturing barricades of ice. He had not given himself over to the beast in too long. The violence of his time in Moscow was marked beneath his skin, and the only way to endure it – to regain his fragmented control – was to hit something or bed someone.

When it came to the second choice, there was nothing but brutal desire. Gabriel had only kissed Lydia once, and he'd been ready to rip off that pretty pink dress. Set his teeth to her skin. Bite her. Make her his. Bend her over and take her hard and fast until his mind purged itself of her.

Instead, he'd killed two men and ruined that pretty pink dress just the same.

Behind him, Wentworth rose from his desk with a long sigh. "Listen," he said, "I assume you care about this woman in your own way. So let me offer you some advice: if anything happens to her, you'll regret it for the rest of your life."

Gabriel gripped the window frame, his shoulders tensing. Beneath his shirt, he could still feel the damp blood he'd had no time to wash off properly. It was his fault those men were in that garden. His fault that Mikhail had held a knife to Lydia's throat. His fault Lydia's memory of her childhood friend was destroyed.

"Are you speaking of Lydia now or your wife?" Gabriel asked.

Wentworth made a soft noise. "You don't have to like my opinion, Monty. If you think coming home to find your Miss Cecil bleeding and dead at the base of the stairs is something you can live with, then disregard me."

Gabriel couldn't help but imagine Wentworth arriving home to find Mrs Wentworth stabbed a dozen times. Searching for the culprit and finding nothing. If someone butchered Lydia, Gabriel would hunt that person to the ends of the earth. He wouldn't stop until he located them, tore them apart, buried them where they would never be found.

He also knew he could never be the husband she deserved. But there was little help for it now – his fate was directly tied to hers.

And she'd pay the price.

Gabriel shut his eyes. "I'll seek permission for a special licence. Make sure the archbishop complies."

8

Lydia ordinarily enjoyed Lady Derby's afternoon visits from the other matrons.

On Tuesdays and Thursdays, her aunt's house in Mayfair became a hive of activity as ladies called in to socialise. These occasions allowed Lydia to converse in the comfort of her own home, without the intrusion of ballroom noise.

But that day, the laughter and calm normality of the sitting room did not soothe her nerves; it irritated her. The established ritual left Lydia restless. How could she be expected to sit there and chat about the season while her entire life was unravelling? While everything she *thought* she understood turned out to be false? A deception?

Envy flared in her. They were oblivious, while her mind was a tempest. She longed to return to her bedchamber and pace its length, an activity better suited to her turmoil.

She'd heard no word from Gabriel for three days.

Perhaps she shouldn't have been surprised. Lydia ought to have grown used to his silences. *I'll call on you*, was an easy falsehood. And from one who masqueraded as a gentleman while operating as an assassin, it was effortless.

With each passing hour and day, her dismay over Gabriel's murder of the two men changed into a surge of fury that vibrated across Lydia's nerves. A short message would have been better than this intolerable silence. An apology consisted of two words that ought to have been easy enough to pen. Even liars knew how to say, *I'm sorry*.

But there she was, enduring Gabriel's silence once more. The reticence that said more loudly than words what he thought of her. After so many years, it shouldn't have ached like a blow to the chest. Maybe time had corroded Lydia's armour. Or possibly his kiss had fractured it.

She'd been so stupid.

"But perhaps Lydia and I will visit Cornwall at the end of the season," Lady Derby said, momentarily distracting Lydia from her angry thoughts. "I do love the coast. I haven't been there since before Lord Derby's passing."

"Quite lovely," Lady Forsyth replied.

"Just so," Mrs Calloway agreed.

The former then announced that her daughter planned to honeymoon on the coast after marrying her duke.

At that point, Lydia made the wise decision to ignore them. Mental images of a serene coastline and festive weddings did not suit her mood. If she were to visit the Cornish coast, let it be during a storm, when the waves battered the cliffs.

Lydia set her jaw and stared down at her needlepoint. The flowers more closely resembled amorphous blobs – they, at least, matched the turbulence of her thoughts. She didn't know how to navigate the ordinariness of her life now. Even an activity as routine as needlepoint – something to keep her hands occupied – confounded Lydia. She was as unbalanced in that drawing room as she would be on the cliffs of Cornwall during a squall. Her life with Gabriel needed to be re-examined. Held up to the light and amended. She could no longer count on her memories of him, of her whole childhood in Surrey.

As her past crumbled to ruins, Lydia was forced to sew calmly while the source of her misfortune wandered the city, oblivious to his part in shattering her. It was no different from his kiss in the Bromes' garden: it was a punishment for Lydia's idiocy.

Stupid, stupid girl.

"Lydia, darling?" Lady Derby's calm voice jolted Lydia from her thoughts.

"Mmm?" Lydia raised her head and found the three older women staring at her. "Did you ask something, Aunt?"

"Mrs Calloway asked how you're enjoying the season. Twice."

The blobs of Lydia's needlepoint flowers mocked her. Like her failure to answer questions by rote, they were a reminder that her life was in tatters. It occurred to Lydia that appearances held power: these matrons would only think of her as a distracted girl, not one who was fraying at the seams. They would never know the thoughts that troubled her.

Lydia swallowed. "Quite well. Thank you for asking, my lady," she murmured.

"Oh, that reminds me," Lady Forsyth said. "My daughter requires a chaperone for the Viscountess of Firth's ball

Monday next. I'm otherwise engaged for the evening. Miss Cecil, would you mind accompanying her in my place?"

Lydia's grip on her needlepoint tightened. At seven-and-twenty, she was now old enough to serve as a debutante's chaperone. The world simply accepted that Lydia would never marry, but would be left to the uncertain destiny of unwed ladies. They were put into the care of other relatives or took work as companions and governesses. And once Lady Derby passed...

Lydia would have no one. The role Lady Forsyth now proposed was to be her fate indefinitely.

Lydia gazed down the long years of her existence with a new perspective. This was the future carelessly left to her by a man who told lies too smoothly ever to be trusted again.

Wait for me.

"Lydia?" Aunt Frances prompted. "Is that agreeable to you?"

Lydia uncurled her fingers from the needlepoint frame. "Of course," she said, forcing a warm smile. "I would be happy to accompany dear Violet."

The matrons beamed. Guilt pulsed through Lydia. There she was, resenting the future they offered out of kindness. The only one open to her as an unmarried lady with no talent other than the perfect deportment she'd been taught since childhood. Now that same talent confined her to one existence. One path.

The only one Gabriel had left her.

Stupid, stupid, stupid girl.

Lady Derby's butler arrived at the doorway. "My lady," he said, presenting her with a silver plate carrying a single card. "You have a gentleman caller."

Gabriel.

Gooseflesh broke out across Lydia's skin. So he'd come, after all.

Lady Forsyth straightened. "A gentleman?" she asked with an eagerness of a hound scenting a fox. It wasn't often that a gentleman appeared during at-home visits, and Lady Forsyth had a second daughter to marry off.

Lady Derby glanced at the card. She froze and cast Lydia an unreadable look. Lydia knew what that unspoken message conveyed: Lady Derby was torn between the etiquette that prevented her from turning Gabriel away in front of her friends and loyalty to a niece who'd had her heart broken.

Lydia gave her aunt a slight nod. She might as well get this over with.

"Send him in," Lady Derby said to the butler calmly. As he left to do her bidding, Lady Derby told the other matrons, "It's Lord Montgomery. I've known him since he was a boy."

The other ladies sat up with delighted interest. Gabriel, after all, was considered one of the season's great catches. With his handsome looks and exceptional fortune, many debutantes were vying to become his countess.

Lydia, meanwhile, put her needlepoint in her lap to conceal her trembling hands. Gabriel's timing was spectacularly unfortunate. She could hardly think of a worse moment to show up on her doorstep and justify murder.

As Lydia agonised over how he planned to explain his appearance *and* speak to her without rousing gossip, Gabriel breezed into the room. He was impeccably dressed in a coal-coloured suit perfectly tailored to his trim physique. A body she now knew was both beautiful and lethal. She had never considered his physique as a weapon. But now she knew it was honed and balanced as a dagger.

Gabriel's dark auburn hair gleamed in the afternoon sunlight that shone through the bay windows. His charming smile held enough wickedness to make Lady Forsyth and Mrs Calloway blush and titter.

It was an astonishing transformation. Lydia almost respected the skill of his duplicity. He had shed the assassin beneath as soon as the sun came up.

He killed two men only a few nights ago, Lydia reminded herself. And yet, not a shred of embarrassment showed on his face.

Gabriel's attention fell on her. Lydia didn't return his smile, and his expression darkened imperceptibly. Had she not been looking for it, she might have missed it.

He shifted his focus to the matrons. "Ladies." He gave a short bow. "Good afternoon. I was nearby on business and wanted to pay a call on my favourite childhood friend."

Lady Derby's smile was courteous, if a bit distant. "You're always welcome to a visit, my lord. Even if it has been... quite some time. Will you sit and join us for tea?"

The other ladies didn't detect the strain between Lydia, Lady Derby, and Gabriel. Perhaps they were too distracted by his dazzling good looks as he settled in the chair opposite Lydia.

Lydia had to break that tension before the other women noticed. She quickly set aside her needlepoint to reach for the tea service.

"No sugar, no milk," he murmured.

Their fingers brushed as Lydia passed him the tea. His

gaze met hers briefly, and that moment seemed to stretch into infinity. "Thank you."

She lowered her eyes and settled herself once more on the divan, expecting him to ask Lady Derby for permission to take her walking in the park. Devise a clever reason that wouldn't encourage gossip.

But Gabriel remained in his seat, as if they had nothing to discuss about the two assassins that left Lydia so restless and troubled that she'd hardly slept for days. He didn't look at her again. Instead, he conversed comfortably with Lady Forsyth and Mrs Calloway as if he had all the time in the world.

The clock ticked on.

Lydia passed the time by watching Gabriel, marvelling at his charm. Despite giving Lydia the occasional bewildered glance, even Lady Derby was persuaded by his amiable demeanour. She began to laugh just as easily as the other women.

Lydia, on the other hand, had no aptitude for the role he cultivated so smoothly. Anger tore through her with sharp claws. Had he *toyed* with her all those years before he'd left? Or was this skill acquired since then? Had Lydia not witnessed Gabriel's talent with a blade, she might have been just as deceived. He was a confidence trickster, performing for his marks.

"Ah, my lady," he said to Lady Forsyth in that smooth, cordial tone. "I have yet to go sailing this season, but you may have just convinced me."

"Oh, but you should! My daughter Violet adores sailing," she said, with no subtlety. "Perhaps you might join us for an afternoon."

"What a lovely invitation," he said warmly. "I'll consider it when I'm confident I won't fall into the water and drown on you. I'm more at ease in drawing rooms."

The ladies laughed. The clock on the mantelpiece chimed. He had been there the requisite quarter of an hour now – any longer would be considered a breach of etiquette.

Worse, he'd left Lydia even more agitated. Her needlepoint had long since been abandoned. Instead, she focused on him with a rage that spread heat across her skin. She was incandescent. She was *furious*. Perhaps he had been right the other night, after all: she didn't know the rules.

Because he was a damned cheat.

Lady Derby gave the clock a subtle glance. "Please feel welcome to call again, my lord," she said politely. "We shall next be at home this Thursday."

"My daughter accompanies me on Thursdays," Lady Forsyth added. The woman was utterly shameless. "She can reassure you about the delights of sailing."

Gabriel sighed dramatically, and Lydia wanted to roll her eyes. "While I've enjoyed your company, I confess to having an ulterior motive for my visit."

Lady Derby considered Lydia with interest. Her aunt would be sorely disappointed if she expected a marriage proposal.

"Pray, do tell us," Lady Derby said to him.

Gabriel's gaze settled on Lydia and left her motionless, utterly frozen in place. How had she forgotten how penetrating his eyes were? He used them without mercy.

"May I speak to Miss Cecil alone for a few minutes?" he asked her aunt.

Lydia almost dropped her needlepoint in shock. Had he lost his bloody mind? Had he—

Mrs Calloway and Lady Forsyth inhaled sharply, and Lady Derby ignored them. Instead, she gave Lydia a thoughtful look. "Lydia, would you like to speak to Montgomery?"

Lady Derby's words were courteous, but Lydia understood the implied message: *Tell me no, and I will come up with a reason to send him away.*

But Lydia dropped her gaze. She wanted an answer for the other night; she *deserved* one after everything she'd witnessed.

She would endure the consequences later.

"Of course, Aunt," she murmured.

"Then take him to the Blue Room," Lady Derby said. "And return to us in precisely fifteen minutes. No longer."

"Of course," Gabriel said politely. He rose to his feet and bowed to the matrons.

Lydia led him down the hall to the Blue Room, shutting the door so the servants wouldn't overhear. She whirled on him. "*Are you out of your bloody mind?*"

Gabriel leaned against the slim writing desk in the corner of the room, all charm now absent. Here was his honest face – the one with the calm focus of a killer. Now she'd seen the truth behind his deception, she wondered how people believed it. Didn't they notice the way his muscles tensed like a predator? That his stare held the same menace as a loaded pistol?

"I'm certain some will say that I am," he said, his weapon-like stare on her. He looked so fierce now.

Lydia gripped the doorframe behind her for balance; his presence threatened her entire equilibrium. "The women in that room think you're here to propose," she said through her teeth. "Not to explain yourself after assassinating two men at Lady Brome's ball."

Gabriel's lip twitched. "I'm aware of what happened. I was there."

Lydia scowled. "I had to throw my gown out with the rubbish and tell my maid that a rosebush tore it beyond mending. Now I'll have to give my aunt a credible excuse in precisely thirteen minutes."

His hand trailed across the surface of the desk. "Poor, poor Lydia," he murmured. "You'll just have to learn to lie, won't you?"

The fury in her chest burned as hot as a dying star. Lydia pushed herself away from the door and strode over to him. Their chests were almost touching as she said, "Listen to me, *Montgomery*." She spat the name like an insult. "This might be a game to you, but it isn't to me. This is my *life*."

His features softened slightly. "You mistake me." She went still as he reached for her, sliding fingertips across her cheekbone. He watched the motion with an almost puzzled look. "I don't think of your life as a game," he murmured. "If I did, I wouldn't be here."

Lydia hated the feelings those words awoke in her. How they doused her wrath like rain on a forest fire. She wasn't ready to lose her anger yet. She couldn't abandon it, not after ten years. Not in minutes.

"Then tell me who Bear is," she said softly.

Gabriel's lips tightened, and he dropped his hand. "Bear is the codename for Boris Medvedev, the leader of an international crime ring called the Syndicate. Apart from engaging in illegal smuggling with a high human cost, they target and assassinate foreign diplomats for a price. My superior in Kabul was one of them."

Lydia's breath caught. "Kabul was when you stopped responding to my letters."

He gave a curt nod. "I was tasked with infiltrating the Syndicate in Moscow, reporting on their movements, and eventually assassinating Medvedev and his inner circle. They knew me as Alexei Borislov Zhelyabov."

Lydia's gaze wavered. "How long were you in Moscow?"

"Four years. When my father and brother died, I returned to England and terminated my employment." His expression turned bitter. "Not that I excelled at being a diplomat. If I wasn't killing to maintain my cover, I did so with the authorisation of Her Majesty."

Lydia's entire world tilted. All those years she had spent thinking he had ignored her, that her letters had gone unanswered because he'd decided he didn't want her. And this was the answer. The secret behind Lord Montgomery's much-lauded smile dripped with blood. He was a sheep unbuttoning its fleece to reveal a ravenous wolf.

Lydia swallowed. "And you failed to assassinate this Medvedev?"

A muscle in Gabriel's jaw twitched. "I put a blade through his skull. It seems he survived it."

She wondered if he had given her that gruesome detail on purpose. It seemed almost intentional, a subtle rebuke for her ever thinking he was harmless. Forever looking at him and picturing the boy she had grown up with.

"Then he's come for revenge?" Lydia's voice trembled. His revelations left her unsteady.

He nodded. "Dimitri managed to escape the Bromes'

garden. By now, Medvedev knows about the noblewoman I was seen kissing. When he looks into our background, he'll discover our past."

A memory of that kiss eclipsed Lydia's jumbled thoughts. Not his attempts at control, or hers at wresting it away – but the moment afterwards, when that kiss shifted. When it came to represent ten years of longing. Ten years of separation.

She wished it hadn't been their first. That she'd dared to kiss him all those years ago before he'd left and become someone she hardly recognised.

As if he read her thoughts, Gabriel's face softened. He studied her with something akin to bewilderment, as if she were a mystery he was trying to unravel.

If Lydia let herself read too much into that, she would forget herself. She had to guard her heart. He broke it too easily. "You think I'm in danger," she said, attempting to gather herself again.

"I don't have any living family," Gabriel said, still examining her with that quiet intensity. "So yes, I think he'll use you. He'd use anyone I might care for."

"Then I appreciate you sending someone to watch over me." Lydia glanced at the clock. They didn't have long now. "I'll think of an excuse for my aunt and the other matrons."

She had precisely five minutes to summon an excuse for being alone with Gabriel in that room. Five minutes to enjoy what remained of her relatively immaculate – if staid – reputation. Even Mrs Calloway and Lady Forsyth couldn't resist the allure of gossiping about a spinster who spent time alone in a room with a gentleman without collecting a marriage proposal.

Cornwall. She had Cornwall to look forward to. A place on the edge of her small world, where she would go and attempt to forget him again.

But Gabriel didn't nod. Instead, his features hardened. This was the shrewd assassin in the body of a rogue. "Tell her we're to marry."

Her head snapped back. "I – sorry?"

"Marriage," he said, his lip curling. "Tell her I offered."

A renewed fury ignited Lydia's veins. Of course he would think nothing of her reputation. To a man, a woman's standing accounted for so little.

For a woman, it meant everything. Entire lives. Entire futures. They depended on it.

"So we'll pretend to be engaged? Then what?" she snapped. "Say you find Boris Medvedev and I'm safe again. What do I say to my Aunt Frances when you ultimately call things off? You've already enraged her by jilting me. And society? I suppose my reputation means nothing to you. How keen you are to save my life, only to ruin it again."

Did he think so poorly of her? Was she just another person for him to destroy? He might not end her life with a blade, but he had sliced it apart all the same. And here he was, offering to do it again – survival at the cost of ruin.

His look was harsh. "You misunderstood me. We *will* marry. The only falsehood I require is that you imply to your aunt that we anticipated our vows. I've already obtained a special licence."

A breath exploded out of her. He'd already obtained…?

So that's where he had been for days – making legal arrangements without consulting her. Ten years ago, the prospect of marrying Gabriel St Clair would have thrilled her. Now it left Lydia uncertain. It didn't help that his expression was as unyielding as steel; suddenly, that kiss three nights ago seemed a figment of her imagination – the desire of a girl who still missed him.

"No." Her voice could be steel, too.

Gabriel made an impatient noise. "You spoke so passionately of your reputation before. Here I am, offering to spare it."

Lydia curled her fingers into her palm. "I won't marry a man offering out of obligation. You don't want me."

Something flickered in his gaze – an intensity as hot as molten metal.

Then his lips came against hers. Lydia gasped in surprise as he kissed her, her hands seeking purchase on his shoulders for balance. Then he made a noise in his throat that changed her.

It was a growl of raw need.

Her own desire blazed to life. But before she could return the kiss, he pulled back with a rough sound, his lips at her ear. "I want you, Lydia Cecil. I've wanted you every single day of my life."

A breath shuddered out of her as she tried to find her balance. "But you don't want to marry me."

His body was rigid beneath her touch. He was silent for a moment. Then: "No. I'm offering you my protection and my name. If you'll take it."

The clock chimed a quarter past the hour. She had to give him her answer now or suffer the consequences of refusal. She valued her life. And with him, she would learn to guard her heart.

She pulled away, forcing her breathing to slow. "Very well. Then I'll marry you."

He studied her intently for a moment, but then he nodded once. "Three days hence." Then he stepped away from her, his countenance as impassive as a statue's. "Our marriage will be legal, and before all of society, we'll act as besotted newlyweds. But it won't be real, Lydia. I can't be a husband to you. Understand me?"

Sadness pricked her. She mourned for the boy he'd been. For the man he had become.

"I understand," she murmured.

In truth, her future husband would be a stranger.

∞ 9 ∞

Gabriel's control over his future was tumbling from his grasp.

Command over his life was all he'd had after Moscow. Gabriel carefully planned every hour of his social life down to the last detail. That was how he dealt with nightmares of his past: with preparation and indifference – defences against his memories.

Now his emotions were too discordant. It was as if he were untethered from the earth, spinning erratically while he waited for gravity to bring him down again.

But Lydia's power over his existence defied physics. She had upended him.

After his proposal, Mrs Calloway and Lady Forsyth left in a flurry of skirts and delighted giggles to circulate the gossip. Lady Derby, meanwhile, had pressed Lydia on Gabriel's unexpected proposal. Lydia demurely lowered her eyes. The falsehood that they'd anticipated their vows left her stammering uneasily.

Not to be outdone, Gabriel perfected the role of a gentleman wedding the adored childhood friend who had always held his heart. Of course, it was all entirely fictional – intended only to conceal his unease.

But desire? *That*, he did not have to fabricate. During Lady Derby's interrogation, he'd let his eyes rest on Lydia with the heat that had consumed him since their first confrontation in Lord Coningsby's study. Their brief kisses had only reignited him; his icy walls thawed when his lips touched hers. His final vestiges of control were all that prevented him from pushing her onto the chaise longue, lifting her skirts, and sinking his fingers into her pussy.

He wanted to know what she looked like when she climaxed.

The direction of his thoughts must have been obvious, because Lady Derby had cleared her throat and promptly agreed to a speedy wedding.

After leaving Lydia to make preparations with her aunt, Gabriel returned to his house with those lurid fantasies still fresh in his mind. In the solitude of his bedchamber, he'd leaned against the wall for balance. Lydia's kiss flickered through his mind again. He was helpless against the surge of thoughts that imagined just what she could do with those lips. With a frustrated noise, he unfastened his trousers, took out his cock, and pumped it with a hand as he thought about pounding into her. The rough, animal sound he'd made as he climaxed was a moment of honesty for himself alone. A reminder that he could not be tender with her – what he imagined was pure fantasy.

He would never allow himself to consummate their pretend marriage.

News of Gabriel and Lydia's betrothal circulated from

sitting rooms to ballrooms in the days that followed. It wasn't every day, after all, that an old maid became affianced to an earl who was the catch of the season. And for a wedding performed in such haste? For that reason alone, an undercurrent of suspicion tarnished the news. Whispers speculated on the number of months before a child emerged from this impulsive union.

Lady Derby attempted to damp down speculation with the love story of two childhood friends whose paths had diverged but were finally reunited. She declared they were simply overeager to begin their lives together after so many years apart.

Gabriel's shoulders tensed as he stood before the vicar in the parlour of his home, with only Wentworth and Lady Derby as witnesses. Lady Derby dabbed at her eyes, her cheeks glistening with tears before Gabriel and Lydia had even exchanged their vows.

Lydia entered the room.

Gabriel's breath caught in his throat. A strange sensation of weightlessness suffused his body as she came to stand beside him. He lost all sense of gravity when she was near, of his place in the world. She was a force of nature, a woman whose very presence could topple kingdoms and shatter worlds.

But if he had ever dared to dream of a wife for himself, that woman had always borne Lydia's face. She was the wife he wanted and couldn't have.

And now, she was the wife he didn't deserve.

You're my plague, he thought as he stared down at her. *A symptom of how far I've fallen.*

Lydia was pale. Her skin nearly matched the modest white

lace gown she had selected from her existing wardrobe; they'd had no time for her to procure a suitable wedding dress.

Her hand trembled when she placed it in his.

Look at me, he thought. But her lashes remained lowered. Gabriel wanted to know what she was feeling. If she dreaded this marriage. If she went into it with the knowledge that he could never be the husband she chose ten years ago.

A husband who could love her. Whose only skill wasn't in breaking people. Who wouldn't put her life at risk.

After the bidding prayer, the vicar added, "I'm required to ask if anyone here present knows of any cause or just impediment why these persons may not be lawfully joined together in holy matrimony. Ye are to declare it now or forever hold your peace."

Lydia raised her eyes and fixed them on Gabriel with an almost fierce intensity. Her gaze was like the edge of a blade set between them. She, too, had the aim of an assassin.

For a moment, Gabriel wondered if she would object. He had been the one to pledge her a future and leave her dejected on his doorstep. He had been the one to destroy her chance of marriage with a gentleman who would have suited her better.

Now she was marrying a bastard and a killer who was beneath her in every way.

But she lifted her chin and said nothing. Even as Gabriel spoke his vows, Lydia's gaze remained as unyielding and steady as steel.

When it was her turn, Lydia's voice was equally firm. Perhaps they ought to have performed some act of affection for Lady Derby's sake, but one peek at that corner of the parlour confirmed it was unnecessary. Lydia's aunt maintained the misty smile of a proud guardian who adored her ward. She did not notice that Gabriel and Lydia stared at each other as if they were forming a reluctant truce from opposing ends of a battlefield.

I'm going to ruin you, Gabriel thought to himself as Lydia spoke the final lines of her vows. Their future was now as inevitable as death. *And I think you're going to ruin me.*

As if she read his thoughts, her lips flattened, and she looked away.

And the vicar proclaimed them husband and wife.

On an indrawn breath, Gabriel leaned forward and pressed a soft kiss on her forehead. That single point of contact – only a brush of his lips – left him unsteady. Lydia caught her breath. Her skin was warm, and Gabriel found himself wishing he had kissed her on the lips again. Now that he'd tasted her, he yearned for her touch.

He craved *her*.

They separated all too quickly, and Lady Derby stepped forward to embrace the newlyweds. Wentworth shook Gabriel's hand. Gabriel maintained his smile for the sake of Lydia's aunt, but his mind was chaos. He needed space to breathe.

Gabriel gently took Lydia aside while Wentworth conferred with Lady Derby. "I'll send my footmen with you to collect your things. I need a few minutes alone with Wentworth."

Lydia gave Wentworth a sidelong glance. "He's someone you know from... your work?"

His work. Such a strange way of describing the things he'd done. Without the crown's authorisation, he'd be no better than the criminals he'd lived among for four years.

Gabriel forced a nod. "My former superior."

"I see." Her voice was quiet. "Very well, then."

"And I imagine you'll want to say goodbye to your aunt and her staff before we leave for Meadowcroft this evening."

Surprise flared. "We're to leave so soon?"

"I don't want to give Medvedev the chance to attack. Any further delay in our departure puts you in danger."

Lydia was silent, her delicate features more ashen and drawn now. Her throat worked as she swallowed. "I understand. Then yes, I'd like to say goodbye."

Gabriel was struck by a sudden wild impulse to soothe her. He instantly rejected the sentiment. That was what real husbands did when their wives needed comforting.

You're not a real husband.

Gabriel stepped away. "I'll see you this evening."

After escorting Lydia and Lady Derby to their carriage, Gabriel returned to his study to find Wentworth pouring himself a brandy. "To your wedding, old man," he said.

Gabriel scowled. "I'm not in the celebrating mood."

"No?" Wentworth snorted. "Come now. She'll make you a fine wife."

Gabriel's face hardened. "Her suitability was not a question, if you'll recall." When Wentworth just smiled, Gabriel made a faint noise. "Tell me about Medvedev. Any word on his whereabouts?"

Wentworth set down his glass, his expression sombre now. When Wentworth had a mind to be charming, Gabriel almost forgot that he ran a secret department from the Home Office. "We intercepted a coded message and I have someone solving it. But watch your wife carefully at Meadowcroft. If Medvedev senses an opening, he'll take it."

"My estate in Surrey has enough land to hold him up if

he attempts to come for me there," Gabriel said. "By then, I expect you to have done your job."

"Oh, you *expect* me to?"

Gabriel scowled. "Meadowcroft is close enough for me to get to London by carriage within two hours. If you find Medvedev, I expect a cable."

Wentworth considered his drink again. "I have a few people who can take Medvedev out without even being seen. Perhaps I ought to hire one of them for the assignment."

Gabriel straightened. "This is personal for me, and you know it."

Medvedev had been the one to take a gentleman and make him into an animal. This time, Gabriel would make sure the bastard was dead.

Wentworth gave a short nod. "As you say. And after we handle Medvedev? What then?"

"I'm not sure what you mean."

His friend rolled his eyes. "Of course you know what I mean. With your new wife."

Gabriel shrugged. "Lydia can do what she'd like. I've twelve properties to choose from and enough money at her disposal to see her through an extended holiday on the Continent. I don't care what she does."

"No?" Wentworth smiled. "You still haven't told me what you were doing in the garden alone with her."

Gabriel moved away from the door. "None of your business. Now, if you'll excuse me, I need to have a word with my solicitor."

"Congratulations, Gabriel."

"Get out of my house, Wentworth."

10

Lydia supervised the maids as they packed her belongings. She took a shaky breath. The edges of her vision blurred, and her balance teetered on a plank bridge between two cliffs. Even with the bedpost's aid, she felt as if she were close to toppling over. To Lydia, watching the trunks accumulate was like staring down at a raging maelstrom from a dizzying height. This was all Gabriel's fault; he had been her one comfort after the passing of her parents, yet here she was – balancing on the precipice between life and death.

All because of him.

She hadn't felt like this since…

If you return to this address again, you will be refused entry.

Yes, since his butler notified her that she wasn't welcome at Gabriel's residence. She'd remained on the step and stared at his shut door; it might as well have represented his heart: inaccessible and entirely closed to her.

So she had forged her own protections.

Gabriel wanted to shut her out? Very well, let the battle commence. Her heart would guard itself with something more impenetrable than timber; Lydia would smelt it from iron so he'd never hurt her again. Reinforce that barrier with iron, day by day, year by year. Nobody would know her heart had never healed.

And now...

She was wed to him. He had kissed her, and the steel that encased her heart clashed against his frigid ramparts, and she felt its weakening. Her shelter had become vulnerable.

Gabriel still had power over her, even after all these years.

A soft knock sounded on the doorframe. Lydia looked over to find Lady Derby on the landing outside her room, her hands twisting in agitation. "Lydia, may I speak with you?"

"Of course, Aunt." They settled into Lydia's sitting room. Tea had already been set out, and Lydia sat down in her favourite chair. "Is something the matter?"

"Yes."

Lydia paused in alarm. "Yes?"

Lady Derby exhaled. "That is... I should have come to you last night, but I was too restless. I've hardly had time to grow accustomed to the idea of you leaving."

Lydia focused on pouring out tea, hoping that her discordant thoughts didn't show on her face. "I'm sorry. I know this must be an adjustment for you."

"And for you."

Lydia lifted her head in surprise. "For me?"

"Yes." Lady Derby regarded her severely. "I should have

asked last night before you stood in front of that vicar... I ought to have inquired if this was what you really want."

Was it what Lydia wanted? When it came to Gabriel, it was difficult to tell. Lydia's memories and emotions were a tangle of briars, full of barbs that pricked all her vulnerable places. She knew first-hand that Gabriel didn't need words in order to reject her. He simply disappeared like a spectre.

But it was too late to change her future. She had made her decision, and now she would share Gabriel's life. "Of course it is," she said now to Lady Derby. "You know I've been in love with Gabriel for years."

Like an imbecile.

Her aunt set aside her teacup and reached for Lydia's hands. "I know. But I was with you when he broke your heart. I still haven't forgiven him for that."

Lady Derby had held Lydia so many times while she cried. When Gabriel's letters ceased, Lydia tried to convince herself the post had been delayed. After he'd returned home and refused to see her, she excused it as grief. Lady Derby had attempted to conceal her pity and failed utterly.

When Gabriel noticed Lydia at a ball and turned his back on her, Lady Derby had taken her home and blotted her tears.

Lydia couldn't forget the sting of those memories, either. They stuck beneath her skin, as painful as lacerations from broken glass. And now Gabriel was Lydia's husband, and she was leaving the aunt who had helped repair the mess he'd made.

"I understand," Lydia said. Then, before tears came, she added, "I'm sorry to leave you so quickly. Now you won't have a companion on your trip to Cornwall."

Lady Derby made a dismissive noise. "It was never my intention for you to end up as my companion, dear. I wanted to see you with someone worthy of you." She drew her shoulders back. "Montgomery had better earn you. If I don't think you're happy, I have a poison garden not far from Meadowcroft and the skill to slip some in his tea, do you understand?"

Lydia pressed her lips together. *Could* she be happy with the man Gabriel had become? He said his wedding vows out of obligation, after all. When he wasn't kissing her, he might as well have been a continent away. If she put her ear to his chest, she wondered if she'd hear anything beating at all.

She didn't know how to be a wife to a stranger who wore the face of the man she loved. If he hurt her again, she would have to recover without Lady Derby to help her restore the pieces of her shattered soul.

"Thank you," she whispered. "For everything."

Lady Derby's eyes filled, and she waved a hand in front of her face. "Oh, dear. Now, look at me."

Lydia set down her tea and moved to embrace the other woman. "I love you, Aunt Frances."

"Come to me if you need anything," she said. "I mean it, Lydia. If that boy breaks your heart, I will not stand by this time and let it happen."

Lydia tightened her arms around Lady Derby. She wanted to reassure her aunt that she intended to protect herself this time.

She would be the perfect wife to Gabriel. She would try her best to make their marriage work.

But she would never let herself love him again.

★ ★ ★

Their carriage sped down the country road.

Lydia couldn't bring herself to look at her new husband. Instead, she watched the landscape change as they drew closer to Surrey. Outside, the clouds gathered overhead, and rain fell softly. The grey sky suited Lydia's mood. In that carriage, she did not have to pretend to be the infatuated, happy bride. She and Gabriel had done their best to pacify society's suspicions; there was no need to continue the deception once they were alone.

The verdant landscape shifted to rolling hills the farther they drove from London. Lydia was almost relieved that night was beginning to fall; the places in Surrey she'd explored with Gabriel when they were children would be swallowed by the darkness and hidden from her view before their arrival. She didn't want to be confronted by those places they had explored for hours and all the fields in which they'd picnicked. So many memories that lanced at her like tiny needles.

"How long has it been since you've been to Meadowcroft?" Lydia asked. The question was out of her mouth before she could stop it.

Opposite her, Gabriel went still. "Two years."

His voice was quiet in the small enclosure of their carriage. It occurred to Lydia that they'd had so little time alone in the last decade; she used to savour the sound of his voice. The deep resonance of it in her ear as they lounged on blankets in the sun.

Lydia kept her attention on the landscape. Long shadows extended across the hills as the last vestige of light vanished from the sky. Soon she would have nothing to look at except him.

She cleared her throat. "I was never able to offer my condolences on the loss of your brother and father. I'm very sorry they're gone."

She hadn't often visited the former Lord Montgomery or Thomas St Clair, Gabriel's elder brother. Both were frequently absent from Meadowcroft, whereas Gabriel remained under the care of his governess and tutors until he was old enough to attend Eton.

Lydia could feel his eyes on her, focused and intent. Even in the darkness of the carriage, they seemed to pierce through her. "We both know you tried to tell me."

The night outside the window was oppressive and dark, the world beyond the carriage little more than a blur of shadows and shifting shapes. Lydia watched as the last glimmer of crimson drained from the sky, feeling the weight of their silence settling between them.

"And I was rejected on your doorstep. I remember." They said nothing for several long minutes. The view became lost to Lydia, and she had no other choice but to return her attention to the husband who did not want her. "What happened in Kabul?" she asked quietly.

She wasn't certain he would answer. His indecision pressed against her like stacked stones, each one heavier than the last. She wondered if he deliberately used the silence to his advantage – that, too, could be a weapon.

When he spoke again, his voice vibrated through the dark interior. "I was stationed in Kabul under my direct superior, Mr Charles Langdon. I had a passing familiarity with the Pashto languages promoted by the new emir, and my colleagues in Switzerland believed I might be of some assistance to the British resident. An internecine war between the emir and his brother lengthened my stay. While I was there, Charles received intelligence that an international crime ring originating in Moscow was targeting foreign delegates." His jaw tightened. "Contract killings."

Lydia twisted her fingers together. "Do you know the source of the contracts?"

"No." He lifted a shoulder. "It could have been the Russian tsar. It could have been the emir. It could have been anyone with enough money and a penchant for diplomatic unrest. As long as it gets paid, the Syndicate doesn't particularly care where the money comes from." He paused again as if to gather himself. But when he continued, his voice was so neutral as to be flat. "Medvedev's men attacked the residence while I was out attempting to secure our immediate departure. When I returned, it was to find Charles, his wife, their son, and every servant in the lodging slaughtered." Lydia felt his eyes turn away from her to the murky landscape beyond the carriage. "That's what happened in Kabul."

Lydia held her breath. She didn't think she'd ever been more motionless in her life – afraid that if she shifted even slightly that he might withdraw from her. Choose deception.

"And after Kabul?" Her words were even.

Gabriel made a soft noise. "Why do you want to know?"

Because now she wanted to understand everything about him. She spent so long consumed with fury over his abandonment that she had managed to convince herself she didn't give a damn what happened to him when he left Kabul. Her unanswered letters, after all, were the same as a rejection – the silent refusal of either a coward, or a man who didn't care enough to send even a single note in consideration of their former friendship.

But things were different now. His façade as Lord Montgomery had crumbled, and she witnessed the man who hid in the gloom and moved like smoke. That man had killed in front of her. Had kissed her.

Had married her to protect her.

"Because I sent you over three hundred letters after Kabul," she said, swallowing when her voice threatened to tremble. She could not reveal how much it pained her. "I dispatched them to the Home Office direct and any consulate I could find an address for – including your old offices in Vienna, Paris, and Zürich – hoping to find *anyone* who could forward it to your place of residence. And I didn't know what became of you until the day your butler shut the door in my face three years ago."

A part of her wished she could see his expression now. She wondered if he thought her a fool for continuing to write him even after he had made it abundantly clear that he'd had no wish to hear from her. But perhaps she ought to have been grateful for the shadows. The darkness made it easier.

She heard the rustle of material as Gabriel shifted in his seat. The dim moonlight filtering through the carriage window permitted Lydia a glimpse of his profile; he'd turned away from her. "I was assigned to infiltrate the Syndicate in Moscow," he said tightly. "And I became a different man from the one you wrote letters to." Before she could respond, he moved again. "We're here."

Lydia was surprised the time had passed so swiftly. Sure enough, when she peered out of the carriage window, she noticed the familiar silhouette of Meadowcroft. She'd always thought it looked like something out of a fairytale, with its yellow colouring and generous windows. In late spring, extensive blooms of wisteria and honeysuckle shrouded the front façade, a lovely complement to its cheerful exterior.

But somehow, at that moment, Meadowcroft seemed to loom out of the mist. Or perhaps it was the dense rainclouds that suited Lydia's mood, her nervousness at being in that vast house with only her new husband and his staff for company.

"Welcome home," she said to him softly.

She felt his gaze fall on her. There was an almost animal intensity to him that rendered her breathless, uncertain of the direction of his thoughts. She could no longer read him. The only time she'd trusted his honesty had been...

An image of Gabriel's kiss came to Lydia, unbidden. He'd pressed against her in the Blue Room as if he were ravenous. As if he craved her touch like oxygen. The ragged, animal noise from him made her desire flare for a reason: it was the first sincere thing she'd heard from him in years.

I want you, Lydia Cecil. I've wanted you every single day of my life.

The carriage halted, and the footman opened the door, sparing Lydia from her thoughts. Her husband stepped out and gently helped her down.

The drive was lined with servants carrying lanterns who had been sent word of their master's belated arrival.

"I'll introduce you later to the servants you haven't met," he said. "You must be tired. I'll have a meal sent to your room if you'd like."

Lydia wasn't tired; she was uneasy. She didn't think she

could sleep. But perhaps he was eager to dispense with her company. "Very well," she said.

"Mrs Marshall," he called. A woman bustled from the front of the line with a jingle of keys. The lantern light revealed the craggy features of an older woman with kind eyes whom Lydia had not seen since her youth. "Mrs Marshall, perhaps you remember Miss Lydia Cecil?"

"Lady Montgomery now," Mrs Marshall said with a delighted smile. "I'm so pleased to have you with us again."

If Lydia hadn't been studying Gabriel in the dim lantern glow, she might not have noticed how his lips tightened at the woman's use of her new title.

But then he forced a winsome smile and leaned forward to kiss the older woman's cheek. "And any word for me, or have you already discarded me in favour of my new wife?"

Mrs Marshall waved a hand. "Oh, stop. Of course I missed you, dear boy." She grasped Lydia's hand. "But you must wish to rest from your trip. Come with me, and I'll have you all set in your rooms."

"Goodnight, Lady Montgomery," Gabriel said as Lydia was led away.

11

Gabriel reclined before the fire in one of the library's overstuffed chairs. A snifter of whisky hung loosely from his fingers, his third in the last hour alone.

Earlier, he had wandered the vast halls of Meadowcroft, orienting himself once more with the residence of his youth. While the Montgomery seat was far beyond Surrey – located in a remote part of Devon – Gabriel's father had preferred the bright outer façade and lighting of Meadowcroft after the death of his countess. Gabriel recalled dashing through the halls with Lydia, eating scones with jam and clotted cream on rainy days. Those memories were perforated into the very walls of Meadowcroft.

He'd taken to drink once his efforts to relax had failed; the agricultural tome intended to induce sleep had long since been discarded on the table beside him.

Instead, he stared into the blazing fire that crackled in the hearth as his thoughts raced. There was little he could do to distract himself from fantasies of Lydia under his roof.

They would spend extended time alone together for the first time in years.

And now she was married to him.

It's not a real marriage, he reminded himself. *It requires no consummation or intimacy.*

Yet for hours, Gabriel had imagined a thousand different ways and places around Meadowcroft he wanted to pleasure her. He longed to push off her clothes, press his mouth to her quim, and devour her.

He drew a harsh breath, and downed his whisky. The convenient bottle beside his book beckoned, and he poured himself another glass – his fourth. Perhaps if he drank enough, his daydreams would fade into a haze of intoxication. The clock on the mantelpiece ticked away, reminding him of how long he had attempted to preoccupy himself since their arrival.

A sound just beyond the library door made him freeze. The whisper of slippers on the carpet stopped at the library entrance, and he knew even without looking that it was Lydia.

"Hello," she said. A pause. "Are you all right?"

He longed to shut his eyes and revel in her voice. Ask her to speak again so he could savour the smooth cadences that caressed his skin like silk.

Say something else, he wanted to say. *Anything. Anything at all.*

Gabriel missed listening to her. After a year in Vienna, he'd noticed that his memories of her voice were fading. In Zürich, when he read her letters, it was as if she were whispering in his ear. In Kabul, he'd lost the ability to hear her entirely. In Moscow, he had wholly forgotten how her voice once tempted him. The way it soothed him like the stroke of a soft hand down his spine.

So when Gabriel returned to London and heard Lydia at the door of his townhouse, his entire body had gone still. *Will you please inform Lord Montgomery that Miss Lydia Cecil is here to see him?*

The ice around his heart had splintered by small degrees. He had very nearly forgotten that he was a monster. When he saw Lydia for the first time in seven years at a ball a few months later, the ice had nearly melted. She compromised the protective barriers he had assembled in Moscow. She was too dangerous to know.

So he'd turned his back on her.

But now she was his wife, and Gabriel didn't have the option to abandon her. So he was reduced to avoiding her.

Gabriel concentrated on the flames in the hearth, watching how the golden whisky in his glass radiated in the light. If he turned and looked at Lydia now, he'd lose command over his desire. She shattered him far too easily.

"I'm quite well." A veneer of control remained in his voice. She couldn't know that it was beginning to fray. "Is there anything you need? Are your rooms comfortable?"

She was silent for a long time. The force of her gaze weighed almost tangibly on Gabriel's skin. What did she see when she looked at him? Was his performance holding up? Or did she see a broken man struggling to maintain the coldness in his heart for her protection?

"Yes," she replied. "My rooms are lovely. I'd wondered if you would visit them."

Gabriel's fingers scraped against the chair's upholstery as

his cock hardened. He needed her to get away from him. "No," he said, a touch too sharply.

He wondered at her slight intake of breath. Was she upset? Relieved? He catalogued every sound and movement of her body, turning them over in his mind as he pondered what each meant. Then his thoughts coalesced with painful force: she couldn't stay. He couldn't keep himself together if she stayed.

Please go.

But Lydia's slippers padded across the carpet and she approached his chair. In Gabriel's peripheral vision, he could see her reach for his discarded book, graceful fingers tracing the gilded letters on the cover.

What would those hands feel like on his skin? What would they look like wrapped around his cock?

Gabriel's teeth ground together. Fractures formed along the frost beneath his skin, splintering at her nearness. She threatened the order of him – safeguards he had erected since Moscow and Kabul.

"So you're reading this tome on agriculture to put yourself to sleep," Lydia murmured. "Rather than visit me."

Gabriel inhaled sharply. "Perhaps I'm not in the mood to fuck you. I told you this would not be a real marriage."

He'd used coarse language deliberately, hoping to shock her into leaving. But he ought to have known that it would take more than a crude word to send her fleeing; she was the most stubborn woman he'd ever met.

In the corner of his eye, he saw her fingers curl into her palm. "You don't intend on consummating this marriage?" Emotion strained her voice. Was she hurt?

You can't help but hurt her. You were always going to, no matter what you did.

"No." His pretence of control was going to fragment. He craved the sight of her face, the sensation of her skin. He'd caressed so little of it, kissed even less. He wanted to rend her nightdress in his haste to set his lips against her.

She made a soft noise. "Fine. If you won't visit me tonight, I'll see to my own pleasure. Besides, I've heard few men care about a woman's release."

Gabriel couldn't prevent the onslaught of images: Lydia, pushing up her nightdress to slide her fingers into her slick cunny. Lydia, with her head flung back in ecstasy as she brought herself to climax. Whose name would she call at that moment? Whose face would she picture as she pleasured herself?

He wanted it to be him. *He wanted it to be him.*

Something snapped inside Gabriel. His hand shot out to grasp Lydia's wrist, and her soft gasp made him soften his grip.

His eyes met hers for the first time since she'd entered the room. God in heaven, he would never get that memory of her out of his mind: her dark hair loose and falling around her shoulders, her pale skin flushed pink with desire and anger, and her gaze defiant.

Gabriel slowly rose from the chair. Lydia watched him, alert now. Then, when he raised her wrist and pressed it to his lips, her eyes flared with need.

For him.

He ought to give her a memory to use when she pleasured herself. When she went to bed alone at night, it had better be his face she pictured in the darkness. Let him plague her thoughts, as well.

Tit for tat.

Gabriel brushed his lips over her fluttering pulse. The texture of her skin was like velvet. "Is that all you want? For me to make you come?"

A tremor went through Lydia. The pulse at her wrist quickened against Gabriel's mouth. "Yes."

That answer was all it took to shatter his final traces of restraint. He pushed Lydia into the chair he'd just vacated and dropped to his knees before her. A shuddering breath left her, but it wasn't enough.

Gabriel wanted her to lose as much control as he. He wanted her shattered. Wanted her sleepless, afflicted with the same temptations that had him roaming the halls of Meadowcroft. When she closed her eyes at night and set her weary head against a pillow, he wanted her to dream only of him.

Tit. For. Tat.

Desire burned hot within him. Gabriel pushed up her nightdress and took hold of her underclothes. He was impatient – a savage need pounding through him to touch and taste her. To feel her bare skin.

He gripped her underclothes and tore, rending delicate fabric.

She made a soft, surprised noise – but Gabriel hardly heard it over the blood rushing through his ears. She lay open to him, her beautiful quim glistening. And Gabriel lost control. He shoved her legs wider and put his mouth to her pussy.

Lydia's cry of pleasure only further frayed his control. He

craved her vulnerability – a reciprocal longing. He yearned to mark himself so deep in her bones that she'd never see anyone's face but his every time she touched herself. He wanted her body to ache with the memory.

Gabriel devoured her. He moved his lips and his tongue across the peaks and valleys of her cunny and relished the taste of her, the soft, shuddering breaths she made as she shivered against his touch. She tasted of salt, like the sea. Of something else that was so uniquely her that he would never forget it for as long as he lived. And when he thrust his fingers inside her, Lydia's gasp embedded itself somewhere deep inside him. Set itself in his heart, with all the other memories of her. He wanted to remember this, remember how her leg hooked around his shoulder to urge him closer. The way her hand gripped his hair and her fingernails scraped across his scalp. She came undone with the same animal desire reflected within him; he understood it on a basic, intrinsic level. Understood *her*.

I'm going to claim every inch of you, he thought. *The way you've claimed me.*

She shuddered beneath his lips. When she whispered his name, he heard it echo deep inside his soul: "Gabriel. *Gabriel.*"

Then she came apart with a harsh sound, a gasp that vibrated through her entire body. And Gabriel did not stop until she had collapsed against the back of the chair, her body shivering.

Only then did he pull away so that he could kiss her. So she could taste her pleasure against his lips. She kissed him back with an urgency that bordered on desperation, her hands grabbing at his clothes.

Gabriel responded by kissing her roughly, nipping at her lips. He was going to tear off her nightdress.

Roll her onto the floor.

Press her face to the carpet.

Thrust into her hard.

Use her body to forget—

His lips tore away from hers. Gabriel forced himself to back off, his hands pressing against the mantelpiece as he tried to gather himself.

"Gabriel?" She stirred behind him. "Is all – are you well?"

Memories pounded through Gabriel's skull, images of every time he'd killed with a knife. His life as Alexei Zhelyabov had been violent; pleasure had blended with brutality. He could so easily become like that with her.

"Quite." His voice came as if from afar. "As I said before, I'm not in the mood to fuck you."

A soft noise left her. "I – very well."

The words were spoken quietly, almost with a glimmer of understanding. Another sliver of pain shot through him, a blade of its own. She might think she knew what he went through in Moscow, but she couldn't imagine. She'd married a monster.

He heard the whisper of clothing as she rose to her feet and padded to the door. Then she paused. "What I said before about pleasuring myself being better... it was inaccurate," she said softly. Then, after a long moment: "Good night, Gabriel."

Gabriel tipped his head back and shut his eyes.

12

Lydia woke at sunrise.

Her bed revealed evidence of another fitful sleep: the twisted sheets and scattered blankets, the pillows that had ended up on the floor. A dozen books at the bedside were arranged in a haphazard stack, and some were overturned with spines up. She recalled attempting to read several and giving up on all of them.

For days now, she had tossed and turned restlessly. Lydia longed to open Gabriel's connecting door and yank off every stitch of his clothing. Rend the fabric to pieces, as he'd done with her undergarments.

She wanted to touch him everywhere.

But Gabriel's reaction in the library confounded Lydia. He brought her to climax and bestowed upon her the kind of scorching kisses she'd only ever fantasised about in her dreams. There had been an urgency to his touch. And then…

He had retreated from her. It had been as sudden as storm clouds cladding the sun's warm rays; indifference dropped over his features like a frigid pall. His desire had shut down, and he changed into someone made of marble. But unlike stone, he had no vulnerabilities.

You shouldn't have been so hasty, she scolded herself. After all, Gabriel's rejection allowed Lydia to reconstruct her own defences. If he was a jagged peak in winter, she could be the ocean at its base. If he thought to touch her again, he would find her guarded by turbulent waters that he couldn't navigate. Let him be just as perplexed by her. Let him experience a cold that matched his own.

Lydia was quiet and contemplative as a maid prepared her for a morning stroll. She donned a wool walking dress for the chilly morning and set out into the gardens. It had been over a decade since she'd explored the grounds of Meadowcroft, and she had almost forgotten the dazzling flowers in spring. The delicate clusters of white cherry blossoms, the vibrant violet-blue of the hyacinths, and the cheerful golden hue of the daffodils. She ambled along a familiar footpath, one that she had often travelled with Gabriel in childhood.

Lydia lingered at the wooden bench, her fingertips skating over the surface coated in cool morning dew. They used to sit there. Gabriel would watch as she gathered flowers. She could not walk the pathways of Meadowcroft without remembering all the days they'd spent together. She had thought she would love him forever.

And now it was too dangerous to give him her heart.

Lydia didn't know how long she stood there, lost in her memories – perhaps it was hours. A crunch of boots along the path roused her from her thoughts, and she knew without looking that it was Gabriel. She remembered his step by heart.

"Lydia."

She shut her eyes, her fingers clenching. Gabriel spoke her name softly. If she had one regret about two nights before, it was that she hadn't heard him say her name during climax. During her fitful sleep, she'd thought about how it might sound when he came undone and called for her in the darkness. Those fantasies had left her unsatisfied and wanting.

Wanting him.

"Lydia."

She had to look at him. She couldn't avoid him now he was her husband.

Bracing herself, Lydia opened her eyes and turned. Had she not been holding her breath, the sight of him might have knocked the wind from her. He was gorgeous in his tweed coat and riding boots, the auburn of his hair gleaming in the morning rays. His severe features were beautiful, carved from shadows and light. He would have been a sculptor or a painter's dream.

When Gabriel's eyes met Lydia's, a ripple crossed his face, as if he read her every thought. It was clear that her admiration was unwelcome. A sharp ache pierced her chest in sudden understanding: she hadn't done enough to reinforce her heart that morning; his kisses wore her down.

She would have to refortify herself.

Lydia pressed her fingernails into her palm and adopted her most aloof expression – one that stopped suitors in their tracks before they could request a dance. The one that gained her a reputation for indifference. "Husband. Is there anything I can do for you?"

Gabriel's gaze searched hers. Perhaps he recognised the swift barricade Lydia had erected, saw that he would not gain access to her heart today. In response, his expression grew more distant. He was more practised at it than she.

"I came to say that you shouldn't freely travel the grounds." His words were flat. "If you want solitude in nature, the greenhouse is protected, and my men won't have to spend their time watching you."

Those words scraped against her skin. Lydia felt like a burden to both him and the men he'd hired to guard her. "I see. Before we left London, you didn't explain that Meadowcroft was to be my cage."

A muscle worked in his jaw, the only sign of emotion in his face. A part of Lydia relished the sight. It was a slip in his façade, a deficiency proving he wasn't nearly as practised a performer as she'd believed.

Lydia longed for other signs that he was every bit as agitated by what had transpired between them. She yearned to unravel him, watch his eyes glaze with pleasure. She wanted to know if his bed had twisted sheets and disorganised piles of pillows. Something she could point to and say was evidence of his vulnerability.

She had no wish to be married to stone or an immovable mountain. She desired flesh and blood and hot lips against hers.

"My men are paid to protect you," he said tightly, "but this property is so vast that Medvedev would take you easily if he found you wandering alone. So I'm asking you to stay in the house for your safety. At least when I'm not with you."

In the distance, one of Gabriel's hired bodyguards stood sentry on the path. He looked away from them, but his body was alert. Still, she had no wish to cause him or any of the other men trouble.

"Then walk with me," Lydia said, her attention falling on Gabriel once more. "I grow restless if I'm indoors for too long. Remember?"

Memories flickered across his features. Lydia wondered what he thought about. Her restlessness, after all, had been the cause of their many adventures – even the governess hired by Lady Derby could hardly keep Lydia indoors. She had a habit of escaping between her lessons to meet Gabriel at the stables.

But then his face became shuttered, and he might as well have been on the other side of the world. "I can't. I've business in London today."

Her fingernails pressed further into her gloves. He was avoiding her. "I see. With Mr Wentworth, yes?"

"That's one item of business," he confirmed. She wondered if the other was to travel as far away from her as possible. "I would prefer I leave here today knowing you're safe."

"And when do you plan to return?"

"I'm not certain. Tomorrow, perhaps."

"Very well." She straightened her shoulders and went to sweep past him. "Then good day to you."

But he stopped her with a hand to her arm. "Lydia. Promise me you'll stay in the house until I return."

She stared down at his hand, marvelling at how she

wanted that hand to touch her everywhere. Even now. But there were so many impediments between them – garments that were as much an obstacle as their past.

"I'm an obligation to you, aren't I?" she whispered, raising her gaze to his. "You wouldn't have married me, and now we're stuck together as if we've been floated out to sea." He said nothing; he only drew in a soft breath, but one that said more than words ever could. Lydia turned away. "I will stay in the house. And see you when you return from London."

She pulled out of his grip and left for the vast, empty house.

13

Gabriel rode to London as if the hounds of hell were at his heels.

He had woken that morning with every molecule of his body on fire for Lydia. As if he were crawling out of his skin. This lack of command over his desire alarmed him; was he safe for her? Would he lose control, or would his mind go blank as it had back in Moscow, when ordered to do terrible deeds to maintain his cover?

For a house as vast as Meadowcroft, he was acutely aware of her presence in every room. He couldn't avoid her. Nor could he escape his thoughts of two nights before in the library.

He had set his mouth to her. He had *tasted* her.

God, but he desperately wanted to do it again.

Shutting himself in his study and poring over his estate ledgers did little to soothe his mind, nor did roaming Meadowcroft's grounds for any sign of Medvedev. He almost wished that bastard *would* attack. Violence, after all, was an ideal distraction from lust.

But Medvedev proved elusive – and Gabriel's passion became a painful barb that kept him too preoccupied.

Last night, Gabriel had been reduced to listening for Lydia's activities in the adjoining room. He'd paused near the door, and the notes of her soft singing as she prepared for bed was like a beckoning finger. Clothing rustled. He couldn't help but imagine the nightgown had been wearing in the library: white, the fabric as insubstantial as gossamer.

So easy to tear until he had her stripped naked.

A frisson of electricity went through him. The soft sigh that reached his ears through the door threatened his composure. He'd retreated to his study, drank until his thoughts swam, and finally dozed in his leather chair. When Gabriel saw Lydia again that morning – amid the flowers, like Persephone before Hades claimed her – his control was dangling by an unravelling thread.

If Gabriel couldn't have her, and Medvedev remained in hiding, then he would use another diversion.

Night had already fallen by the time he reached London. He let himself into his townhouse in Mayfair and greeted the bewildered servants with a smile. One mention of seeking a gift for his new bride dispelled any doubts about his visit. Not even the most talkative of maids would think to question the behaviour of a husband so plainly besotted.

After the house settled for the evening, Gabriel intentionally chose his finest coat, boots, and gloves. Then he left Mayfair with a spring in his step. Every part of his disguise was assembled for a purpose – with a distinct destination in mind.

The East End suited Gabriel's temperament. He'd tried to abandon brutality after Moscow; seeking distraction with a willing woman was a more satisfactory solution to his disturbed sleep. It reminded him that he was still capable of emotions other than wrath. Those nights, he had been like a ghost roaming the world, attempting to find a way back to his old existence. Back to the person he was ten years before.

Back to the man Lydia fell in love with.

But that life was gone, and he could never return to it.

Smoke wafted across the road as he strolled down a narrow lane redolent with the aroma of coal fire. A scream echoed in the distance – perhaps a drunkard or easy prey for a criminal. Who could tell? People watched him with alarmed bafflement. He couldn't blame them; it wasn't every day they saw a gentleman casually strolling through their part of the city, let alone past nightfall. He made sure to greet them with a cheerful voice, his distinctive accent marking him as an outsider.

Every criminal in London assumed a stupid toff made for an easy mark.

Then, in the darkened lanes of Whitechapel, a shadow fell across his back. Gabriel had had years to grow intimately attuned to danger. He honed his instincts for combat. But that night, he wanted them to see the expensive material of his coat and gloves, the gleaming buttons they could filch and sell for a fine price.

That night, he wanted them to think him helpless.

A sharp whistle split the air, and two men strolled out from opposite ends of the lane, effectively closing Gabriel in. One of them smoked a cigar, the lit end glowing in the dark. The other wore a black cap low over his brow.

"Bit far from the posh end of town, guv," the man with the cigar said, exhaling a puff of smoke.

Gabriel's performance was timid and perhaps a touch stupid. "Ah – yes. I'm not sure of my way back. Could you redirect me to Mayfair?"

The smoking man grinned slowly, catching sight of the man in the black hat circling behind Gabriel. Both were confident they'd just stumbled upon the easiest robbery of their lives.

"Maybe," Black Hat said, inching closer.

A violent rhythm pulsed through Gabriel's veins, a song of brutality that had become his enduring companion since Moscow. He cooled it down, needing to perform a bit longer; they were all monsters meeting in a dark alley. These men just hadn't recognised it yet.

He pretended to scoff. "Gentlemen, if you don't intend to offer any assistance, then I bid you—"

"Thinkin' I like that coat, guv," the cigarette man said.

Black Hat made a noise of agreement. "Bet those buttons could fetch a few quid, eh Mitchell?" He gestured to Gabriel's footwear. "And them boots?" He gave a soft whistle. "Reckon those'll keep me cockdeep in whores for a year."

"Aye, that they could," the cigar man said. "Might check to see if he has blunt in his pockets. Eh, guv? Wanna help a lad out?"

"No," Gabriel said. He exuded arrogance, the assurance of an aristocrat secure in his place in the world. Let it provoke them. He was growing tired of their mockery. That fraying thread of control was on its last filament. "Fuck off."

Black Hat shoved him hard into the wall. Gabriel gritted his teeth against the jolt through his bones, but he had endured worse. So much worse.

"Now that wasn't nice, was it, Mitchell?" Black Hat said, pulling a knife from inside his jacket. "Thinkin' you owe us an apology, but we'll take the coat, the boots, the gloves, and might consider leavin' ye with a pair of trousers to find yer way back to yer fancy Mayfair residence."

"I said" – His voice was steady, dangerous – "fuck off."

Black Hat snarled, and both men attacked. Gabriel's remaining fibre of control snapped. Brutality surged through his body. It had been whetted like a blade for worse. For men who had been trained to kill.

His assailants grunted in shock when he fought back. They attempted to coordinate attacks, but Gabriel was faster. He was better trained.

And he had craved a fight all bloody day.

Gabriel let them get a few hits in. God, but this was what he needed to feel alive. His body was a weapon formed from steel, forged in fire, and sharpened without mercy. He knew nothing else. Everything he had become over the last ten years was in that alleyway.

He would do well to remember it if he ever thought he was good enough for Lydia.

By the time Gabriel finished, both men were battered and unconscious on the ground. He plucked their weapons from the pavement and straightened his coat. The tide of violence that had flowed through his veins began to ebb. Then it was gone – and he was empty again. A void where his mind should be. A void where his heart should be.

Ice through his veins.

Just when Gabriel pondered provoking another fight elsewhere, a man stepped into the lane and leaned one shoulder against the building. Gabriel's lips tightened when he realised it was Wentworth.

"You shouldn't be here," Wentworth said.

"Neither should you," Gabriel said with annoyance, wiping one of the blades against his coat. It was a decent weapon. He'd keep that one. "Are you following me?"

Wentworth snorted. "Of course not. I was at the Brimstone playing a game of hazard when Nick Thorne received word that an aristocrat was wandering about his territory like a stray dog. I thought to myself, 'It can't be Gabriel St Clair, who's supposed to be in Surrey with his new bride. Surely not.'" His expression turned hard. "But here you are. Not where you're supposed to be."

Gabriel plucked open the buttons of his coat and deposited his new weapon into the inner pocket. "Can't be the first time a gentleman has found himself lost in the East End."

"Probably not," Wentworth admitted. "But most don't traipse around greeting everyone they pass like a damned dupe. You playing the idiot to instigate a brawl is a ruse I'm familiar with. So I let Thorne know I was acquainted with the halfwit in question and to let me deal with him."

"I wasn't aware you and the King of the East End were on such friendly terms."

If anything, Wentworth's countenance darkened. "We're not. I watch his establishment for the information, and *now* I have the King of the East End's attention. And he'll be curious about the idiot lord who overpowered two criminals with such ease. You might want to rethink making an enemy worse than Medvedev."

Gabriel slid the second criminal's knife into his boot and straightened. "I thought he married the Earl of Kent's sister and went soft."

Wentworth let out a dry laugh. "Soft for her? Yes. Soft

for anyone else? Hell no. And Lady Alexandra is terrifying, clever, inquisitive, and will probably know your entire history by morning."

"Then she's welcome to it. I don't give a damn."

Wentworth's expression didn't change. "Why are you picking fights in the worst streets of London instead of protecting your new wife in Surrey, Monty?" he asked softly.

The mention of Lydia only further inflamed Gabriel's temper. "I'm not interested in an interrogation." He turned on his heel and headed down the lane away from Wentworth.

The other man caught up with him. "You're in a mood."

Gabriel kept walking. "I'm always in a mood."

"Except that when you get like *this*, you become destructive."

"And if I had been another gentleman, your men at the Metropolitan Police would presently be inspecting my corpse. Those criminals seemed all too eager to provide you with the work."

Wentworth made a faint noise. "And you seemed all too eager to leave me two of them."

Gabriel's look was sharp. "I left them alive."

"How fortunate for the criminals. I couldn't say the same for the last time you got like this."

Gabriel stopped abruptly. Three youths watched them with interest at the end of the lane, but whatever they saw in Gabriel's face made them slink away. "The Home Office required an assassin, and I gave them one. Your offices never seemed to mind the corpses as long as there's bureaucracy involved before I kill them."

Something flickered in Wentworth's features, gone in a second. "Then you insisted on retirement, and I agreed. Since then, you get in one of your moods, and you find a woman to bed. You've got a wife now, so go home to her. But don't prowl Nick Thorne's streets looking for reasons to hurt someone."

Mention of bedding Lydia did little to improve Gabriel's mood. He couldn't go to her like this – he was too unpredictable. Violent. A savage. Brutal. He couldn't return to Meadowcroft until his emotions were tightly under control once more.

Gabriel clenched his jaw and looked away. "I told you. It isn't a real marriage."

"It's a legal marriage. That makes it real. Ask your wife if she's willing."

"I don't want your marital advice, Mattias." He was impatient now. He needed to return to Mayfair and clean himself up before the servants woke. "Tell me about Medvedev. Any news since your last telegram?"

Wentworth let out a frustrated breath. "He's hiding from my best men. So far, we've found nothing." Wentworth's face was sombre in the darkness. "I won't offer you marital advice, but I will say this: stay with your wife, Monty. By now, Medvedev will know where you both are. He might even have scouts that know you've left her. Comprehend me?"

Gabriel's chest tightened with fear as he recalled Lydia's restless wander through the garden. He hoped she'd heeded his advice. "I comprehend."

"Good. Then go home."

∽ 14 ∽

A thump from the adjoining room woke Lydia.
A peek at the curtains revealed that it was near dawn, the muted glow of morning light spilling through the gaps of thick textile. Lydia stirred, and the thick book she had been reading slid off her chest. The previous night, she had paced the long corridors of Meadowcroft, wondering how Gabriel fared. Desperate for a distraction, she'd taken a novel from the library and finally managed to exhaust herself enough to sleep.

Rising from the bed, she set the book aside and approached the connecting door. She stared at the panelling, dithering over whether to interrupt Gabriel. But then another thump sounded from inside his room.

Lydia held her breath, twisted the knob, and entered.

Gabriel whirled round in surprise. His thin undershirt was open at the neck, and his hair was slightly damp from the early morning mist. Lydia was momentarily struck by his beauty – that untamed look suited him. He seemed even more untouchable than usual: part feral, part gentleman. But at least it was honest, the state of him. Lord Montgomery was too polished and charming; she preferred him like this, knowing that the world could unravel him.

Lydia spotted faint bruising near his eye.

"What on earth happened to you?" she asked, venturing closer.

But when Lydia reached for Gabriel, he angled his face away. "It's nothing."

"That is *not* nothing," she insisted. "Was it Medvedev?"

Gabriel took off his jacket and tossed it onto the chair. "No. I don't want to discuss it with you. I'm tired."

Lydia curled her lip. "I don't care. When you left yesterday morning, you told me you had *business*." She motioned to his face. "*That* doesn't look like business to me."

A dry laugh escaped him. Gabriel came forward until his chest was nearly touching hers. "Let me tell you something, sweetheart. In my world, brutality *is* business. Understand?" Gabriel breathed heavily. His green eyes were harsh and just a bit wild. Then, at her silence, he made some bitter noise. "No response? And what would you say if I asked for this? If your new husband harboured such a taste for violence that he sought it out intentionally?"

Lydia was utterly motionless as her thoughts raced. Was that what he'd been doing while she paced the corridors of Meadowcroft? She had marvelled at his bestial state without realising that it came at the cost of pain.

Her gaze lingered once more on the faint contusion marking his skin. "Is that why you went to London?" she asked gently. "Was it to hurt yourself or someone else?"

A muscle leaped in his jaw. "Either. I don't know."

She longed to know his mind again. He might share a name and a face with the Gabriel St Clair of her youth, but he was unknown to her. As unfamiliar as the deepest parts of the sea.

Perhaps she ought to have been frightened of this unpredictable man who lied with the ease of breathing, but then she noticed the subtle indications that he was not as in control as he seemed. The slight tremor of his hand, the rigid set of his jaw. Minor signs that indicated vulnerabilities in his defences. Or did she imagine they meant something more?

But she had a test of her own, which might provide the proof she sought: she placed her hand over his chest.

And felt the rapid thump of his heart.

"Or perhaps you left for a different reason," she whispered. "You were running from me."

His heart slammed. Gabriel jerked away from her touch. "I don't run from anyone. Now, if you'll excuse me—"

"No. I'm not finished with you." She gestured to the bed. "Sit there so I can put something cold on your face."

Gabriel stared at her, bemusement flickering across his features. "Why?"

"Why?" she echoed. "To bring down the swelling and spare your pretty face from worse bruising."

He didn't react to her compliment. "Why do you want to take care of me?"

"I hardly know," she muttered in irritation. "You are such an obstinate thorn in my side that I'm starting to empathise with whoever punched you in the face. Just sit down, will you?"

A sudden, unexpected smile broke out across his face.

Lydia marvelled at the sight of it – the first genuine smile she had glimpsed from him in over a decade. Even bruised, his entire face transformed and brightened.

And then – as if he realised what he'd just done – it was gone.

An ache settled in a solid weight against Lydia's chest. She wondered if those smiles would be rationed during their marriage like rare treasures, or if she should even hope to see one again.

He used to smile so often.

Gabriel clenched his jaw and surprised her by sitting on the edge of the bed. Not hesitating in case he changed his mind, Lydia briefly left him to collect a cloth and small basin from her water closet. She soaked the fabric. The brisk evening had chilled her earlier bathwater enough to redden her hands.

Gabriel winced as she pressed the cold cloth to his cheek. Lydia made a soothing noise, her fingers brushing his soft hair aside. They remained quiet for a long time, until the fabric warmed, and Lydia plunged it once more into the cold water.

She cleared her throat. *Say something.* "Lord and Lady Ely have invited us to dine with them," Lydia said, pressing the cloth to his cheek again. "How shall I respond?"

"Decline." His answer came without hesitation.

A twinge went through Lydia as the walls of Meadowcroft grew smaller. She couldn't travel outside them without his company.

"And the Arundells invited us to a party two days hence," she added. "Mr and Mrs Crombie were forced to cancel due to a family emergency, and we've been asked to take their places. Their estate isn't far, and they've invited an opera singer from Italy to perform for Lady Arundell's birthday."

"Polite decline," Gabriel said, his attention on the carpet at her feet. "With a gift."

Lydia removed the cloth from his face and set it again in the cold water. "We've invitations piling up." She couldn't help the acerbity that entered her voice.

"Then I'll have my secretary respond," he said curtly, "if you find it too tedious."

She made an annoyed sound as she wrung out the cloth and pressed it to the other side of his face, where smaller bruises lined his jaw. "That's not my point," she said. "Surely you understand how we must appear to the *ton*. Their most admired and near-unobtainable bachelor married an old maid. We were never seen courting. Your proposal came unexpectedly in the middle of tea, we wed three days later, and then you whisked us off to Meadowcroft that very afternoon. One of these things would be enough to court gossip; the combination of the five has set London on fire."

"How melodramatic," he said dryly.

"*Gabriel.*" She raised his face so that his eyes met hers. "I have managed to send letters pacifying my aunt by assuring her that we are happily enjoying our honeymoon. But even she's sent missives asking questions about our abrupt wedding and your subsequent decision to hide us from society. Understand?"

Gabriel tipped his head back. "In nine months, it won't matter. Unless you care about what society thinks."

Lydia let out a soft breath as she stared down at him. His face was, she realised, perfect for a liar. His features distracted from his words; they were constructed to conceal secrets. In nature, beauty was a lure. A trap for prey. He learned that skill so well that perhaps he forgot some people were not fooled by his falsehoods.

"How easy it must be for you not to care," she murmured, tossing the cloth into the basin. Then she ran her fingertips across the handsome contours of his face. "You've only ever had their admiration. When they speak of us in London, you're the one above reproach. Instead, they wonder what a spinster like me must have done to trap you. Poor, poor Lord Montgomery, yet another victim of a woman's artifice. He could have married anyone, and now he's stuck with that frigid bitch."

Gabriel's eyes flared hot. In a moment, he had Lydia rolled beneath him, his muscular body covering hers. Then his lips came down hard against her own, his kiss fierce. With a helpless moan, Lydia returned his touch with equal ferocity. He was impossible to resist.

Then he dragged his lips from hers, panting. "I've never wanted anyone else," he said to her, grazing her jaw softly with his teeth. "Do you understand me? Not in Vienna or Zürich. Not in Kabul or Moscow. Not in England. I just wanted you." He exhaled raggedly as he pressed his forehead to hers. "But I do not, and will not, ever deserve you." Then, before she could reply, he rolled off her and helped her to her feet. He nudged her towards the connecting door. "We'll attend Lady Arundell's birthday party. Now go back to bed, Lydia."

In the solitude of her room, Lydia touched her lips. Her armour was beginning to crack.

15

Two days later, Lydia and Gabriel left for the Arundells' party.

It had taken a lady's maid over two hours to get Lydia ready; she had wanted to make a suitable impression for her first outing as the Countess of Montgomery. Though she'd had no time to order fresh attire in the short days since her marriage, her wardrobe for the season had gone mainly unworn.

So she selected the loveliest garment in her collection: a pale blue silk gown embellished with lace that displayed her figure to its best advantage. The maid had carefully prepared Lydia's hair into an elegant twist decorated with jewelled hair combs. The emeralds she wore at her neck and wrists were a gift bestowed by Lady Derby when Lydia turned one-and-twenty. Lydia hoped having something of her aunt's would give her courage, but the feeling diminished the farther they journeyed from Meadowcroft.

It was dark as the carriage rounded the drive to Thornfield

House, an hour from Surrey. Husband and wife had spent that hour in relative silence as Lydia fiddled nervously with the emeralds at her wrist.

The carriage pulled to a stop, and the footman opened the door. Gabriel didn't even look at him. "Give us a moment," he said, to Lydia's surprise.

The door immediately shut.

The very air within the shaded interior of the carriage filled with expectation as Lydia waited for Gabriel to explain his sudden desire for privacy. During the last few days, he had again become as remote as the farthest ends of the earth. Entire continents might have divided them. He'd hardly spoken to her since his return from London, and last night, she'd listened to him pacing his bedchamber, back and forth repeatedly. She wondered what preoccupied him at night. Was it Medvedev? Or perhaps he fretted over the future of their marriage.

His thoughts were hidden, even when he was about to play the role of the ideal husband. The flickering torches outside the carriage provided just enough light to illuminate his features while he stared at her, his expression as unfathomable as the spaces between stars.

Then Gabriel stunned her by reaching out and placing his hands over hers. Lydia had been fidgeting again with her emerald bracelet. "You're nervous," he said, his voice gentle.

Lydia studied their hands, wishing their skin was not separated by layers of gloves. When she touched him, he did not seem so remote. He became real. "Am I that obvious?"

His lip twisted in a ghost of a smile. "If you tug at that

bracelet any harder, you're going to break it." His eyes dropped, and he lifted her wrist to study the glittering gems. "It would be a shame, I think. You seemed so delighted when Lady Derby gave it to you."

The shock of his words made Lydia's body go still. "You read that letter?"

Something flickered across his face, and his hand tightened over hers. "It made its way to me," he said. "So I read it."

"You never responded." Her voice was barely above a whisper. "You hadn't written to me for over a year by then. I requested that the Home Office forward it to you but never heard anything back."

"I wasn't in a position to respond," he said simply. "Why are you nervous?"

She suddenly wished they weren't in front of the Arundells' residence, moments away from re-entering society. She longed to be back at Meadowcroft, where she might get an answer to the queries that plagued her. *Why didn't you write me? What happened to you after Kabul?*

What did the world do to you?

But Lydia swallowed her questions. She let herself trail her gloved fingertips across the back of his hand, gratified by his sudden intake of breath. "I hardly knew what to say the day you found me in Lord Coningsby's study. I don't know how to be Lord Montgomery's wife."

His thumb stroked her palm, intercepting her touch. "What's your worry? That they won't like you?"

Gabriel's caress was distracting her. It made her think of kisses. Of his lips between her thighs in the library. She wanted him to touch her like that again.

Lydia let out a long breath to calm herself. "Perhaps I'm worried they'll think I'm not good enough for you."

His fingers skimmed her wrist. "Wouldn't that make them look foolish?" he murmured. "If they had any sense, they would understand that you're too good for me."

"Gabriel…"

He raised her hand to his lips and pressed a kiss to her gloved palm. "You're the perfect Lady Montgomery," he said, "because you're you. Yes?" Lydia couldn't respond; his touch had robbed her of words. "May I open the door now, or shall we court further scandal?"

Lydia let out a laugh. "I think we've courted enough scandal, don't you?"

Another slight smile touched his face. It warmed her. It was small, but it was real. "Never," he said.

But then he opened the door and stepped outside to help Lydia down. The grip of his hand sent another shiver through her. His touch was a gift bestowed in small increments, and she longed for more.

As if he read her thoughts, heat flared in Gabriel's eyes. Nearby chatter drew his attention to their surroundings – to the people stepping down from their own carriages – and his expression changed. That small, genuine smile he'd given her had switched into the pleasant but aloof façade of Lord Montgomery, a role as effective as a boundary around his heart.

But then his head dipped toward hers. "Just breathe, sweetheart," he murmured in a voice as smooth as honey.

A few people outside glanced at them curiously as Gabriel led her up the front steps and gave their name to the footman. As Gabriel and Lydia entered, they caught the attention of the other guests.

It was strange to be the focus of so many inquisitive stares. For years, Lydia had lingered in her remote corner of the ballroom, avoiding everyone but Lady Derby and the other matrons. She had unconsciously telegraphed a message of inaccessibility: *My heart has been claimed. I'm not available.*

So she became known for being aloof. An ice queen.

But now…

"They're all staring at me," Lydia whispered to Gabriel.

"Of course they're staring at you," he said. Then he dipped his head indecently close to her ear. "Let them appreciate how beautiful you look, Lydia."

The words, spoken for her alone, brought a smile to her face. He thought she looked beautiful? Nearby, she heard a few ladies gasp and whisper to each other.

Gabriel was deliberate in his methods – every touch and lingering look conveyed a husband utterly enchanted with his new wife. He cradled Lydia's hand in his. The way his thumb brushed across the wrist of her gloved hand drew numerous inquisitive stares.

Do you admire me? she wanted to ask him. *Am I really the only woman you've ever wanted? Or am I just another mark to perform for, like everyone in this room?*

She had so many questions she longed to ask. Each was further evidence that her armour was growing more rusted each time he looked at her. She needed to remember that this smile, too, was false. She shouldn't let herself love someone who lived so much of his existence as a performer.

"Lord and Lady Montgomery!" Lydia and Gabriel turned as Lady Arundell bustled over, smiling widely. "Welcome. I'm so glad you could replace the Crombies at such short notice."

"We're delighted," Gabriel said warmly. His grin was so dazzling it almost hurt to look at him directly. "And a very happy birthday to you, Lady Arundell. You're as radiant as a debutante."

The older woman blushed, and Lydia could hardly blame her. When Gabriel played the high society game, he could sell seawater to fishermen.

"You're such a flatterer, my lord," Lady Arundell tittered. "We've missed you since your departure to Meadowcroft." Lady Arundell's attention fell on Lydia, as if just noticing her. "But you've married. My congratulations to you both."

Lydia forced her own smile. "Thank you."

"We were all quite surprised by your sudden nuptials," Lady Arundell continued. "Why, many of us didn't even know you were walking out."

Gabriel's smile remained in place, but Lydia felt his hand close around hers. A harshness entered his expression. How had she not seen it before, in the years since his return to England? Perhaps, like everyone else, she had been too blinded by his beauty.

"My dear wife and I were friends in childhood," he said easily. His voice did not give any hint of the minor flaws she'd noticed in his performance. "Weren't we, Lady Montgomery?"

"Since I was five," Lydia said, relieved that she could give an honest response. She wondered if Gabriel had intentionally spared her from lying. "My aunt, Lady Derby, maintains a property nearby in East Clandon. I grew up there."

"And we met again quite by accident," Gabriel continued. He let his gaze linger on her, every sinful thought evident in his slow perusal. His beautiful smile held a hint of wickedness Lydia supposed was calculated to convince Lady Arundell that theirs was not a marriage of convenience. "And I kicked myself for letting her get away once. I couldn't do it again."

The matron fanned herself. "Oh. Oh my goodness. I had no idea."

A blush rose in Lydia's cheeks at his hot stare. If he kept it up, he'd set the room ablaze.

She was rescued from this moment of discomfiture when someone called her name across the room. Caroline Stafford, Duchess of Hastings, hurried over.

Lydia smiled in welcome. "Duchess, how lovely to see you."

"You infuriating girl," Caroline said, laughing as she took Lydia's hands in greeting. "Imagine my surprise when I saw your wedding announcement in the broadsheet." The duchess glanced over at Gabriel. "And you? Not even a note, cousin? *Neither* of you invited me?"

"I was just about to relay the story of our quick nuptials to Lady Arundell," Gabriel said smoothly. His smile for his cousin was genuine; it softened around the edges. To Lydia, it was even more beautiful. "I didn't want to risk Lady Montgomery marrying another man, or worse still: turning me down."

Lady Arundell laughed as though the very notion was absurd.

Lydia's mood dimmed somewhat, because it was.

Certainly, she was pleasant to look at, but her age and lack of fortune had long ago guaranteed her limited prospects. "Forgive my husband," she said lightly. "I believe he might have indulged in a quick libation before our arrival."

His tender regard was so convincing, she almost believed it. "It was one whisky, and you're utterly enchanting."

Lydia forced herself to smile. "See? He's lost his senses."

Caroline glanced from one to the other, her polite expression darkening with an understandable touch of suspicion. She had, after all, helped Lydia solve Gabriel's mysterious cryptogram, and – mere days later – Lydia married him and left the city.

"Well, I think it's wonderful," Caroline said finally. "I love it when my favourite people marry each other. Monty, will you allow me to steal Lydia for a moment? I'd like to catch up before the recital begins."

"Of course," Gabriel said. He pressed a quick kiss on Lydia's knuckles. "Don't gossip for too long, my lady."

Lydia understood. Any information she gave Caroline must be kept to a minimum.

Lydia followed the duchess into a quiet alcove, where Caroline's face turned serious. "What's happened?" she asked without preamble.

Lydia tried to keep her expression neutral. The other woman was perceptive and clever, and her sharp regard saw too much. "I'm not sure what you mean."

Carline's gaze probed hers. "Don't avoid the question," she said calmly. "Days ago, you visited me with Monty's cryptogram. Now I've discovered that you hastily married, and he whisked you away to Meadowcroft without even a letter of explanation."

Lydia curled her fingers into her palm. A part of her longed to tell Caroline everything, but the secret of Gabriel's past was not hers to share. Now it was one they carried together. "I can't tell you," she said in a low voice. "I wish I could, but I can't."

The duchess was the closest thing Lydia had to a friend; Caroline had been there for her when everyone else in society shunned or ignored her. To every other person at the Arundells', Lydia was a curiosity. She was a spinster of seven-and-twenty who had unexpectedly wedded their most eligible bachelor. How had she succeeded where the most beautiful debutantes of the season had failed? Why her? Why *that* one?

And the answer to their question was simple: duty and deception. She was not such an exception to their rules as they imagined.

Caroline must have noticed Lydia's uncertainty. She gave a soft sigh. "Just tell me you are safe."

"I'm safe," Lydia confirmed. "That's one thing you need not worry about with Gabriel." Lydia paused, noting for the first time that the duchess seemed more weary than usual. There were smudges of blue beneath her eyes. "Are *you* well?"

The other woman glanced at the people around them, her composure less steady than before. "Is it noticeable that I'm not?"

"No. You just seem a bit fatigued. What's the matter?"

Caroline's lips twisted. "My husband is in London. And with Julian's other apartments being let until the end of the season, he'll be staying at Hastings House until the next session of Parliament."

Lydia winced. She knew intimately the heartbreak of childhood love developing into estrangement. But Caroline was not open about how she fell out with her duke, who spent much of his time travelling, unless the House of Lords was sitting. He never even visited his wife.

"Will you be departing for Ravenhill, then?" Lydia asked, referring to the duke and duchess's estate in the country.

Caroline looked annoyed. "No. I'm not letting Julian run me out of London. I'll endure it until *he* leaves."

Though she sounded confident, Lydia perceived an undercurrent of frustration. Caroline was more upset than she let on. But there was no time for Lydia to inquire further – at that moment, Lady Arundell clapped her hands and let everyone know that the recital was about to commence.

Gabriel approached and gently took Lydia's arm. "I apologise for interrupting, but Lady Montgomery and I will take our seats."

Caroline nodded graciously. "Of course. I shall see you for tea when you return to London, Lydia."

As Gabriel led her into their seats, he murmured, "Is all well?"

"Yes."

He helped her to a chair in the ballroom, requisitioned tonight for the singer's performance. The candlelight was low, filling the room with a dim, pleasant glow. As Gabriel settled beside her, his thigh pressed to hers. Even through layers of clothing, she could feel his warmth and solidity.

Lydia used the rare opportunity of proximity and circumstance to shift closer. "This is my first time hearing an opera singer," she whispered.

He glanced at her in surprise. "Is it?"

"Aunt Frances preferred the theatre."

Gabriel nodded. "Is that why you plucked this particular invitation from the pile?"

"Perhaps." She fidgeted with her reticule. "Do you enjoy the opera?"

The low light obscured everyone's features. Gabriel didn't have to play the charming gentleman now; his façade could drop. It had been easy to forget, until this moment, that the real Gabriel operated in the shadows.

"I don't enjoy anything," Gabriel said in a low voice.

"No?" She whispered. "Nothing at all?"

He seemed to consider her question. Then he whispered, "I enjoy you."

Lydia smiled at that. It softened something inside her as the opera singer stepped into a halo of candlelight and began to sing.

16

G abriel couldn't focus on the recital.

Instead, he watched Lydia as she leaned forward, so captivated that her whole body reacted to the singer's voice like a reed surrendering to the wind. Tears glistened in her eyes. Some strange emotion surged within Gabriel – yearning, yes. But it was combined with a sort of envy at seeing her thus moved by a performance for which he felt so little. What would it be like to share that unabashed enjoyment again? To experience emotions so fully?

Lydia reached over to grasp his hand as if it were the most natural thing in the world. Gabriel was startled by the gesture, his jealousy suddenly replaced by an overwhelming desire. This woman smoothed the serrated edges of his soul and trusted him enough to seek the comfort of his touch. She tended to injuries he had only previously nursed himself. For so long, he had existed only in terms of his title – but Lord Montgomery was a man with no dark past, while Gabriel St Clair's was as black as the deepest ocean. She alone glimpsed the truth of him.

And still, she reached for his hand.

Still, she had kissed him two nights before.

Her lips parted in concentration. Gabriel focused on those luscious lips, all too aware of their petal-soft texture. He regretted not kissing her before he'd left England – he'd squandered so many things with her. It was miraculous that she didn't hate him.

Lydia moved. The flickering candlelight stroked along her cheekbone, exposing the flushed skin of her face. Gabriel's breath caught in his throat. He envisioned her like that in his bedchamber, naked and writhing as he took her. The image was so potent that a peculiar dizziness overcame Gabriel and left him unsteady.

His expression turned sharp, assessing. Did he affect *her*? Or was he alone in this madness?

He was already tugging at his evening glove before he finished the thought.

With that barrier gone, Gabriel experimentally slid his hand up Lydia's arm to brush his bare fingertips against the exposed skin above her own long evening glove.

Lydia caught her breath, and her eyes shifted to meet his. They stared at each other in the low candlelight, and it was as if they were the only people in that room. Gabriel's entire body was attuned to Lydia. To the heat of her, to every reaction at his touch. She trembled as his thumb glided down that little square patch of bare skin in a teasing caress. Her response gratified him. More: it dissolved the ice in his blood, leaving heat in its path.

So this was what it was like to be alive. He'd believed his

soul dead for so long that he'd almost forgotten what it was like to hunger for Lydia. She was the only thing he had ever coveted in his entire life.

Suddenly, that ballroom became an impediment. All the people in it were obstacles. Here, he couldn't touch her freely. He couldn't lean forward and nip at those full pink lips until she kissed him. He couldn't push up that pretty skirt she wore and set his mouth against her just to hear her scream his name.

A shuddering breath left Lydia. In her gaze, Gabriel glimpsed a need that echoed his own. The aria faded to background noise, and all that remained was the texture of her skin against his fingertips, gooseflesh puckering at his touch. Did she respond like that everywhere? He hadn't seen her without clothes.

A flash of desire in her eyes indicated that his thoughts were not secret. Her teeth snagged her lower lip, and his attention fixated on the movement. Such a small gesture that betrayed a great deal.

You shouldn't want me, he thought to her. *Broken man that I am. You can't fix shattered glass.*

Then the singing ceased, and the spell was broken. The audience around Gabriel and Lydia broke into applause, and servants rushed to light more candles in their sconces. Gabriel quickly dropped his hand from Lydia's arm and slid his glove back on.

The room became ablaze with golden light, and the din of chatter increased as guests left their chairs to congregate before dinner.

Gabriel helped Lydia to her feet. "Must we stay for dinner?" she whispered.

He paused. He shouldn't indulge her – shouldn't give her pleasure when he couldn't be a proper husband – but all his thoughts fixated on the lingering sensation of her skin at his fingertips. At the meagre access he'd been granted and the strange lightness in his chest that he hadn't experienced for years.

"It might be considered rude to leave," he said.

"Us? Newlyweds on our honeymoon? I think we're considered the exception."

"Here I was thinking you were growing bored of Meadowcroft."

She leaned in, her voice for his ears alone. "Bored of Meadowcroft. Not of my husband."

Her smile was contagious, an adorable twist of her lips. She wanted to be alone. *With him.* Despite everything. The buoyancy spread even further through his chest.

Before he could squash it down, he said, "You inform Lady Arundell, and I'll retrieve our coats."

Her grin was brighter than the candlelight.

As Gabriel accepted their garments from the servant and waited for Lydia to apologise for their premature departure, the Duchess of Hastings approached. "Leaving so soon?"

"It seems Lady Montgomery is eager to return home, and so am I."

Caroline assessed him, her gaze as piercing as a needle. Gabriel's cousin had always been profoundly clever; after Moscow, she was one of the few people he couldn't fool. He imagined she recognised the loneliness in his soul as matching hers.

"You seem different," she said softly.

"Do I?"

"Happy." Her regard was relentless. "Or the closest thing to it since your return."

Something about that disconcerted him. Yes, he supposed the strange levity he'd identified earlier was the first twinge of joy he'd experienced in years – a feeling that had become as foreign as a new language.

But he detested it; that thrill left him too vulnerable to his enemies. It left *Lydia* vulnerable.

What was happiness in the hands of an assassin but a weapon to be wielded like a blade?

Caroline made a faint noise. "And now you're thinking too much."

"You're a romantic." His voice was almost harsh. "I would have thought your own marriage might have disabused you of the notion."

Caroline's expression hardened. "It's not romanticism. I know what it looks like when someone is trying to shut another person out."

"Leave it alone, Caro."

"Monty," Caroline said in a low voice. "Consider how rare it is to be given a second chance with someone." Her lips twisted. "Many are not so fortunate."

Lydia said her last goodbye to Lady Arundell and started toward Gabriel. Her eyes met his, and that abnormal joy rose inside him again. This time, he suppressed it. Caroline was right – many people weren't so fortunate.

But he had to choose Lydia's life over his own happiness.

17

Lydia stared at her husband, sitting on the other side of the carriage as they travelled back to Meadowcroft.

The lone swaying lamp near the window cast deep shadows across Gabriel's austere face, leaving no softened edges. Instead, his harsh features communicated a warning as clear as the stare of a lethal animal: *Stay away. Approach me at your risk.*

What on earth happened while Lydia was saying goodbye to Lady Arundell? She'd noticed Gabriel's aloofness when she rejoined him in the hall, where he waited with the Duchess of Hastings. Oh, he was still polite – as they said their farewells to the other guests, his smile had been as bright and dazzling as a spring day. Lydia, too, had almost been convinced she'd imagined it.

But when he took her arm, Gabriel's touch hadn't lingered. There were no scorching glances. When he shepherded her into the carriage with a hand on her back, the contact was brief and impersonal.

And once the door shut, Gabriel's deceitful smile had vanished, and he settled into his seat with the cold immobility of a statue.

The transformation left Lydia's thoughts discordant. Each passing mile of their journey matched the distance between them. How could he be a mere arm's length from her and still seem so far away? He was as isolated as a ship anchored in the broadest ocean.

How was this the same man who'd gazed at Lydia earlier as if she were a strange and beautiful treasure?

Now, she was left with her armour shattered. He'd impaired her defences and left her vulnerable to the elements. Open to harm.

Utterly, utterly exposed.

A surge of anger and frustration flared within her. How could Gabriel sit there so calmly while she was frayed and damaged? Her fingernails curled into her dress. She wanted to smash through Gabriel's own fortifications, crack him apart, leave him unguarded. Let him know how it felt to be raw and exposed.

An idea came to her as she stared at him in the dimmed carriage. She did not have to bear the weight of her vulnerability alone; the darkness could give her courage.

Lydia leaned forward and put her palm on his trouser-clad knee. His sharp intake of breath gratified her as she ran her fingers slowly up his muscular thigh.

Gabriel's hand came down over hers. "What are you doing?" His voice was as cold as tundra, but she had heard the involuntary intake of breath, and knew her husband was a consummate actor.

"Touching you. I should think that was obvious."

But when she tried to move again, he gripped her. "Lydia."

Very well, she had other means. Lydia pulled his hand towards her and pressed her lips to his knuckles. "Gabriel."

She grazed the back of his wrist with her teeth, and Gabriel made a faint noise. "When I married you, I hadn't realised I'd wedded the most concupiscent woman in the country."

Lydia wondered if he intended these sharp words to drive her away. Instead, it only hardened her resolve. She leaned forward, her lips finding his with unerring accuracy.

Gabriel gripped her arms and broke the kiss. "*Lydia*."

Her chest rose and fell in agitation. "If I'm lustful, perhaps it's because my husband implied earlier that I might expect something other than a frigid reception in this carriage."

Gabriel's regard was sharp, those shadowed eyes searching hers. For a moment, she wondered if he would reject her. If he would push her to the other side of the carriage as if sending her in a boat out to sea.

"Then tell me what you want," he said, his voice ragged. Proof of his icy defences splintering. "Speak plain."

She comprehended then that she could shatter him. "I want your hand beneath my skirts," she whispered. "I want you to touch me back."

Gabriel gave a rough, savage growl and slammed his lips against hers. Lydia groaned as he pressed her against the side of the carriage and shoved her knees apart.

He pulled his lips back from hers. "You want me to fuck you with my fingers until you come? Is that it?"

"Yes," she said, reaching for him again. "*Yes*."

He released a harsh breath and kissed her again, his hand shoving at her petticoats until he found her drawers. She groaned into his mouth as he located the slit in her garment. Spurred by his touch, she moved for the front of his trousers.

Gabriel's free hand caught her wrist, his message clear: *Your pleasure, not mine.*

Then his fingers thrust inside her. Lydia arched her neck with a gasp as Gabriel's fingers slid in and out. He timed his movements with the speed of her breath, increasing with every uneven exhalation. The rough cadence of his breathing matched hers. She kissed the length of his stubbled jawline, wishing they were not in that carriage. Wishing she could have him bare. Wishing she could extend that moment beyond her fleeting pleasure.

But she couldn't. Lydia came with a harsh cry that seemed to echo in the confined space.

As her climax subsided, she clung to him and kept her lips pressed against his neck. That single point of contact gave her access to his pulse, which pounded in a discordant beat mirroring her own.

Stay with me, she wanted to say. *Stay with me. Let me have you for a moment longer.*

But Gabriel pulled away from Lydia and settled on the opposite seat. Then he extracted a handkerchief from his pocket, cleaning his fingers with almost punishing swipes of the fabric. He was withdrawing from her, his heart unreachable now.

The interior of the carriage felt as cold as a winter landscape.

"I hope that met with your satisfaction," he said flatly as he gazed out the window.

Lydia's face burned with humiliation and shame. She

shoved down her skirts and looked away from him, toward the dark scenery outside. Their moment was over.

He'd crushed her armour and left her with a thousand tiny cuts.

ᴄᴍꜱ 18 ᴄᴍꜱ

G abriel crossed the hallway, searching for his wife.

Lydia was usually in the solarium writing long letters to her aunt at this hour. But he opened the door and found it empty, the desk scattered with uneven stacks of stationery and crumpled paper. That evidence of her unease hooked his chest like a claw.

He'd wondered what she put in those notes to her aunt; if she had developed a talent for lying in her letters. But the crushed, half-written missives were proof it did not come as naturally to her as it did to him.

He picked up a crumpled paper, gently smoothing the edges.

We attended a gathering at the Arundells yesterday evening. My first time hearing an opera singer! Aunt, I think I held Lord Montgomery's hand the entire time. What a lovely husband he is, to

We had such a marvellous time

I was so overcome that we left early. I—

She had scratched ebony streaks of ink across the entire letter, blemishes that echoed across his heart. He'd hurt her last night. He'd been intentionally cruel to push her away, but rather than feeling relief, the proof of her dismay only choked the breath from his lungs.

Gabriel caught Lydia's scent as he turned towards the door, and the fist around his heart tightened its grip. "Mrs Marshall," he said when he spotted the housekeeper heading across the hall. He set down the crumpled letter. "Have you seen Lady Montgomery?"

"I believe she's in the greenhouse, my lord," Mrs Marshall said.

The greenhouse. The place Gabriel had suggested might give her a feeling of outdoors while keeping her secluded within Meadowcroft's house. Limitations for which he was responsible. The location alone suggested she didn't want his company.

"Thank you," he said.

He needed to find Lydia and apologise for being a fool. He almost let out a bitter laugh at the thought – he hadn't apologised for anything in years, and he owed her a hell of a lot more than the words, *I'm sorry.*

The greenhouse was silent. The air was redolent with the sharp aroma of botanicals, the fragrance of exotic blooms, and damp air. The glass ceiling arched above him, a view of the clouds beyond obscured by vegetation that thrived in the heat. His father had imported everything from abroad in Gabriel's absence.

The temperature reminded Gabriel too much of Kabul.

He wandered down the main aisle of the greenhouse. He didn't have to walk far before he located Lydia near a stone bench. She was admiring a crimson flower, and her dark hair was curling at the back of her neck from the humidity. God, but he longed to press his lips there. Kiss his way down the arch of her spine. He wanted to see her bare.

"It doesn't have a strong scent," he said. Lydia straightened. When she said nothing, Gabriel edged closer. "You'll find other flowers with stronger perfume, if that's what you want."

Her fingers curled into her palms. "Perhaps I'd just like to admire this lovely one."

Gabriel paused as hot shame snaked through him. He cleared his throat. "*Lilium lancifolium*," he said, reaching to caress its spotted petals. "I noticed it on my travels in the east of Russia. It's indigenous to that part of the world."

If anything, her expression only hardened. "Then I ought to pity this poor flower for being taken from its home and confined in a greenhouse."

"Pity it if you'd like." His voice was sober. "The owner deserves your censure."

Lydia's chin raised a notch, and her lips took on a determined line. "You are not here to discuss flowers with me," she said sharply. "If you want to monitor my well-being, I can tell you it's unnecessary. One of your men is stationed directly outside the glasshouse. Callahan, I believe his name was."

He had not seen her like this since the Duchess of

Hastings' house party. Then, as now, her fury had battered him like jagged stones. A year ago, he'd built the armour to defend himself from her condemnation; now, he let those sharp edges penetrate his skin as punishments for hurting her.

"That's not why I'm here, either."

"No?" She arched an eyebrow. "I can't imagine it was for me. You desire my company as much as you desired a wife."

Gabriel pressed his teeth together. *You deserve this*, he said to himself. Hell, he deserved worse. She ought to hate him. Why *was* he here? He'd succeeded in pushing her away; that would keep her safe.

Wasn't her indifference what he wanted?

But those motives became unthinkable the moment he'd seen her humiliation the previous evening. He had given her pleasure and then made her feel shame for it. *That* was unforgivable.

"I'm sorry," he told her. When she did nothing but stare at him, he let out a breath. "I was a bastard to you last night, and I'm sorry for it." Her scrutiny was like a stone pressing against his lungs. Gabriel felt compelled to fill the silence. "Will you walk with me?"

Her silence was the longest moment of his life. Then she nodded wordlessly and grabbed her shawl. She draped it around her shoulders.

Gabriel noticed Callahan in his watchful position in the gardens and gave the guard a subtle gesture to indicate all was well. Callahan flashed a grin and promptly walked away to provide husband and wife with privacy.

It was mid-afternoon, and the slight chill to the air tinged Lydia's cheeks with rouge. She gripped her shawl more tightly around her shoulders, and Gabriel wondered if it was because of the cold or for protection. Last night she'd reached for him, and Gabriel had rejected her in the most vicious way possible.

"You're pushing me away," she said finally, as if she heard his thoughts.

Gabriel made a noise and gazed up at the trees lining the garden path. "I only know how to push people away. I'm afraid you're not an exception."

"When you proposed, you told me this wouldn't be a real marriage." Her voice was quiet; it didn't seem to fit such a sombre topic. It was a voice made for whispering to Gabriel in the darkness, when he needed her most. "Last night felt real to me."

He wanted to tell her that, for a blissful few hours, it felt real to him, too. That he couldn't help but think of the life they might have had if he'd stayed ten years ago. If he had decided to marry her then. Upon arrival in Kabul, the conflicts between the emir and his brother ought to have been a warning for Gabriel to hand in his notice and return to England. But he foolishly remained, then he had taken the assignment in Russia and become a man unworthy of her.

"I said that because I'm not capable of being a good husband," he said quietly. "Not since Moscow. Perhaps not since Kabul."

She fidgeted with her shawl. "You never told me what happened in Moscow."

Memories flickered through his mind. He'd spent four long years there reminding himself that he was not the man he pretended to be. That his name was not Alexei Borislov

Zhelyabov and that his mission served a purpose. He vowed to return to England one day and pick up the pieces of the life he only dimly remembered.

But he'd returned, and those pieces had been shattered beyond repair. He had no life left to rebuild.

Gabriel stopped on the path. Lydia stared up at him with an expression that was a touch guarded, for she had come to expect rejection. And for that, he would never forgive himself.

"I did unspeakable things," he said softly. "And last night, you looked at me as if I had never done them."

Lydia's expression softened slightly. "You were wrong before. You didn't say what you did because you're incapable of being a good husband. You told me that because you intend to spend the rest of your life punishing yourself for Moscow."

"What's the difference?" he asked tiredly.

"The difference is that you've proved you *can* be a good husband." Her eyes held his. "It's just that you don't think you deserve to try."

Gabriel lifted a hand to her face, marvelling at the softness of her skin. Regretting all the years he'd wasted without her. He ought to have asked to touch her years before; perhaps then he would never have left. "Just think of what gentlemen would say if they knew the woman notorious for her iciness had such a soft heart," he told her. "They would have offered for her long ago."

"Tell me what happened in Moscow," she said, her voice quiet.

Her mind had the unerring precision of a hunter's arrow. She had honed her skill in his absence.

"Why?" Why did she want to know everything he wanted so badly to forget?

"Because," she said. "I want to know what made you turn me away from your door three years ago."

"Then I'll tell you one day. Perhaps as a reminder of why I'm not fit to be your husband."

She stared at him for a long moment and then turned and started down the path again. Gabriel quickly followed her. "And when you catch Medvedev, what then?" She spoke as briskly as she walked. That tender look she'd given him was gone now; her anger had renewed purpose. "Shall we cohabitate at Meadowcroft, or do you intend to leave Surrey at the first opportunity?"

When Gabriel married her, he thought it would be easy to decide his future: he would leave her at one of his estates, and they would live in separate locations. No one would think twice about an estranged husband and wife. It was the way of the nobility.

But now that he had spent time with her – had kissed her, heard her laugh, made her smile – his old plans were receding from his mind. And that was too dangerous for her. After all, Medvedev was not the only enemy he had made over the years.

A breath left him. "I don't know what my plans are anymore."

Her jaw tightened. "Then tell me what you intended when you asked me to marry you."

"I would return to London." His words rang hollow, much like his life would be without her in it. "Reside in my townhouse. Encourage you to do what you like."

"What I like?" she echoed softly. "And where, in this hypothetical scene, did you place me? Meadowcroft?"

He paused again, taking that moment to take his fill of her. Her hair had come loose from its chignon, coiling around her face in soft mahogany ringlets. Such an innocent countenance; it didn't match her eyes. Those watched him with a circumspection that scraped at his soul. He wanted to take that look from her and make her laugh again.

But he had not earned it.

"In my mind, I always place you in Meadowcroft," he told her. Too tempted to touch her, Gabriel pushed his hands into his pockets. "Every memory I have of you is here, with the wind in your hair and a smile on your face."

"But you're never with me, are you?" Her question was faint, spoken like a whispering breeze.

He shook his head. He couldn't help himself now; he lifted a hand to feel one of her soft curls. "When I think of myself with you, it's in the Bromes' garden. Near the men I killed."

She flinched. "What if I don't want to be here without you? Does it matter that all my memories of you are at Meadowcroft?"

"Yes." He held her hair to the light. He had yet to see it cascading down her naked back. He never would. "Your memories were of another man."

Her regard was challenging. "Were they? Very well, then. Maybe I won't stay at Meadowcroft if you've decided I ought to do whatever I want."

Of course she wouldn't want to stay. Perhaps those memories of their childhood carried some pain. "Stay wherever you like. I've fifteen other properties if this one doesn't suit. If you want distance, I even have one in Scotland."

Her expression grew more severe, but she didn't recoil from his touch. Rather, she kept her attention on him unwaveringly. "And what if Scotland doesn't satisfy? What if I desired to go somewhere further? In your mind we're already still as far apart as England is from Russia."

Lydia's voice scraped in Gabriel's ears like a blade over rough stone. If she had made this a test, he was failing it. But maybe she wanted to hurt him back; perhaps she understood that the mere notion of her leaving chafed at him. Even Scotland now seemed too far. He wanted her somewhere close.

"Where do you have in mind?"

She blinked as if the question surprised her. Then she lifted her chin. "I've never been to Paris. Or Spain. Parts of America, I hear, are quite lovely. Lady Derby has friends in New York I could stay with for an extended visit."

America.

Across the entire ocean.

Leagues of water between them.

Already, he imagined the space between them growing; she was slipping through his grasp like water.

"Of course." His words sounded hollow to his ears. "Travel wherever you like."

"And if this is not to be a real marriage, then what of lovers?" she continued.

His jaw clenched so hard that he swore he heard it crack. "Lovers," he repeated.

"Yes. Lovers." She stepped away from him then, shying from his touch. "Had you considered them in your original plan for us, or did you mean me to remain alone and unloved for the rest of our sham of a marriage?" Her eyes flashed with anger. "I already spent years waiting for you. Will you demand that I spend the rest of it being faithful?"

Gabriel was consumed by a searing shame that writhed within him like a serpent. But in an instant, that feeling was supplanted by a vision that was even more agonising. He saw her surrendering herself to another man, crying out his name in ecstasy. The image clawed at Gabriel's insides.

"Is there someone you want to fuck?" he asked flatly.

Her lips tightened at his blunt, vulgar question. "You. But since you have no interest—"

Gabriel snapped. He grabbed the front of her dress and yanked her against him. His mouth covered hers in a hard kiss. A rough sound left Lydia's lips, her hand coming up to grip his hair. Her nails dug into his scalp as she kissed him back.

"I have an interest," he said, dragging his lips from hers. "Whenever I see you, I have to stop myself from pulling you into any available room and pleasuring you until neither one of us can move. I want you every damn hour of every damn day, so badly I can't even think straight."

"Then be my first," she whispered against his lips. "I've always wanted you to be my first."

First and only and last, he wanted to say. His thoughts shifted into something uncivilised and savage, pulsing with a need to claim her. He already wore her mark on him.

He pushed her against a nearby tree. The moment of indecision – had he hurt her? Was he too forceful? – passed as Lydia seized his jacket in a hard grasp and returned his kiss with equal ferocity. Her hand found courage, those clever fingers dancing down the buttons of his waistcoat. Gabriel's kiss was artless; his emotions warred within him as she plucked at his shirt. His thoughts were a maelstrom, a cacophony of unruly feelings. All he knew was that he craved the heat of her. Something tangible. Something he could think about when his mind became mired in memories of Moscow, of Kabul, of all the things he'd done. His past was like a great black pit with which he was always backsliding until he heard her voice.

Until he touched her.

She gave him courage enough to move again.

As his fingertips skimmed the neckline of her dress, a shot split the air. A bullet whizzed past and smashed into the bark next to Lydia's head.

Gabriel reacted on instinct. He pushed Lydia to the ground and used his body to shield her. Then, he looked up to see someone running away from them – one of Medvedev's men.

"*Montgomery!*" The voice belonged to Callahan – he must have heard the shot. The guard raced up, his breath heaving.

Gabriel hauled Lydia to her feet, fear tightening his grip. "Take her," he ordered Callahan, nudging Lydia toward the other man. "I want her inside the house and guarded at all times."

Lydia started to protest. "But—"

"Go with him," Gabriel said, speeding away. "Take care of my wife, Callahan."

Gabriel sprinted out of the gardens after the gunman. He panted, his throat burning with the effort to catch up with the other man. His lead narrowed, but he still couldn't determine the attacker's identity. Feodor, perhaps – Medvedev's best sharpshooter. Or Boris, who had a proven skill with a rifle. There were dozens of men employed by Medvedev with the talent to shoot with such precision that –

Cold fear increased his pace. Lydia had almost died. That man had nearly murdered her.

But just as they reached a clearing, the sharpshooter launched himself into the saddle of a waiting horse and raced away.

Gabriel stopped, panting, gazing after the rider as he sped off.

He was finished with waiting for Medvedev. He would find the Russian himself.

CRR 19 CRR

G abriel returned to the house and found Lydia with
Callahan in the sitting room. She paced anxiously
near the fireplace. Callahan, in contrast, leaned against the
window frame with a sombre expression.

Lydia halted when she noticed Gabriel, her chest rising
and falling in agitation. "Did you find him?"

Gabriel could barely face looking at Lydia – his mind
fixated on the memory of the bullet striking the tree next
to her. Medvedev's sharpshooter had merely been off by
the length of Gabriel's shortest finger. Divine intervention
in the form of a sudden breeze could easily have altered
the bullet's trajectory. Such small details made the ultimate
difference between her life and death.

"He had a horse saddled and waiting," Gabriel said, his
voice tight.

Lydia fidgeted with her shawl. "And now?"

"I'm leaving for London directly. Callahan and the other
men will watch over you while I'm gone."

The guard gave a nod. Callahan wouldn't fail; he had a reputation almost as violent as Gabriel's.

Lydia cast a meaningful look at Callahan. Understanding her unspoken message, the bodyguard cleared his throat and left the room. Knowing Callahan, he would be just out of earshot.

"How long will you be gone this time?" Lydia asked. Gabriel stood utterly still as she gently brushed the leaves and dirt from his jacket. He almost wished she wouldn't; the wild state of his appearance mirrored his jumbled thoughts. It seemed appropriate, somehow, to maintain it.

"I don't know," he answered honestly.

Gabriel kept his attention fixed over Lydia's shoulder, lest he be tempted to kiss her again. Back in the garden, he had forgotten himself. He had let her overwhelm his mind with such a maelstrom of feelings, memories, and desire that he'd forgotten his forced indifference was in order to protect *her*.

His past would always catch up with him. Always.

Lydia put her hand over his heart, and Gabriel curled his fingers into fists.

"Look at me," she whispered.

He clenched his jaw and met her gaze. Her eyes softened, but Gabriel saw beyond her lovely, dear face. Leaves and twigs had become tangled in her coiffure. Grass stained her pretty dress, and a splatter of mud smudged one of her sleeves. Each imperfection was yet another indictment of his failures.

Next time, the bullet might not miss.

Abruptly, Gabriel turned to the door. "I'll see you when I return," he said.

He left without looking back.

* * *

Wentworth raised an eyebrow as Gabriel entered his study hours later.

Gabriel was aware that his appearance had not improved during the carriage ride to London. His boots were still splattered with mud from pursuing Medvedev's sharpshooter, and his hair was tousled from running his hands through it.

Still, he had no wish to return to his house for a bath. His journey had given him enough time to plan how he'd confront his enemy. To picture his revenge. After all, Gabriel had learned brutality under Medvedev's vigilant guidance. He understood how to deploy it without mercy.

There would be no compassion for the man who threatened Lydia's safety.

"A second visit so soon," Wentworth said, leaning back in his chair. "Here I was assuming you might take my advice and attempt to enjoy your honeymoon. How foolish of me."

"One of Medvedev's men almost killed Lydia," Gabriel said curtly. "Because you haven't done your job."

Wentworth leaned forward, alert now. "When?"

"This morning, on the grounds just outside the house. If there's one sharpshooter near Meadowcroft, there might be more. Tell me you have a lead on where Medvedev is hiding."

Something flickered across Wentworth's face.

"You know something." Gabriel took a step forward, his entire body taut with barely contained violence. "Tell me now."

The other man took a sharp breath. "Fine. There's a bawdy house by the dockyards," he said. "The dockworkers there tend to get chatty after buying a woman. One of them is a man of interest for the Home Office named Rafferty; he runs a smuggling ring that might have been in contact with members of the Syndicate. I'd planned to question him tonight."

"Then I'm coming with you."

Wentworth sat back with an intent look. "If you come with me, you follow my lead. I've no interest in leaving this man dead at the brothel. Prostitutes already have enough shit to deal with. Understand?"

Gabriel gave a nod. "Fine. But know that I intend to do whatever it takes to get my answers."

Hours later, after scouting the brothel's entrance, Gabriel and Wentworth watched dockworkers begin to enter the establishment. Wentworth's eyes focused on an older man strolling through the alleyway, then knocking on the door of the bawdy house for admittance.

"There's our quarry," Wentworth murmured. "We'll wait for him to hire a woman."

Gabriel's limbs were stiff from loitering in an adjacent side alley. The misting rain had long since begun to penetrate his wool overcoat. But he ignored these discomforts and concentrated on what he was about to do; the anger during his earlier carriage ride had changed into a cold rage. The weight of the pistol hidden beneath his clothes was a reminder of how far his control had stretched. The bullet that nearly killed Lydia had been his limit.

After a few long minutes, Wentworth gave the signal, and the men crossed the road. Once inside, Gabriel's senses were overwhelmed by the smell of perfume intended to mask the sweat, body odour, and stale stench of tupping.

The prostitutes immediately began preening themselves. Gabriel and Wentworth might have dressed down for the evening, but their attire bore unmistakable evidence that they had money enough to spend. An evening with one of them might enable a prostitute to keep a few coins after she paid the landlord and the bawd.

The madam came forward to greet them. She scrutinised their clothes and clean, handsome faces. "Welcome," she said in a thick, throaty voice. "Come to purchase a girl for the evenin'?"

Before Gabriel or Wentworth could respond, one of the women approached, her dress displaying a generous amount of cleavage. "I'm free, ma'am," she said, eyeing Gabriel with a hungry look. "Be happy to service this one. Maybe even his friend, as well."

Wentworth ignored the doxy and held up a roll of notes to the madam. "For you and your girls, if you tell me which room the man in the red cap went into, and you don't come upstairs even if you hear him scream."

The madam's attention was fixed on the money, but she made no move to take it. "If ye hurt my girl in there with him—"

"No harm will come to her. Upon my honour."

"Can't depend on a man's honour." Nevertheless, she plucked the wad out of his hand. "But I can depend on this. He's on the second floor, the third door on the right. Ye leave a corpse up there, yer takin' care of it yerself."

Wentworth bowed before heading to the stairwell. Gabriel followed him, catching the eye of the earlier prostitute, who gave a wink and wiggled her fingers as if to say, *Come back anytime*.

Gabriel and Wentworth climbed the stairs and stopped at the correct door. Inside, a man was moaning with pleasure. Wentworth didn't wait – he raised a booted foot and kicked open the door.

The prostitute rose from her knees with a startled screech. Rafferty whirled, his trousers around his ankles.

Unfortunate timing, indeed.

Gabriel tossed the woman a dressing gown left discarded over a chair. "Out."

The prostitute fled.

"What the?" Rafferty sputtered, his mouth opening and closing like a fish. "You can't just come in here and—"

"For God's sake," Wentworth said in disgust. "Pull up your trousers."

"Sod off and wait your turn!"

Gabriel grabbed the pistol concealed within his overcoat and aimed it at Rafferty. "He said to pull up your trousers."

The other man gaped at the pistol. Gabriel motioned impatiently with the weapon, and Rafferty quickly bent to pull up the garment, his hands shaking as he fastened the buttons. "I – I don't..."

Wentworth exchanged a sharp glance with Gabriel, who understood the unspoken message: *Do not shoot this man in a bawdy house, you absolute lackwit*. But Gabriel knew how to interrogate a man until he broke. He had been trained for it.

"Now... now, I don't want any trouble..."

"No, I don't expect so," Gabriel said, with deadly calm.

"Not when you have cargo that still needs to be unloaded for the Syndicate and money to collect. Yes?"

Fear distorted Rafferty's features. He lunged for the door, but Gabriel was too fast. He had one of his throwing knives out in a blink. The blade sliced through the other man's hand just as he reached for the doorknob.

The man shouted. Blood spattered on the carpet at his feet. Something went quiet in Gabriel's mind – a dark, cavernous mental space. A place where Gabriel St Clair ceased to exist, and guilt did not impair his work.

"Monty," Wentworth said quietly. "You promised."

"Not to worry," Gabriel said, approaching a whimpering Rafferty. He slid his pistol back into his coat; he'd always preferred knives. "I'm not going to kill him. As long as he cooperates."

Gabriel seized the hilt of the blade, and Rafferty hollered again. "Shh. That's enough. We're in a business establishment, and the girls here still have to work. So let me make one thing clear. I take this blade out now, and you may still have use of your hand. I twist it, and you learn how to function left-handed. Understand me?"

The man gave another pathetic mewl, but nodded. His chest rose and fell with his breathing.

"Good." Gabriel's features settled into an icy disdain. It was a look many men had seen before their deaths, one that he knew was as cold as a Russian winter. "You've done dealings with someone for your new shipment. I'm uncertain of the name he goes by, but you might know him as a man with one eye."

Rafferty's breathing became erratic. "No," he said. "No, no, no, no. Not someone I can cross, mate. You don't—"

"Oh, I comprehend perfectly. You're aware of his reputation, and he's paying you a lot of money. Not the sort of man you betray."

Rafferty nodded eagerly. "That's it. Can't help you, mate."

"No, you misunderstand me." Gabriel leaned in and whispered, "Who do you think took his eye?"

The other man gaped at him, his body going utterly, utterly still. "I can't," the man whispered.

Gabriel twisted his dagger slightly. The man shouted, and Gabriel felt that animal part of him stir in response. It found satisfaction in violence. It had been Gabriel's language for too long.

"Remember what I told you about this blade," he said to Rafferty. "Either this man is worth your hand, or you tell me where to find him."

"I don't—"

"He has people with him," Wentworth interrupted. "They would be seeking either shelter or entertainment within the East End. Where would they go?"

They would not be found at the more upscale establishments like the Brimstone. Nicholas Thorne was not a man even the Syndicate would cross – he commanded the territory of the East End, after all. But even those involved in the Syndicate had needs.

Rafferty wavered, but then Gabriel turned the knife ever so slightly, and he gave a cry. "Stop. *Stop!* There's the underground fights. The location moves every time, but I've heard a few make bets."

Wentworth and Gabriel exchanged glances. They had both heard of the underground fighting rings. Bareknuckle boxing was the lifeblood of certain families in the East End.

Fighters made enough to feed their wives and children. It was the only way some people survived in the streets.

"When does the next fight take place?" Gabriel asked.

"Tomorrow," Rafferty said. "In a warehouse by the docks. Ask if the doorman knows where you can find the butcher. He'll take you down the stairs. I've heard the one-eyed man has men who fight there."

Gabriel's mind worked, forming a plan and deciding what he would need to do to keep Lydia safe. He would do anything.

Anything.

With a rough jerk, he pulled the knife out of Rafferty's hand. The man's shout rang in his ears. Panting, Rafferty held up the quivering, bloody evidence of how far Medvedev had pushed Gabriel. The stained carpet at their feet would need replacing.

Gabriel calmly removed a handkerchief from his pocket and handed it to Rafferty. The other man swayed from blood loss, whimpering in pain as he wrapped his wound. Gabriel took mercy on the old man and set a coin down on the prostitute's nightstand. "For the doctor," he said. "And if I find out you've told your associate about this meeting, I won't be so merciful."

Wentworth and Gabriel left the brothel. As they strolled down the street, Wentworth said, "That wasn't necessary."

"I got the answer out of him."

"And I wouldn't blame Rafferty if he told Medvedev because you stabbed him in the hand, Monty."

"I left him money for the doctor."

"You still damn well stabbed him in the hand."

Gabriel looked at Wentworth sharply. "And if Rafferty

tells Medvedev anything, I'll visit him in the night and slit his throat. I believe I made that abundantly clear back at the brothel."

Wentworth sighed, flicking up the collar of his overcoat. "I thought you didn't enjoy killing."

"I don't," Gabriel said. "But your office never seemed to mind that when you gave me a target."

He was like a blade, wasn't he? He might have other uses, but in the end, he was employed as a weapon. He would do well to remember that when it came to Lydia, tempting him to think he deserved something better.

Back in Moscow, the Queen's approval was the only difference between him and Medvedev.

"I'll meet you tomorrow night before the fights," he told Wentworth.

But before he could leave, Wentworth grasped him by the arm. "We find Medvedev's men, you leave them alive, Monty."

"I'll consider it," he said. "But I still have some names other than Medvedev to strike from my ledger."

20

Lydia stared down at her needlepoint, her mind a maelstrom of anxiety.

Gabriel hadn't returned home the previous night, and he'd sent no messages from London. *It's only been a day*, she told herself. *Only a day.*

But she couldn't help worrying absently whether or not Medvedev had harmed him, or if that gunman in the forest had undone the small gains she had made with her husband.

The minutes before that bullet...

Lydia vividly recalled the rough scratch of the bark as Gabriel pressed her against the tree. That minor discomfort ceased to matter the moment his lips touched hers, seeking her kiss with an urgency bordering on desperation. A victorious thrill had shot through her when Gabriel lost control. *She* had done that. For a moment, she had torn down the walls he'd built to keep her out, and he had been her husband in truth.

There was no denying it any longer: Lydia loved Gabriel.

She'd loved him since she was a child. She'd loved him the day he left her for the diplomatic service. She'd loved him when she stood on his doorstep and endured his icy rejection.

She loved him now, despite all her efforts at guarding herself. Her heart was as fragile as his control – one push, and it shattered.

Lydia brushed her fingertips over the delicate stitches, the vines of florals she sewed to calm her inner tumult. They hadn't helped; if anything, the mundanity of the activity encouraged her thoughts to wander. Where was Gabriel while Lydia sat in the sunny sitting room? What did he—

A rustle of fabric drew her attention. Lydia looked up to see Mr Callahan clasp his hands behind his back as he gazed out the window. Her new bodyguard had the bearing of a former soldier, and she wondered about his background. His family. Did they not miss him while he was forced to protect ladies from assassins?

A strand of brown hair fell across his brow, but Mr Callahan made no move to push it back. It struck her that this man was as handsome as her husband. His features had the same austere quality making him seem remote and inaccessible. Who was this man her husband had entrusted with her safety?

"Mr Callahan," Lydia said. "You've been at that window for hours now. Won't you sit down?"

His eyes flickered towards her, and she noted they were a pale shade of grey – the colour of a bullet. "I'm content to stand."

She wondered about his subtle accent. It betrayed a

background camouflaged beneath polite Englishness. Lydia set aside her needlework. "Would you like tea, then?"

"No, thank you."

"Mr Callahan, I understand my husband has tasked you with this position, but it wouldn't be polite if I didn't at least invite you to rest your feet for a moment."

His focus returned to the landscape beyond the window. "As kind as your offer is, I'm used to not resting my feet."

Lydia made a frustrated noise. "I see why my husband hired you; you're just as stubborn as he is." She thought she saw his lip twitch. Progress. Lydia leaned back and studied him. "Do you have a wife somewhere who might be missing you?"

He gave a wry smile. "I'm unwed."

"A family, perhaps?"

Mr Callahan raised an eyebrow. "If you'll beg my pardon, Lady Montgomery, I'm not here for conversation. I'm hired to be your protection."

"Yes, I'm well aware of that. But since I'm deprived of company, you're the nearest thing to it. How did you meet my husband?"

Mr Callahan gave a quick, dry laugh. "Tenacious, aren't you?"

"Did you expect the wife of Gabriel St Clair to be anything else?"

That drew his attention. Callahan's perusal of her was slow and thoughtful. "A few of us had bets back at the Home Office that he would either marry a hellion or the stupidest woman alive."

Lydia leaned forward with interest, setting her teacup on the table. "And what was your bet, Mr Callahan?"

"Oh, I expected him to marry a fool out for his fortune. A woman who would have no interest in a husband beyond what he puts into her purse."

Lydia smiled. "And now?"

Mr Callahan's regard was astute. Her previous assessment had been wrong – he did not have eyes like a bullet, but like the sharpest blade. "Now I'm wondering what the hell he was thinking, wedding a woman who will delve so far into a man's past that she might as well be digging her own grave."

Lydia's smile faded. Was that what she was doing by wanting to stay with Gabriel? Digging her own grave? "You have quite a cynical view of romance and matrimony, Mr Callahan."

Mr Callahan lifted a shoulder. "Men in my position often do."

"I thought it might be a result of your upbringing. I notice you have a subtle accent. Is it Irish?"

He straightened, a sound escaping him. "You really can't help but dig, can you?"

"No." She picked up her tea again. "But my view of romance is not so cynical. How much did you lose in your bet?"

"Ten pounds."

"Then let that be a lesson to you, Mr Callahan. Never gamble against a tenacious woman."

⤢ 21 ⤢

Gabriel dressed himself like a dockworker and met Wentworth punctually in a hired hack. The other man had donned equally threadbare garments with a hat angled low over his brow, covering his pale blond hair.

"Any word from your men?" Gabriel asked as the conveyance lurched forward and began its journey through the London streets. Home Office agents had been tasked to watch the fight's location before Gabriel and Wentworth's arrival.

"They confirmed what we knew," Wentworth said, gazing out the window as the hack rounded into the East End. "Tonight's fight is being held at a warehouse in Spitalfields. Our informant said one of the competitors was a man known simply as the Russian."

"What else did your informant say?"

Wentworth lifted a shoulder. "That the Russian won his last three fights and more than one brawl has broken out over the betting. It seems some London pride has been bruised."

"It's not Medvedev," Gabriel said, confident in his knowledge of the Syndicate leader. "He would never put himself in the ring unless he was guaranteed to win.

Wentworth dipped his head in agreement. "Then we'll use this man to find Medvedev's location and interrogate him about the sharpshooter at Meadowcroft." He rapped on the roof with his fist. "We'll get off here."

After Wentworth paid the driver, he and Gabriel walked the remaining distance to the warehouse. At the end of the street, the hazy glow of the flickering gaslights illuminated the other spectators.

Wentworth passed Gabriel a coin. "For your admittance."

Gabriel peered down at the token, a slim piece about the size of a sovereign with etchings he couldn't make out in the dark street. "Where did you get this?"

Wentworth gave a slight smile. "I have more resources available to me than most," he said easily. "Including you." The spymaster knocked on the warehouse door, and the panel slid open. "Do you know where I might find the butcher?" Wentworth asked, his accent a perfect imitation of a Spitalfields local.

The door opened, and the massive man guarding the entry gestured with his fingers. "Coins."

Both men flashed their coins, and the guard examined them. Then, with a quick gesture, he invited them to enter. "Down the stairs."

The warehouse was dark and appeared vacant; it might have been a repository for a nearby tavern or used to hide smuggled goods. The only indication of its purpose tonight was the clamour that echoed beneath their feet. Wentworth and Gabriel felt their way along the wall until they reached a stone staircase that descended to the below-ground fighting ring. Torches flickered along the walls.

The shouting intensified as Wentworth and Gabriel progressed farther beneath the streets of the East End. As they rounded the last bend, Wentworth and Gabriel faced an unruly crowd as dense as fire smoke. The heat of the below-ground room assailed Gabriel with the force of a blunt instrument. Worse: the sudden, foul stench of sweat and body odour assailed his senses, churning the contents of his stomach until he had to swallow back a heave. People pressed together, hollering encouragements and profanities at the makeshift ring in the middle of the room, where two shirtless men were locked in a violent, bloody bare-knuckle fight.

Gabriel wasn't familiar with London's underground fighting rings, but he had frequented some in Moscow. It was there he'd first understood that he would forge his new identity in blood. Fighting became a release. Pain was a punishment.

He had learned new lessons.

One of the men in the ring knocked the other out with a punch that sent blood flying.

"*Get up!*" someone in the crowd near Gabriel roared. "*Don't let that bastard win!*"

Gabriel's attention fixed on the victor – a man with a body of pure muscle who towered over his opponent. Gabriel hadn't seen Vladimir since he'd left Moscow, but Medvedev's second-in-command had been on Gabriel's death list. Vladimir fled after rumours of Medvedev's murder spread; he knew how to disappear in Moscow's streets. It would have taken Gabriel too much time to search for him – time he couldn't spare after the deaths of his father and brother.

Vladimir had been Gabriel's rival within the Syndicate. He was distrustful by nature, governed by petty jealousy. As Gabriel rose within the organisation, Vladimir's position became threatened. They'd frequently battled for supremacy – and Gabriel had to do terrible things to prove himself loyal enough to join Medvedev's inner circle.

"You know him?" Wentworth had to shout in Gabriel's ear to be heard. At Gabriel's nod, he added, "We'll wait until after the fights are over, then we'll grab him outside the warehouse."

Gabriel didn't respond. He watched as the unconscious opponent was hauled away, and the next contender stepped into the ring.

That man lasted only a few minutes.

On and on it went: Vladimir dominated competition after competition and never seemed to falter. Bookmakers collected bets, and the crowd shouted more profanities as Vladimir thrashed their local competitors. Wagers were made and lost as men gambled the money they needed for food, clothes, shelter, families.

Finally, Vladimir turned to the assemblage, and as yet another opponent was dragged from the ring. "Who's next?"

People tried to convince others to take up the challenge. Money was on the line, after all. Livelihoods were being ruined. Vladimir was about to walk away with a fortune.

"I have a better idea," Gabriel told Wentworth, pulling off his overcoat.

Wentworth's eyes widened. "Don't even th—*Gabriel!*"

Gabriel shoved his coat at Wentworth and headed toward the announcer, flicking open the buttons of his shirt.

"English," he said crisply. "Not interested in giving a name." After tonight, he would vanish, after all. He had no reason to achieve notoriety in Spitalfields.

"We've got a new challenger!" the announcer said. "A mystery Englishman!"

The crowd roared as Gabriel shrugged off his shirt and entered the ring. The mat was specked with the blood of Vladimir's other rivals.

Vladimir's countenance hardened when he saw Gabriel's face. His lip lifted in a sneer. "Alexei Borislov Zhelyabov. The fucking traitor," he said in Russian.

Gabriel kept his hands loose at his sides. "Volodya," he said, circling the other man. Then, in Russian: "You're a long way from home."

"We came here just for you, *Lord Montgomery*."

Vladimir lunged, his fist striking with the speed of a bullet. Gabriel dodged, but only just in time. The man was fast for being the size of a mountain.

"You've got quicker since we last fought," Gabriel remarked, circling again.

"You're slower," the Russian replied. He came for him again, but Gabriel dodged and spun out of the way.

"If you're here for me, then tell me where I can find Medvedev."

Vladimir gave him a disgusted look. "I won't betray the brotherhood."

"Loyal to the very end, Volodya." Gabriel dodged another hit and sent his fist into the other man's gut. Vladimir backed away with a grunt – evidence that he wasn't as invincible as he seemed. The audience cheered. "Medvedev can fight his own battles."

"But he's got plans for you and that wife of yours," Vladimir said.

Anger scorched through Gabriel, but he suppressed it. He couldn't afford to lose focus. "Tell me where he is, and I'll consider letting you live, Volodya. You remember I had a talent for killing."

The Russian snarled and lunged. His fist caught Gabriel in the middle with the force of a boulder. Gabriel moved quickly, but the Russian was faster. He slammed his fist into Gabriel's face. Gabriel staggered, and Vladimir came at him again with another blow. Another. A fourth.

Shouts echoed across the cellar – men encouraging Gabriel to fight back. Gabriel had endured this sort of pain before; a part of him welcomed it. It gave him a moment's salvation from the dark place in his mind where memories of Moscow erupted in visions of torment. His body, after all, was a destructive instrument. He knew how to use it.

Vladimir put an arm around Gabriel's throat, pressing hard. "Listen to me, you English piece of shit," he hissed. "I won't kill you tonight – Medvedev wants that pleasure for himself. But word spread about that little wife of yours, and the men and I keep taking bets on what we'll do with her." His arm tightened until stars exploded behind Gabriel's eyes. "Some say we should kill her. I say we force you to watch us while we share her. But Medvedev suggests otherwise. He's thinking he'll have you watch as he takes out her eyes and carves into her pretty flesh, so the last thing you ever see is the nightmare of your wife's face before you die."

A savage growl left Gabriel's throat. His past rose like a great beast within him, fire flickering through his blood. Gabriel focused on the vision Vladimir had conjured up:

what Medvedev would do to Lydia. How he would break her.

Gabriel snapped. He struck with an elbow to Vladimir's gut and whirled, his fists flying. Vladimir twisted to dodge, but Gabriel slammed his fist into the Russian's face. Came forward, did it again. Vladimir tried to land another blow, but Gabriel was too fast. Muscle memory was a miraculous thing; his body knew the way of things. He had fought his memories for so long in London, hidden them behind false smiles. Hidden them from Lydia.

But right now, he gave violence free rein. He let it roar through his veins, yielding to the animal desire to hurt something. To protect Lydia.

Gabriel would kill any man who came near her.

He struck Vladimir's face again and the other man staggered. The crowd cheered. They shouted for Gabriel, but he barely heard them over the blood pounding through his ears.

"You ought to have remembered what I was like in Moscow," Gabriel said, coming forward again. His fist rocked the Russian back. "The name Medvedev's men gave me. You know what they used to call me, Volodya. Or do you need reminding?" He wrapped a hand around the other man's throat and squeezed. The Russian staggered against him, his face mottled red and bloody. Gabriel leaned forward and whispered the name in Vladimir's ear as the other man struggled against him. "*Zver*. The Beast."

Then he broke Vladimir's windpipe.

The crowd roared as the Russian went down – not yet realising Gabriel's defeated challenger was dead. Gabriel left the ring before the announcer could check on the other man or declare a winner. As he pushed through the crowd, hands smacked him on the back. Money was passed around. Men shouted and cheered him as he left the building. Gabriel had made them all plenty of coin – and in a few moments, they'd know he'd also left them with a corpse.

Outside, Wentworth caught up with him. "Did you leave him alive? I couldn't tell."

Something calm settled over Gabriel, the same repose he always felt after a kill.

"No," Gabriel said simply.

Wentworth flattened his lips. "You *idiot*."

Gabriel grabbed his coat from Wentworth and yanked it on as he swung into an alley. "That was an authorised assassination. Unfinished business from Moscow."

"I don't give a damn. I would have liked to question him before you finished your assignment three years late."

"Vladimir wasn't going to betray Medvedev's location. He'd die before crossing the *vory*," he said, using the Russian word for *thief*. Every Syndicate member followed that code, although inconsistently.

Gabriel plucked a handkerchief from his pocket and wiped the blood from his face. He strode as fast as he could through the streets without running; he had no desire to draw any more attention to himself.

"I know how to interrogate criminals, Monty," Wentworth said sharply.

"He threatened Lydia," Gabriel snapped. The beast inside him was still near the surface, too easily freed. "If you found the bastard who murdered your wife – if you'd had the chance to stop him before it happened – would you have taken it?"

Wentworth flinched. Gabriel watched as memories flitted across the other man's face, the grief he suppressed by immersing himself in work. Then, after a long moment, he said, "Yes. I would."

"Then you understand why snapping that man's windpipe was more merciful than he deserved." Gabriel straightened. "Prepare your men. Once Medvedev hears of this, he'll plan an attack."

Wentworth nodded. "And you?"

"I'm moving Lydia from Meadowcroft. She's not safe there anymore."

22

Lydia was reading by the fire – preoccupying herself during another restless night – when she heard boots pounding down the hall.

Gabriel.

She shot to her feet as he opened her bedchamber door and closed it behind him with a backwards kick. Lydia flinched at the sight of his face. A laceration split his lower lip, a ruddy bruise was developing on one cheek, and the other had a slim gash near the corner of his eye. His clothing was sodden. The fabric of his overcoat was threadbare, made of coarse wool she had only ever seen on factory workers. Lydia notice the buttons left open to show a triangle of bare, tanned skin. What on earth had happened to his shirt? Where had he been?

Lydia pressed the book to her chest, her grip tightening on the leather spine. A poor substitute for what she really wanted: to caress him. Tend to him. Take care of him.

But this man before her was different from the Gabriel

she knew. This was not the tender husband or even the cold assassin she had witnessed in the Bromes' garden. No, his wild, almost fierce expression matched his unfamiliar attire.

"What happened?" she asked. "Is Medvedev—"

"Still alive." His interruption was terse, his breathing uneven as he looked her over, as if checking to make sure no harm had come to her in his absence. "I fought one of his men."

Killed him, she knew he meant. She had seen him kill before – in the Bromes' garden, but then he had possessed such utter composure. He had carefully restrained every emotion as he scrubbed the blood from her face. This time, Lydia sensed Gabriel's control fraying as if it were a tattered rope barely holding him together.

This time…

Her attention fell on his hands, and she sucked in a breath. "Oh, my," she breathed.

The book fell to the carpet as she rushed to him. Gently, she lifted his swollen hands, examining the patchwork of cuts, bruises, and dried blood. Those fists were proof of his brutality, and yet all she wanted was to press her lips to every blemish.

"Let me bandage these," Lydia whispered. Gabriel had done this to protect her.

"No."

Before she could argue, he took his hands from hers and put his palms on either side of her face, cradling her as if she were made of delicate glass. His expression was soft, but it couldn't erase the ferocity she had sensed before. She shivered at his sudden focused attention.

Even bruised and bleeding, he was the most beautiful man she had ever seen.

"You asked me what happened in Moscow," he whispered.

Lydia was afraid to breathe – fearful that even the slightest movement might prompt him to retreat behind the icy shield he donned so easily. It was absent now, replaced by heat and flame. And vulnerability.

She took the risk: "Yes."

Gabriel's thumb slid across her cheekbone, the texture of his finger rough. The surface of his hands was proof that his life of leisure had ended the moment he'd left her drawing room ten years before. "Ask me again."

Lydia leaned into his touch, letting her eyes meet his. "What happened in Moscow?"

Gabriel bent forward and his lips skimmed across her forehead. When he spoke, his voice was low, barely above a whisper. "After the Syndicate began targeting foreign diplomats, I was tasked with infiltrating their inner circle in Moscow and finding out more about their leadership. I would send coded messages back to England to root out Syndicate allies planning to target members of Parliament." His lips kissed down her cheek, his breath warm against her skin. "My Russian was fluent, but I spent time among labourers in Moscow to better imitate their accent. Once I joined the Syndicate, my performance had to be flawless."

Gabriel fell silent.

Lydia worried he wouldn't continue, that he had reconsidered confiding in her. "Tell me," she said quietly, resting her hands on his shoulders. She, too, could use her touch.

"The lowest levels of the Syndicate consist of petty thieves," Gabriel said. He finally moved again, his fingertips coasting down her jawline. "They're hardly in contact with

Medvedev's inner circle, except to hand over a portion of their take. To climb the ranks of the Syndicate, I had to do worse than steal. My superiors in the British government told me to do whatever was necessary to gain Medvedev's trust. So I earned a reputation for violence."

Lydia slid her hands under his overcoat, grazing the bare skin of his torso. This was no caress of desire but one of comfort. Of reassurance. She wanted him to feel her solidity, the press of her fingertips as his memories drew him back to Moscow. And she wanted to rage over what had been done to him – over what he'd had to do.

He whispered, "They called me zver – the Beast. For years, I was Medvedev's instrument: seemingly resistant to guilt or softness. I followed the thieves' code, the ponyatiya, and allowed myself no vulnerabilities they could exploit. Meanwhile, if I caught word of a diplomat targeted by the Syndicate, I sent a coded warning to the Home Office." His cheek pressed to hers. "After a while, I requested a transfer."

"Did the Home Office grant it?" she asked, her fingers gliding down the firm surface of his chest.

A muscle leaped in his jaw. "No. My life was not in immediate danger, and my cover wasn't threatened. Nightmares weren't a good enough reason to surrender the information that saved allied diplomats and members of Parliament."

She stared at the deepening bruise across his jaw as the silence deepened. A part of her was furious at herself for thinking he had forgotten her. That when he hadn't responded to her letters, it was because he had found a life beyond England – to which she was no longer suited.

If only she had known that he had been by himself all

those years. With no one in whom to confide. Pretending to be someone he wasn't.

"And what about your life," she whispered, nuzzling her cheek against his. "Didn't they care at all about your life?"

Gabriel let out a breath. "Men like me aren't given that luxury. Once extracted from Moscow, I would have found myself with a new name somewhere else."

"But you didn't go somewhere else," she said, lifting her gaze to meet his. "You returned to England as Gabriel St Clair."

His dry, humourless laugh made her wince. "You misunderstand. No one cared about Gabriel St Clair. The new Earl of Montgomery was a different matter."

Lydia went still as her mind made sense of his return. As the new Earl of Montgomery, he would have had to take his father's seat in the House of Lords. Second sons often went into the civil service or politics – positions of prestige gained through familial connections. But it was the heirs who mattered in English society.

She brushed her lips over his bruised skin and whispered, "I care about Gabriel St Clair."

She heard his breath catch. "I know." His voice was quiet. "That's why I turned you away when you came to my door. I wanted you to stop caring."

Lydia said nothing. She kissed his bruises again, let her lips linger over his skin. His breathing quickened, and she was gratified by the way his hands trembled. She stepped back from him and began to untie her wrapper, casting it from her shoulders. All she now wore was the gossamer-thin night rail that barely covered the contours of her breasts.

Gabriel made a sound in his throat as his hot gaze fell

on that translucent garment. "God, you curse of a girl," he said, his voice low and rough.

Lydia had been insulted the first time he'd said those words. But now, she saw them as an admission of her power and as a confession of his vulnerability. She'd had that influence over him for years and never knew it. Now she did. Now she understood that her touch made him tremble – that she occupied his thoughts in just the same way he did hers.

And that was all the encouragement she needed.

Lydia reached up and began untying the ribbon at her throat. "I'm not going to stop caring about you. I won't be like those men at the Home Office. Let them worry over the diplomats and members of Parliament." The ribbon that held up her nightgown yielded. "It's your life that occupies my mind, Gabriel St Clair."

"Lydia," he said again. He said nothing else, as if torn between saying, Lydia, stop. Or Lydia, continue. But then he focused on the single finger holding up her nightgown. "Drop it," he said softly.

Lydia lowered her hand. The silk nightgown fell to the floor, revealing the naked length of her body. She watched Gabriel's fingers curl into his palms as he looked his fill of her.

"You are fortunate that I'm too battered to do all the things I want right now."

"Describe them to me."

Gabriel came forward, the muscles beneath his unbuttoned overcoat flexing. When his eyes met hers the expression in them was almost fevered. "Not yet. Tonight…" He dropped to his knees. "I want to taste you."

Then he leaned forward and pressed his mouth to her quim.

G abriel revelled in the taste of Lydia's wet cunny.

She bucked against him. The only thing that kept her balanced was her back against the door and Gabriel's firm grip on her hips.

"Gabriel," she panted. "*Please—*"

He slid his tongue inside her.

Lydia's head tipped against the door, and his name left her lips in a rough groan. That small encouragement was its own message: he could satisfy her as long as he liked. He could indulge. He could manipulate time and make this moment last. Whatever came tomorrow no longer mattered; just this once, Gabriel would let himself drown in her.

His cock strained against his trousers, but he disregarded the ache of his desire. A slight discomfort was a price he was willing to pay to make her writhe beneath his touch.

Pleasure, after all, was an ambition. It required attention and effort. When they woke the next day, and he was forced to shut her out, he wanted this memory to savour in the quietness of solitude. When Moscow overwhelmed him, Gabriel wanted to recall the sharp, salty taste of her. Her moments of ecstasy, when she gained the courage to dominate.

But that dominance was not one-sided. He lifted her leg and set her foot against his shoulder to improve his angle. Lydia arched her hips as Gabriel used his tongue to possess her, to mark her with the heat of his mouth.

She burned him.

She made him feel alive.

She made him yearn to exist only for this: pleasuring her. He would prostrate himself at her altar if she wanted it.

The sudden constriction in her grip indicated her release was near. Her nails scrabbled over his scalp in an almost punishing hold, but the discomfort gratified Gabriel. It was proof of her need. Evidence that she was lost to this as he.

She came with a sharp cry. Then, as she stammered his name in shaky breaths, a strange emotion went through him – and he had a vision of a life spent in bed with her.

Mornings with Lydia in his arms.

Afternoons where he would steal her away for a brief interlude.

Nights pounding her into the bed until she climaxed again and again and again.

But that life wasn't for him. No matter how much Gabriel yearned for her, one part of his mind would always be buried firmly in the past – where she could never follow.

Gabriel lowered her foot to the ground and rose to his feet. When Lydia's eyes met his, another peculiar sensation passed through him – her expression was so genuine, so sincere. So full of trust.

She'd looked at him like that the day he left England ten years before.

Don't, his mind thought sharply. *Telling you what I did doesn't erase it. I can't be that man for you.*

"Where are you going?" Lydia whispered. "Moscow?"

He frowned at her words. "No. I've no intention of returning—"

Lydia shook her head. "Up here," she said, gently skimming her fingers through his hair. "You're no longer with me up here." A breath vibrated through her. "So, are you in Moscow or Kabul?"

Gabriel placed his hands on her shoulders, on the delicate wings of her naked collarbones. He let himself marvel at her beauty, at the open honesty of her features. All that trust he did not deserve. She was his lodestar, his one constant as he navigated the tumult of his past. But like Polaris, she would always be out of reach – a shining beacon in the distance.

"What does it say about me," he asked her, "that I can have you right in front of me, and part of my mind will always be thousands of miles away?"

Lydia reached up and slowly pushed the overcoat from his shoulders. "Then let us be in Moscow," she said softly, grazing her fingers against his bare skin. "Let us be in Kabul. Imagine me there with you, as if you had taken me with you that day ten years ago."

Just tonight, he thought to himself.

Couldn't he have tonight? Tomorrow, he would consider how he had sullied her. Tomorrow, he would relearn how to exist without her. Hadn't he learned to live with his sins before? This was no different.

But tonight, she was offering herself to him, dragging him towards her like a force of gravity.

She trailed a hand across his shoulders as if she were memorising him. Cataloguing every feature with her clever mind.

Then, after a moment's hesitation, she reached for his trousers. He held his breath as she flicked open the buttons and pushed the garment down. He kicked them off the rest of the way, waiting as she took her fill. Her eyes studied him in a way that felt like the soft touch of fingertips skimming across his naked skin.

Heat flared in Lydia's eyes. That fire matched the conflagration within Gabriel; his blaze recognised its equal in her. A savage urge to take her flared to life, but he damped it down. He wouldn't subject her to the pleasure-pain he typically employed to forget himself. He needed to be tender with her.

Gabriel lowered his lips to hers, kissing her with a soft, searching caress. He realised then that he had not kissed her enough. That he would have to fit all their kisses into the span of a single evening because he could not do this again.

All they had was tonight.

"Not Moscow, nor Kabul," he whispered against her lips as he swept her into his arms. He set her onto the bed and fitted his body against hers. "But Vienna, Zürich, Paris? I'll take you with me, just as I should have done ten years ago."

⌒ 24 ⌒

G abriel gazed down at Lydia in wonder.
His muscular body was pressed hard against hers, the physique so different from her own. Lydia let her fingertips trail down the sinewy line of his torso to the curve of his hip. She held her breath as her hand came to rest over the strong arch of his buttocks.

She longed to admire Gabriel in the light, to spend endless time exploring his shape, the dips and valleys that comprised his lean form. She longed to slide her hands over the entire terrain of his body and marvel at how his muscles moved when he shifted.

He was a work of art.

But then he kissed her, and that changed the course of her thoughts. His lips were their own revelation, the pressure soft and light and searching. But she had skill at it now; she could use this intimacy for her own purposes. Lydia slid her hand back up and sank her fingers into his hair, deepening the kiss.

Gabriel groaned into her mouth. Lydia teased him with her tongue, coaxing him from those places where she couldn't follow. Her caresses summoned him from the abyss of his memories, travelled with him across the landscape of his thoughts. She could take up residence there, burn that kiss into his recollections like a brand.

Take me with you to Kabul. Take me with you to Moscow. And I can bring you back to England. I can take you home with me every night, if you need me to.

She pulled his face away from hers. "Your name is Gabriel St Clair," she whispered. "And this is real. Understand?"

His eyes closed briefly at the pressure of her touch, as if it grounded him. Dragged him away from his memories. Returned him from the distance in his mind.

Then he leaned down and kissed her again.

This time, Lydia let Gabriel set the pace. His kiss was tender, lips sipping as if hers were sweet nectar. Gabriel trembled above her as though that kiss left him unsteady. His hips sought purchase against her own, and Lydia gasped at his arousal sliding along her wet quim. Gabriel made a soft noise – every bit as lost to that sudden contact of their bodies. They were two forces colliding.

"Please," she said. She held him close, pushed her knees to his hips. "*Please.* Give me more." *Give me everything.*

"You want me inside you?" he murmured, his lips gently grazing her nipple.

"*Yes.*"

Gabriel lifted his head, his gaze meeting hers. "How deep do you want me to be?"

The intensity of that look rendered her speechless. Her thoughts were chaotic – he was already beneath her skin, embedded in her soul. But she craved his love, his heart, the parts he kept from her.

Words she couldn't say.

"I want all of you, Gabriel St Clair," she whispered. "I want everything."

Something constricted in his face. But when she thought he might pull away, he leaned down and kissed her fiercely. Then he slid inside her until he found resistance – proof that she had never done this before. Lydia sensed his hesitation, that this man who had become an instrument of violence did not want to hurt her. No, he treated her as if she were infinitely precious.

Lydia held his sides between her thigh in silent encouragement.

And then he pushed inside her to the hilt.

Lydia sucked in a breath at the sting of pain. Gabriel watched her, his gaze intent, as if counting every second of her discomfort. Lydia dragged him closer for another hard kiss.

I want this, she said with her lips. *I want you.*

Gabriel muttered something against her lips that sounded like, "Thank God."

Then his entire body came alive. He dragged his lips from hers, sliding his hot tongue along the pulse at her neck. Then he pulled his cock out of her and thrust it back in.

Lydia gasped at the pleasure of it. He noticed her response, the way her hips rose to meet him, and took that as encouragement. His pace increased, his hips pushing against hers with a force that rocked the bed. That slight burn she'd experienced earlier seemed eternities ago. All that remained was...

Pleasure.

God, but Lydia burned with it. Now she understood what she'd longed for as she thought of him in the privacy of her room. What she wished for when she slid her fingers into her cunny and imagined it was him. She wanted this: the rocking of his hips, the intense focus of his gaze, his tongue tracing the shell of her ear as he tupped her.

"Where are we?" she whispered, brushing his hair back from his face. "In your mind, where are we?"

"Vienna," he replied, his breath coming fast. "I had a little apartment in Alsergrund where I read your letters. I used to imagine you with me in the cramped bedroom. We would drink wine, and I would pleasure you until sunrise." He shut his eyes and groaned, his cock slamming into her. "God, Lydia. Tell me you want it like this."

"Yes," she said. At that moment, it was the only word she was capable of uttering. *Yes, yes, yes, yes.*

"You feel so good," he said, moving faster. "So. Damn. Good."

God, but he was beautiful like this. His muscles strained above her, and his entire face looked... unburdened.

She scraped her nails across his back, raising her hips to match his pace.

"Again," he whispered in her ear. "Keep doing that."

Lydia's release tore through her, and she arched against him with a soft cry.

And then Gabriel came, his hands gripping the blankets on either side of Lydia as his climax tore through him. A rough groan escaped his lips as he collapsed, panting against her shoulder.

In a sudden surge of tenderness, Lydia wrapped her arms

around him and held his body against her own. Felt the beat of his heart as his pulse rate came down and his breathing began to slow.

She didn't know how long they lay like that, their bodies fitted together like two rocks sanded into the shape of each other. It might have been epochs. Time ceased to matter when he touched her.

Stay with me like this, she wanted to say. *Give me tonight. Give me tomorrow.*

But just when she wondered if she might convince him, Gabriel gently pulled away from her, dropped a kiss on her hand, and rose from the bed. The absence of his warmth brought a cold reminiscent of a winter morning.

When he turned to her, his countenance had gone distant.

"You're no longer in the little apartment in Alsergrund with me," she said. An ache spread through her chest. "Nor are you here in this room."

Gabriel paused. "When I sleep, I go where you can't follow." Then, with a sigh, he padded to the connecting door. "Get some rest. Tomorrow, we'll be leaving Meadowcroft for Devon. For your safety."

When he closed the connecting door, Lydia felt its echo in her heart. That connecting door might as well have been the entire distance to Russia.

The following afternoon came and went as Gabriel prepared for their journey to Devon.

Servants had spent the better part of the day packing trunks, and Gabriel used the time to scout the estate. Past an outcropping of trees, he'd discovered discarded cigar butts, but there was no indication of how recently they had been smoked. His exploration yielded nothing else, but he felt watched, and he couldn't tell if the sensation was entirely in his mind or if his wholly reliable instincts were warning him like a peal of bells.

Wentworth travelled from London with his men to ensure a secure departure. The carriage ride to Devon would take until the early morning hours, and there would be little time to rest. Gabriel was used to the discomfort of long journeys, but Lydia would be in for a difficult night.

Gabriel's mind strayed to the previous evening as he supervised the servants loading the carriages. He had told her about Moscow, and she'd still looked at him as if he were a man worthy of her affection.

It's your life that occupies my mind, Gabriel St Clair.

God, but he had so few defences left against her. She had overpowered every fortification to inscribe herself an intaglio across his heart.

He could no longer rely on the iciness that once protected him. Now, he would have to come up with something else – some new defence against her.

One day soon, he was going to have to leave her.

A noise distracted him. Wentworth was standing beside him at the window in his study, watching the servants on the drive. "You're sure about this?"

Gabriel dipped his head in assent and took a sip of whisky. "Medvedev knows a challenge when he sees one. With Vladimir gone, he's missing an enforcer in a foreign city."

"You don't think he'll wait to regroup?"

"No." Gabriel watched Callahan direct the packing of a trunk atop one of the three waiting carriages. "Medvedev will say he's through with waiting. If his sharpshooter was confident enough to take a shot at Lydia and flee through my property, then they'll return. I can't keep her here."

Even the few hours they had spent preparing to travel had set Gabriel on edge. Wentworth's men were scouting the premises, but the next assassin's bullet might not miss.

Lydia would never be safe as long as Gabriel was near.

You brought this disorder into her life, he reminded himself. *That's why you have to let her go. You can't have her.*

"I understand," Wentworth said quietly.

Guilt flared hot in Gabriel's stomach. What Wentworth had gone through was Gabriel's worst imagined torment: to find his wife murdered. To grieve her loss and wonder if he could have done more.

No, he couldn't keep Lydia at Meadowcroft. He didn't give a damn anymore about killing Medvedev; he just wanted her safe.

"Any word on Medvedev's movements?" Gabriel asked, taking another drink. The spirits burned his throat on the way down. It matched the fire in his bloodstream.

"Nothing yet," Wentworth said. "I've had my men keep their ears open, and there have been some whispers of a man matching Medvedev's description, but nothing I can verify. I've allocated more spies to the East End; it's only a matter of time before they find something."

"Keep me apprised while I'm gone," Gabriel said, setting his empty snifter on the table. That half-finger of whisky was all he could allow himself before their journey. "I'll have my staff visit the telegraph office."

"Will do."

Fabric rustled just beyond the door. A moment later, Lydia strolled into the room, wearing a wool travelling dress fastened at the base of her throat. Gabriel's gaze lingered on the long, orderly row of buttons that made her look so prim. An intense surge of lust flared hot through his body. Those neat little buttons were just waiting to be flicked open to reveal the pretty floral corset and undergarments she favoured. Beneath that lay the smooth expanse of skin he had yet to acquaint himself with properly. He still needed to kiss her everywhere.

The awareness of what she looked like under all those layers of tidy clothes was a privilege granted to him alone. He nearly smiled at the thought.

Lydia's gaze caught his, and a faint blush crept over her face.

He wondered how far that blush spread beneath her dress.

She softly cleared her throat. "Mr Wentworth," she said. He took her hand and kissed her knuckles. "First, you see us before we left London, and now here at Meadowcroft. I regret that our acquaintance has yet to extend beyond a swift exit."

Wentworth smiled politely. "When you're back in London, you must visit my house for dinner. It hasn't had guests for years."

Lydia laughed and then cast Gabriel another glance. The flare of desire in her face compromised his balance. He wanted her again. He longed to carry her back up to the bedchamber. If he had the choice, she wouldn't leave his arms until morning.

Lydia's blush deepened. Gabriel almost smiled as he pictured the rest of her pale skin going pink at the thought of bedding him.

Gabriel's wife forced her attention away.

"Goodness," she murmured, her attention on the army of servants out the window. "I wasn't aware the maids had packed me enough for three carriages."

"The others are decoys," Gabriel told her. "Wentworth and his team will be on one, Callahan on the other. After what I did to Vladimir, Medvedev will be planning his counter-attack."

"You think they'll attack us on the way?"

"Perhaps not," Wentworth assured her. "My men are watching the roads. But Lord Montgomery wants to assure your safety."

Lydia let out a breath. "Then thank you, Mr Wentworth, for helping us today."

Outside, Callahan lifted a hand to signal that the staff had finished. Gabriel fought the urge to rush Lydia into the carriage. The faster he took her to Devon, the sooner she would be out of immediate danger.

"You're ready?" he asked her.

His wife swallowed but nodded. "Yes."

"Good. Prepare for a long journey. Any rests between here and Devon will be short."

And once he got her there, he would do whatever it took to keep her safe.

The carriage rolled down the uneven country road. Gabriel attempted to conceal his apprehension – but he wondered if the woman sitting across from him noticed the tense way he gripped the lapels of his overcoat. The distance between them in that cramped carriage seemed so small and yet so vast at the same time.

Every part of him ached to be closer.

Lydia fidgeted, her hands resting in the folds of her dress. Gabriel was aware that her unease matched his, but he could do nothing to soothe her. The boy she had grown up with knew how; when she cried over a skinned knee, he knew to hold her and whisper calming words in her ear.

But Gabriel was not a man trained to comfort. That had

been obliterated in Moscow. Reassurance, after all, had little value in his work there. It was worth nothing.

"How long will it take to get there?" Her voice jolted him from his thoughts. He looked up to find her watching him, and he wondered if she spoke to fill the silence. "My aunt has always longed to holiday in Cornwall, but I've never been farther than Bath."

Gabriel cleared his throat. "The entire night. We'll arrive before sunrise."

An image, unbidden, rose from his mind: her beneath him as he pounded into her. The taste of her skin as he kissed her.

Last night, she had asked him to stay.

"Gabriel," she said, still fidgeting. "Are you worried?"

Why could he kill a man and feel nothing, but the barest hint that she might be terrified made him want to bundle her up and hold her close?

"No." His voice was cold. He had learned to use that voice for effect during his operations.

She twisted her hands tighter, and Gabriel wished he hadn't noticed. He wished he could focus on the dark landscape outside the windows. On anything but her. But he was aware of her every movement and the evidence of her unease. It struck him like a blunt instrument.

Lydia took a shaky breath. "I don't recall you telling me about the property in Devon."

"Langdon Manor," Gabriel said. "It was my mother's favourite house, but my father had difficulty visiting after she passed. I haven't been there for years."

She nodded, staring down at her trembling hands. Gabriel couldn't bear it anymore; he could not feign indifference while she sat opposite him, fearful about their journey. That his usually calm wife trembled at all left him furious.

Gabriel reached over and covered her hands with his. "You're afraid," he said softly.

She swallowed. "Yes." Then she made a noise. "And I'm worried about Mr Wentworth and Mr Callahan in the other carriages."

The three carriages had left Meadowcroft at the same time in different directions, each one packed with plenty of luggage to maintain the ruse. "Don't be," he told her. "They're armed and trained."

"So are you, and yet both times after you left for London, I didn't sleep."

More of his façade dissolved as he envisioned her pacing the bedchamber at Meadowcroft while he roamed the streets of London doing foolish things to avoid her. She had lost sleep over his choices.

Over *him*.

Gabriel slowly lifted Lydia's hand and pressed his lips to the inside of her wrist, along the bare skin between her glove and travelling dress. A part of him resented these garments – impediments to access; he wanted to kiss every naked inch of her. But another part was possessive and exultant: only he had been granted the privilege of kissing her. Only he would know the texture of her skin. These were gifts bestowed upon him alone.

"You're distracting me," she whispered.

"Trying to." He gave a slight smile. "Is it working?"

"Yes."

"Good."

But as he leaned forward to kiss her on the lips, a shout

echoed from outside. The carriage shuddered to a halt. Lydia smacked against him, and Gabriel gripped her shoulders to steady her. One of the horses reared up and jolted the carriage again, but they weren't going anywhere. And if they weren't going anywhere, then—

Bang! The gunshot echoed across the country landscape. *Bang!* A second. *Bang, bang, bang!* Somewhere behind the carriage, Gabriel heard the thump of a body hitting the dirt, and a horse screamed.

Lydia choked, her hand covering her mouth. Gabriel's lips tightened. They both knew the driver and the bodyguard – Wentworth's men – riding with them must be dead, and the horses as well.

"Get out of the carriage." The voice spoke in Russian, but it was no one Gabriel recognised. Not Medvedev.

Gabriel pulled away from Lydia. Her breath came faster, chest rising and falling in agitation. "Listen to me," he told her in a low voice. "When I say your name, get down under the carriage, and don't come out until I tell you to. Do not hesitate. Understand?"

Lydia shut her eyes and gave a nod.

"*Get out of the carriage!*" their assailant shouted again.

Gabriel opened the carriage door and helped Lydia down. A short distance away, the bodies of his footman, coachman, and horses had collapsed in the dirt, their silhouettes exposed by the bright moonlight.

Five men had their guns drawn and pointed right at Gabriel and Lydia.

Shit.

"I see Medvedev hasn't come," he said in Russian.

"Went after one of the other carriages," one of the men

said, coming forward. "You might have been fortunate, Alyosha. Some of us think he's still fond enough of you to offer mercy."

"Andrei, is that you?" Gabriel gave a grim smile. "Leading your own *vory*? I didn't think Medvedev would promote a lackwit like you."

"Shut the hell up," Andrei snarled.

"I don't recognise your companions," Gabriel continued easily, readying himself. "All the way from Russia? Or is Medvedev so desperate that he's hired help from my fellow Englishmen?"

Andrei snarled and pulled back the hammer of his pistol with a *click*.

"Lydia, now!" Gabriel shouted.

Lydia dropped to the ground and rolled beneath the carriage.

Good girl.

Gabriel launched himself at Andrei. The sudden movement surprised the other man, allowing Gabriel to seize the pistol. He broke Andrei's kneecap with a swift kick, and the man went sprawling. Gabriel used Andrei's body for cover as the other men fired their pistols into their ally. Then, before they could correct their aim, Gabriel raised Andrei's gun with the skill of a sharpshooter: one down. Two. Three. Four.

All dead with a bullet to the head.

Gabriel panted as everything went silent. The gunshots still rang in his ears – or was that his blood? It didn't matter. All that mattered was...

Lydia.

Gabriel dropped to his knees near the carriage and

found his wife there. Her eyes were tightly shut, and her small hands clenched into fists.

"Lydia," he whispered. She didn't move. Did she hear him at all? "Lydia, love." He gently touched her hair.

Lydia's eyes opened slowly. "You're all right?" Her voice trembled.

He didn't answer her. "Come out from under there, love."

He helped her to her feet. When Lydia's head started to turn in the direction of the bodies, an instinct came over Gabriel – a sudden desire to protect her from the things he had done. A part of him wondered if he should do so deliberately, to disabuse her of the notion that he was worthy of her. But it was overshadowed by the part of him that remembered her asking him to stay and wishing he could be a better man for her. The man that the boy she knew would have grown up to be if his choices had been different. But they weren't, and neither could return to being the children they once were.

"No, don't look," he said softly, taking her gently by the shoulders. "I don't want you to see this."

"Gabriel…"

"I don't want you to see this," he repeated, more firmly this time.

She kept her back turned and waited while he grabbed each of the corpses and hauled them to the ditch on the side of the road. The horses, he'd have to leave where they were.

He took note of the markers to indicate their location: the twisting tree to his left, the length of time they had been travelling. In the morning, he would send Wentworth a telegram informing him where he could find Medvedev's men. Someone else would have to dispose of the corpses.

When he looked back at Lydia, he found her hugging herself, her arms wrapped around her middle. Though he couldn't see her face, he hoped it was showing her once and for all he would only ever bring her trouble.

Yet... he hated to lose her again. He had let her go once, and now he would have to do it again.

Lydia cleared her throat. "What will we do about the – about Medvedev's men?"

"Wentworth will have a cleaning crew come for the corpses."

Medvedev's men had left their own horses tied to a tree just beyond the side of the road. Gabriel went over and gently soothed the agitated animals with a soft murmur, releasing them from their tethers. He grabbed the reins of the calmest.

"And if someone steals our luggage?" Lydia asked.

Gabriel patted the horse on its neck and murmured to it softly. It wasn't this creature's fault it was involved in this awful business. "I sent a few small items on a conveyance earlier. The servants at Langdon Manor will know to prepare for our arrival," he said, gently stroking the horse. "In case something like this happened, I didn't want you to be without belongings."

Lydia was quiet for a moment. Then: "And our bodyguards? Will Mr Wentworth notify their families?"

He winced at the catch in her voice and his expression softened. "They had no families," he said gently. "But I'll have Wentworth ensure they're buried properly." He held out a hand to her. "Come. We'll have to make the rest of the journey by horseback."

She allowed him to help her into the saddle. Gabriel

swung up behind her, trying not to notice how warm she was.

How alive she was.

His dead heart beat now only for her.

"Gabriel," Lydia said as she relaxed against him.

"Yes?"

"I'm sorry," she whispered. "For thinking the worst of you all those years. For what happened to you."

He loosed a breath. "You owe me nothing." Before she could argue, he kissed the top of her head. "Sleep now. I'll let you know when the horse needs rest."

He was the one who owed her a lifetime of apologies.

ᖗ 26 ᖕ

Lydia was exhausted.

Gabriel had pushed them both relentlessly through the night, stopping only briefly to water the horses before urging them on again. Lydia's bones felt like they would crumble at any moment, but she kept her complaints to herself, knowing that Gabriel was likely just as weary as she was. Despite his exhaustion, Gabriel was unyielding in his quest to keep moving forward. He haggled fiercely with the innkeeper for fresh horses, wasting no time on small talk or pleasantries. Lydia felt a pang of envy for Gabriel's stamina, as she struggled to stay awake in the saddle.

Yet, even in the face of her weariness, Gabriel remained patient and kind. He never once snapped at her for her clumsy attempts to mount her horse or for her frequent stumbles. Instead, he stayed steady behind her, his touch gentle and reassuring. At some point, Lydia leaned back on his shoulder and passed out.

An hour before their arrival at Langdon Manor, the

rainclouds that had threatened their journey finally broke. The deluge soaked them through in an instant. Gabriel's arm tightened around Lydia – offering her the warmth from his body – but pressed on.

Lydia was shivering so much that by the time they arrived at Langdon Manor, she could barely slide out of the saddle and into Gabriel's waiting arms.

"Just the one horse," Gabriel shouted over the downpour to someone behind Lydia – the stablehand, she gathered. She could barely keep her eyes open.

Gabriel swung her up in his arms and carried her into the house. The sudden chatter of servants echoed through the vestibule, their voices reaching Lydia as if from a great distance. What were they saying? Were they speaking to her? She could hardly concentrate on their words.

"Lady Montgomery needs a fire urgently," Gabriel said. The heels of his boots pounded across the marble floor.

"My lord, did something happen?" The heavy clank of keys indicated that the voice came from the housekeeper.

"Carriage accident," he said shortly, holding Lydia close. "The fire, Mrs Dunford?"

"The maids already laid it in preparation for your arrival. Shall I send someone for the doctor or have the maids draw a bath? Perhaps something cold for your face? The bruising will—"

"Not tonight," Gabriel said. His hand tightened on Lydia's shoulder, and she knew his forbearance was on a short leash. That he managed to communicate with such composure at all was remarkable. "Goodnight, Mrs Dunford."

Lydia heard skirts rustle as the other woman left.

What about you? she wanted to ask Gabriel. When she rested her forehead against his bare neck, his skin was as chilled as hers. He had given all his earlier warmth to her.

She felt him mount the stairs, striding briskly. After a few minutes, he pushed open a door. The heat of the room instantly engulfed Lydia in a warm, welcome wave from the blazing fire in the hearth. Lydia opened her eyes to see the maids gaping at husband and wife in alarm.

Gabriel ignored them. "Get out." Gabriel's tone was brusque and commanding now. The fatigue that had been gnawing at him since they started their journey had shattered any semblance of polite protocol. Lord Montgomery's courteous façade had been obliterated.

"That was rude," Lydia murmured.

"I'll apologise in the morning."

Gently, Gabriel set Lydia down in one of the chairs, his hands steadying her when she threatened to collapse again. His eyes filled with worry as he stripped the sodden gloves from her fingers and attempted to massage the warmth back into her limbs.

"Your lips are blue," he said softly.

"I'll be fine." Lydia's teeth chattered so severely she could barely get the words out.

"I need to get these wet clothes off you."

"You first." He'd already supported her enough.

But Gabriel only gave her an indulgent look and pulled Lydia to her feet. She couldn't even muster a thrill when he stepped behind her and began unbuttoning her dress with deft fingers.

"You really should take care of your own." Her words were slurred with cold and exhaustion.

"I am taking care of my own," he said, voice soft.

Oh, she thought. He was talking about her. If she hadn't been so cold, Lydia would have flushed with pleasure.

Gabriel finished unfastening her soaking gown, which fell to the carpet with a heavy thwap. Then he started on her underthings, his hands shaking as he unlaced her corset. Gabriel's beautiful, pale face was almost severe while he concentrated on removing her remaining garments, tossing each item into a pile on the floor. When Lydia was naked, Gabriel seemed almost indifferent.

"Wait here." Lydia watched as Gabriel pulled the blankets from the bed and built a soft nest in front of the hearth. "The bed would be more comfortable, but this will be warmer for you," he said.

With the makeshift bed in place, Gabriel covered Lydia with the fire-warm blankets. Her skin prickled, the sensation almost painful as warmth suffused her frozen limbs.

Gabriel took her hands to his again to rub feeling back into the tips. Lydia watched him beneath heavy eyelids, studying the damp strands of auburn hair that had begun to curl at the neckline of his wet shirt. The bruising on his face was more prominent, but it did not detract from his beauty. If anything, it lent his features a fitting sort of ferocity.

"When will you see to yourself?" she asked him, hoarse with weariness.

Gabriel's large hands closed over hers, massaging. The prickle of warmth through the cold was painful, but Lydia concentrated on his touch. "When I've seen to you," he said simply.

Lydia fought to keep her eyes open. She wanted to keep

watching him. She was afraid he would leave once she shut her eyes, going where she couldn't follow.

"This marriage feels real to me," she whispered.

Gabriel paused, his gaze meeting hers. Something unreadable passed across his face – a riot of emotions in mere seconds: denial, yearning, hurt. Perhaps more. His feelings toward her were all sifted through his past in Kabul and Moscow. But Lydia's imagination was not so creative; whatever he had endured during those ten years was beyond her.

He looked away and put her hands under the blankets. "Goodnight, Lydia."

Lydia wanted him to stay. When she heard him fighting Medvedev's men in the darkness, she worried that she would lose him. That she would never again kiss or touch him. That their second chance had been so ephemeral it might as well have been a fantasy.

She worried he would be the one lying dead on the roadside instead of Medvedev's men.

"Gabriel," she said softly.

Her husband paused. He seemed so weary now. He had taken care of her, and she had not been able to do the same for him. "Yes?"

"Stay with me." She heard his soft intake of breath. To reject her? She couldn't chance it – so she said the one thing she knew that would keep him there: "Will you hold me until I fall asleep?"

Gabriel shut his eyes briefly. But just when she thought he might still refuse, he took off his sodden wool coat. A tremor went through his hands as he unbuttoned his waistcoat and then yanked his wet shirt over his head. He fumbled with the fastening of his trousers and pushed them to the floor.

God, but he was beautiful. His skin was marbled from the cold, and the firelight was generous to his form. Every angle of him had been crafted by a master sculptor. Lydia relished this moment, the ability to see him in the light, but the instant was all too brief. Gabriel lifted the blankets and settled beside her.

"Come here, you curse of a girl," he said, his voice tender.

He pulled her against his warm body. She could feel every angle, every hard muscle taut against her. And when his arm slipped around her middle, she had never felt so relaxed.

With a sigh, she whispered, "Thank you, Gabriel."

He didn't reply. But as she began to drift into dreams, Lydia thought she felt his lips on her skin.

Gabriel jolted awake.

His breathing heaved as he took in the unfamiliar room, seeking focus and finding none. His mind was a spiked weapon repeating memories of Moscow.

Stab. One victim.

Stab. Another.

Stab. Another.

You are Alexei Borislov Zhelyabov, the Beast of Moscow, and Gabriel St Clair no longer exists. You are—

A soft noise came from behind him, and then Lydia's arm slid around his waist. A breath exploded out of Gabriel. Every luscious, bare inch of Lydia's naked body was pressed against his back, warm and inviting.

A desperate thought came to him: he could lose himself in her. He could have her again, use her body until she reminded him that he was not Alexei Borislov Zhelyabov. He was not the Beast of Moscow – not anymore. All he had to do was turn and wake her up. Then he'd get her permission, push her against the blankets, and thrust his cock inside her until he found his release. Until he remembered his true name. Until—

Gabriel tore himself away from her arms and staggered to his feet. Blood roared in his ears as he grasped the back of a nearby chair to recover his balance. His cock was rigid. His mind pulsed with images – the violence of Moscow thundering through the heat of his arousal. The killings on the road to Devon had flared more memories he'd tried for years to suppress, and the only solution he knew was to make a choice between brutality and hard sex. He hadn't been like this since...

Since his return to England three years before, when Wentworth first found him scouring the streets for a fight. It had been at Wentworth's suggestion that he choose a different physical outlet, harness those memories with intimacies that chilled the raging heat in his blood. When Gabriel bedded a woman, he lost himself in it until the memories of his other life faded in the physical act of pleasure.

On nights like that, he was not capable of being gentle, so the women he'd bedded had a predilection for roughness. Each coupling suited their mutual needs.

But Gabriel did not want another woman. He wanted the one in the blankets, whose features were illuminated in the low glow of the fireplace embers. He wanted to bed his curse of a girl until he recognised his name was Gabriel St Clair, and this was England, and he would never be anyone's weapon again.

But when his hands remembered touching anyone, they were not gentle. Violence was too vivid in his mind, and his hands had been instruments of brutality for too long. He was no husband.

He was an assassin.

Gabriel flinched, his fingernails digging into the upholstery. He'd find another task that demanded punishing his body. He didn't give a damn.

But then Lydia's voice sounded behind him, soft and slurred from sleep. "Gabriel?"

God, but her voice caressed him like soft fingertips dancing along his skin. She'd sounded like that after he'd brought her to climax. Her eyes had gazed at him with an undeniable tenderness, and Gabriel felt the ground beneath him shift. For a man like him, unsteadiness could be fatal.

Gabriel stared at the carpet, trying to gain some command over his body. He could not face Lydia. He might not have the strength to leave; already, he was trembling with the desire to return to the blankets and take her in his arms. Set her on her knees. Take her from behind.

"Time for me to return to my room." His voice was cold, and he knew it. That little sense of control was all he had remaining.

Blankets rustled with her movements. When she spoke again, it was from directly behind him. "Where are you right now?" she whispered. "Kabul or Moscow?"

"Moscow," he whispered.

Tell me you're real, he didn't say. *Please, God, tell me you're real.*

He felt her warm hand against his shoulder, followed by the petal-soft touch of her lips there. "Then take me with you to Moscow, the way you did to Vienna."

Something in him splintered at the thought of her in

Moscow. Her seeing everything he had done as Alexei Borislov – worse than what she had already witnessed.

He whirled on her, seized her by the wrist. Held it in a firm grip. "I told you Moscow is somewhere you can't follow." His tone was harsh; it did not reflect the need that flooded his body.

Her eyes flickered over him, desire flaring in her eyes. That response gratified the animal lust surging through his veins. She was getting under his skin, making him want things he couldn't have and coveting a life he didn't deserve.

Lydia raised her chin. "I won't leave you alone with your memories. Not tonight."

Gabriel's breath heaved as his control unravelled. "You don't know what you're asking. I don't even know if you're real right now."

Her features softened. "I'm real enough to matter," she whispered, taking his hand. She pressed soft kisses on his fingertips. "Real enough to kiss you. Real enough to touch you."

The pressure of her lips fractured him more. "*Lydia*."

"Take me with you, Gabriel," she whispered. "Don't bury yourself in your mind. If I want you to stop, I'll use the word *England*, understand?"

Then she stepped into his arms and pressed her body against his.

And Gabriel shattered.

∽ 28 ∽

Lydia knew the moment Gabriel's control broke. She gasped as his lips met hers in a desperate kiss, plundering her mouth with his tongue. He backed her hard against the bedpost, shoving his hands into her hair.

Lydia accommodated him. His body was hot against hers, his hard cock jutting between them.

Gabriel drew back. "You are not to touch me," he said in a fierce growl.

Then he spun her. Shoved her onto the bed until her backside was facing him, her face pressed to the mattress.

Lydia flushed at the position. At having her body bared to Gabriel in such a vulnerable way. His hands fisted in her hair as he plunged his fingers inside of her.

Lydia gasped with pleasure. She was beyond words. Beyond thoughts of England or Moscow, her entire body was fixated on that point of contact. She heard Gabriel's harsh breathing behind her. He did not speak, not like the other night. Instead, he positioned himself over her with a feral noise.

Gabriel kicked her legs apart as his fingers worked her, coaxing sounds that betrayed her mounting desire. She wanted to beg him. But she could mutter nothing coherent as he pressed her face into the bed. Then she felt the hard heat of his cock as he shoved into her. Lydia would have arched off the bed if he hadn't kept his hand on her back, holding her in that vulnerable position.

Completely at his mercy.

And God, but Lydia liked it. She loved the feel of Gabriel pounding against her, uncontrolled. Of the harsh breath against the nape of her neck. Of the hand that squeezed in her hair. He did not whisper filthy things to her. He did not speak. He was a lover in the dark driven by carnal need, and so was she. She ground back against him as he plunged his cock in and out. He'd said she couldn't touch him, but she could do this small thing. She could touch him this way.

Gabriel's breath caught at the movement, and he quickened his pace. The only sound in the room was the slap of skin, their harsh, ragged breaths.

Then, with a rough groan, he climaxed. His forehead pressed between her shoulder blades as his breathing evened out. And for a moment, he held her like that. Cradled her with a tenderness that stole her breath.

Then he whispered, "Lydia. I'm sorry. God, I'm so sorry."

Then he withdrew from her and crossed the room. Before Lydia could utter a single word, he shut the connecting door.

And she heard the lock slide into place.

ᐧᐧᐧ 29 ᐧᐧᐧ

Gabriel patrolled the grounds of Langdon Manor and tried not to think about Lydia.

He had been riding since before dawn, making his way across the hills of the craggy landscape, a place he had not visited since shortly after his father and brother died. That inspection two years earlier had been brief, but something about the jagged escarpments and persistent moody weather had suited him. His flashes of childhood memories at Langdon had faded around the edges – more dreams than reality. So little of his past self was there to burden his present. Unlike at Meadowcroft, he did not have constant reminders of the life he could have lived with Lydia.

Even so, Gabriel's mind was in uproar over what he'd done to Lydia the night before. A sudden darkness clouded his mind. Had he hurt her? Done worse? *England*, she would say, if he had gone too far. She would remind him they were in England.

But memories of Moscow had been too close to the

surface; he had been stranded in his memories. Had she said the word? Did he fail to hear? In taking her with him to Moscow, Gabriel wondered if he had shattered Lydia's belief he would keep her safe.

Gabriel tipped back his head and shut his eyes. "Shit," he breathed.

Previous lovers had been warned about his predilections. So when he found a woman who enjoyed it rough, he paid her regular visits.

But until a few days ago, Lydia had never been intimate with a man – and last night, he'd shoved her face into the mattress and claimed her like an animal.

Gabriel didn't know how to apologise to her. She might have given him permission, but Lydia deserved the right to change her mind. And he didn't know if he'd given her the chance.

He couldn't bear to remain in that bedroom with her afterwards. The very thought of her coming to understand just how damaged he was had wrecked his already fragmented soul.

He was too broken to be a husband to her.

Too broken to be a proper, gentle lover.

Too. Damned. Broken.

With a weary sigh, Gabriel affectionately patted his horse's neck and rode back to the manor. Earlier that morning, a cable had come from Wentworth with a short message to say he would arrive that afternoon with Callahan. Gabriel's relief that they had both survived Medvedev's men dimmed when he read the second part of the message: *Bear escaped.*

So Medvedev was still a danger, and Lydia...

Gabriel had to apologise to her. Do anything he could to

make it up to her. He'd get down on his knees if she asked it of him.

Lydia was leaving the library when he walked into the hall. She paused, a flicker of apprehension on her face as she looked him over. "Good morning. Were you out for a ride?"

Gabriel set his gloves on the entryway table. "Patrolling. Wentworth sent word earlier that Medvedev managed to get away last night. I wanted to make sure we weren't followed."

"Oh," she said softly. She fidgeted with the lace on her dress, and Gabriel's concern grew. "Despite the reason, did you... have a lovely ride?"

Her faint words were like shards of glass twisting through his chest. She seemed so uncertain.

"I did," he said. "The grounds of Langdon are beautiful. I'll show them to you sometime."

God, but the veneer of politeness he maintained for the servants took every ounce of effort. *I'm sorry*, he wanted to say. *I am so sorry. If you forgave me, I'd be the most fortunate man who ever lived.*

"Wonderful." Lydia's throat bobbed as she swallowed. She glanced over at where a maid was beginning to clean the vases. "May we speak in the library?"

She shut the door behind them.

"Lydia," he said before she could speak. He couldn't touch her; he'd lose his senses if he made physical contact with her right then. "I'm so damn sorry for last night. Christ, I'm—"

Lydia's hands twisted. "You're... sorry."

His mind scarcely functioned. "For the way I treated

you." His words were ragged. "For what I did to you. For not hearing you when you said *England*—"

Lydia's eyes snapped to his. "I never said *England*."

A breath left him. Had he heard correctly? "You didn't?"

Lydia stepped closer. "No. You left before I could tell you that any night you are in Moscow, I will come with you." She pressed her palm to his chest. "I thought you must have regretted it."

His heart squeezed. That muscle in his chest pumping ice through his veins for so many years now came to life. Every part of his body was suddenly still, entirely calm. "I thought I had hurt you."

Her features softened in understanding. "I was with you until the moment you shut the door." She pressed her hand to his cheek, palm warm against his skin. "And I liked it."

Gabriel sought some insincerity in her voice; he had grown too used to liars. But the gleam of desire in her face was unmistakable. Wonder filled him and he marvelled at this beautiful woman who accepted every broken shard of his past and every jagged edge of his thoughts. This woman who would be hurt if his enemies ever came for them.

The thought doused his ardour. There was a reason the thieves, criminals, and killers in the Syndicate had a prejudice against wives. They became liabilities.

Lydia frowned, as if sensing he was distancing himself. But before she could say anything, several carriages drew up outside bearing the Montgomery crest.

"That will be Wentworth and Callahan," Gabriel said, stepping away. "You might be pleased to know that they're carrying some more items from your wardrobe."

Lydia dropped her hand, with an unreadable look. "Of

course." But then her expression changed as she noticed something out the window. "Wait a moment, is that my aunt's carriage?"

Sure enough, one of the carriages stopping in front of the house bore the crest of the Earl of Derby. Gabriel couldn't believe it. The last thing he needed was Lady Derby visiting when Medvedev's men might attack.

"Get rid of her," Gabriel said, striding to the door.

"She's my aunt," Lydia replied sharply.

Gabriel threw open the door. "And if she stays, she might become your murdered aunt."

Lydia winced. "Point well made."

Gabriel watched her rush to welcome Lady Derby.

As the two women exuberantly greeted one another, Gabriel walked over to where Wentworth and Callahan stood with the horses. "Which one of you is responsible for bringing Lady Derby?" he asked with quiet malice. The question might as well have been: *Which one of you am I murdering later?*

"Don't look at me," Callahan said, patting the neck of one of the carriage horses. "I don't bring grannies into my operations."

Wentworth glared at him. "As if I had a choice. She was on the road to Meadowcroft, and I had just been attacked by five of Medvedev's men. Was I supposed to leave her?"

"You could have lied," Callahan said.

"You could have told her Lady Montgomery and I are still on our honeymoon," Gabriel added.

Wentworth's gaze flickered over to where the countess embraced Lydia. "There's one small problem with both those suggestions."

Callahan looked interested. "What's that?"

"Lady Derby is bloody terrifying."

At that precise moment, the matron in question extricated herself from her niece's embrace and approached Gabriel. "Lord Montgomery," she said. "How wonderful to see you. And so far away from where I expected."

Gabriel pasted on a charming smile.

"Lady Derby," he said, kissing the air above her knuckles. "Always a pleasure. My wife was interested in seeing some of my other properties. Would you like the servants to prepare you a room?"

"I haven't decided yet." Her smile was strained. "I'd like to take tea with my niece first and determine how *she* fares." Her grip on his hand tightened. "Her happiness is very, *very* important to me, you see."

She made the benign statement sound like a murder threat.

Gabriel held his smile. "Of course."

She pulled her hand away. "Lydia, dear? Show me to the drawing room."

As Gabriel watched Lydia lead Lady Derby away, Callahan said, "Damn me, but you're right. She is terrifying."

30

"Would you like something to eat, aunt? You must be famished after your journey."

Lydia fidgeted as Lady Derby scanned the sitting room with an unreadable expression on her face. Lydia had noticed earlier that many of the furnishings, rugs, and curtains were dusty and threadbare, their colour faded with age. They were relics of a bygone era – perhaps proof that the Earl of Montgomery had found it painful to return to Langdon after his wife's death.

"I've no appetite just now," Lady Derby said, her eyes finally settling on Lydia. She took a seat on the sofa opposite her niece. "I hardly think I can drink tea, to tell the truth."

Lydia motioned to the maid waiting at the door, dismissing her. "Is something troubling you, aunt? You've come such a long way."

Lady Derby's gaze was frank and assessing. Lydia became acutely aware of the state of her travel dress. The maids had laundered it, but it was still worse for wear after her journey to Gabriel. Lydia had dressed her own hair while hurrying through her toilette, hoping to speak with Gabriel before he left the house again. She knew it looked messy. And, perhaps, her aunt sensed the unsettled state of Lydia's thoughts. Despite her best efforts, Lydia didn't have Gabriel's skill at pretence. She couldn't conceal her fear of Medvedev, her yearning for Gabriel, discontentment with the idea that their marriage might end the moment he caught the Syndicate leader. Gabriel might have taken her to Moscow the previous evening, but he had made no promises to keep her.

"Your letters have been lying to me," Lady Derby said, squaring her shoulders. "And I don't like it."

Lydia feigned a look of puzzlement. "I'm sure I don't know what you mean."

Lady Derby made a soft noise and looked out of the window to where Gabriel still conferred with Mr Wentworth and Mr Callahan. "My dear girl, I've known you and that boy since you were small enough to sit on my knee. I know when you are lying. And I know when *he* is lying."

Lydia pressed her fingernails into her palms. She wanted to tell Lady Derby everything. A part of her wanted to be a child again, resting her head in her aunt's lap to cry while Lady Derby stroked her hair. Her aunt had raised her like a daughter. She had been there all those years when Lydia suffered over Gabriel's silence. Keeping this secret from her seemed, somehow, like a betrayal of trust – a treachery.

But if Lydia told Aunt Frances she was in danger, the other woman would insist on staying. She would put herself in harm's way. So Lydia kept her expression carefully neutral.

"Have you come all this way to see me or to accuse me of making things up?"

Lady Derby looked impatient. "My old bones were prepared for the journey to Meadowcroft, not to Devon. I was surprised to find that detail omitted in your letters after you so prettily described everything else."

Lydia could hardly fault her aunt – she *had* filled her letters with insignificant details of Meadowcroft to conceal her true purpose there. In place of an explanation for her hasty marriage, she had described a blissful honeymoon riding across the estate, enjoying picnics, and exploring paths she had enjoyed as a girl. In the absence of truth, Lydia had drawn entirely on her memories with Gabriel, creating a picture of young love which in hindsight seemed naïve. That love, after all, had never been tested. It hardly reflected the complexity of her marriage now, when ten years of distance and personal pain had fundamentally altered their once uncomplicated relationship.

"Our trip was quite sudden," Lydia said, with an honest, apologetic tone. "Lord Montgomery mentioned that the late earl and countess were quite fond of this property, and I was in a mood to visit somewhere new. Rather like the time we went on holiday to Brighton."

Lydia's effort to coax a smile from her aunt did not work. If anything, her aunt's face grew more severe. "Of course, you're married now – free to have an adventure as you please. But imagine my surprise that *Mr Wentworth* was informed of your abrupt change in plans before I was. He offered to escort me back to London, but I declined when he divulged that he would be journeying to Langdon Manor."

"Mr Wentworth has been a great friend of my husband's," Lydia said, aware the explanation seemed flimsy. "They had planned to fish together."

"Lydia."

"But, of course, I must apologise," she continued hastily. "You shouldn't have had to travel all this way with worry. And—"

Lady Derby reached forward to grasp her hands. "*Lydia.*"

Lydia was horrified to realise her eyes were wet. That all her attempts to suppress her feelings had failed utterly. She was not a natural liar. "Yes, aunt?" she whispered.

"I need to know that you are all right," Lady Derby said. "And I won't leave you here until I'm satisfied with your answer."

"I don't know," Lydia said, blinking back more tears. She didn't know because she loved Gabriel. Perhaps she had never stopped loving him. It was a simple fact of her life: the sun rose, the stars shifted, and she loved Gabriel St Clair.

But she did not know if he loved her back. She did not know if this marriage was destined to end when Medvedev was dealt with. Her future with Gabriel remained as uncertain as the depths of the ocean.

"My sweet girl," Lady Derby murmured sadly. "Does he... not treat you well?"

Lydia knew how it must have seemed to her aunt: keeping secrets, maintaining appearances – all the signs of an acrimonious marriage. But even she couldn't help but express surprise at the notion that Gabriel would hurt her. The very idea had been so repellent to him that he'd locked himself in his room earlier.

Lydia's eyes stung once more. "He is the best husband I

could ask for," she said. She paused to gather herself. "But I don't know if he wants to have the kind of marriage I do."

Lady Derby's face fell. "Oh, Lydia."

"I love him so much," Lydia said, all too conscious that the tears she had so valiantly tried to subdue now fell freely. "And I don't know if he loves me back."

Her aunt sighed and released Lydia's hands. She reached into the pocket of her travel dress and plucked out a handkerchief to dab Lydia's cheeks. "I remember observing the two of you together when you were children. One thing I noticed was how that boy watched you when you weren't looking." Her aunt gave a small smile. "Forgive an old woman for the sentimentality, but it warmed my heart."

Lydia shook her head. "All those years apart, his time in the diplomatic service… things are different now." She wished she could tell her aunt how much.

But Lady Derby made an exasperated sound and continued wiping Lydia's cheeks. "I'm aware that Lord Montgomery isn't the same, don't think I'm not. He might have all society fooled, but I've known him since he was young enough to climb my trees."

Lydia gave a quick smile at the memory. "He and I aren't like we were then."

"That's not the point I was making, my love. I watched him when he returned to England. I noticed how different he was." She smoothed Lydia's cheek affectionately with her thumb. "But he always looked at you the same way. As if you were the brightest star in the sky."

∽ 31 ∽

Gabriel spread the map of the Langdon estate across the table in his study. "If Medvedev's remaining men try to attack, they'd have to scout this area. It's larger than Meadowcroft."

Callahan studied the map, then tapped a rocky outcropping nearby. "Plenty of places for them to hide there."

"Have your men patrol and keep watch in shifts," Gabriel said. "After losing several of his agents, Medvedev will be more determined than ever." He glanced at Wentworth. "Any idea how many people he has working for him?"

Wentworth shook his head. "But you know that doesn't matter. Pay the right man in the rookeries enough, and he'll join Medvedev in trying to murder you and your wife."

"Then he'll be paying the right people to hide him," Gabriel murmured. "Plenty of criminals know how to escape the authorities, and the East End is full of places for him to regroup while his scouts gather information about this property."

Callahan glanced at Wentworth. "You ought to ask Nick Thorne to help. He knows the rookeries better than anyone, and residents might be more willing to talk to him."

Nicholas Thorne was the owner of the Brimstone, a successful London gaming hell that had elevated him from criminal to one of the richest men in England. Residents in the rookeries referred to him as the King of the East End. His marriage to Lady Alexandra Grey, sister to the Earl of Kent, had raised him to something like respectability. Still, Gabriel had heard Nick Thorne wore that respectability like a costume. And Gabriel knew a thing or two about disguises.

Wentworth seemed intrigued. "Thorne cooperates with the authorities on his own terms but doesn't like to involve himself with the business of aristocrats. Until Medvedev causes trouble in the East End, Thorne might not be interested in offering to help."

"Give him my name," Callahan said easily, still studying the map of the grounds. "Remind him he owes me a debt."

Surprise flared in Wentworth's eyes. "*You* know Nick Thorne?"

Callahan didn't even look up. "Who doesn't?"

"There's a difference between knowing him and having the King of the East End in your debt," Gabriel added.

"If I were interested in sharing my history with Thorne, I would," Callahan said impatiently. "Just call in the favour, Wentworth." He pushed away from the table. "If you'll excuse me, I'm off to familiarise myself with the grounds."

Wentworth watched his agent leave with an unreadable expression Gabriel had come to know well.

"Don't scratch at that particular door, Wentworth," Gabriel said. "You don't need to know everyone's business."

"It's my job to know everyone's business," Wentworth murmured.

"Yet you keep a thousand of your own secrets."

"When mine become a problem, perhaps I won't." Wentworth looked thoughtful. "And you?"

Gabriel frowned. "What about me?"

"Medvedev wasn't the only Syndicate leader. There are whispers about internal conflicts, and the missives we've had decoded indicate other major players who are just as dangerous."

"Come to the point, Wentworth."

A ghost of a smile lifted his lips. "You have the most knowledge of the organisation. Have you thought about what you'll do after we deal with Bear?"

Gabriel studied the other man carefully. "Just tell me what you're asking."

"You're one of the best spies we had," Wentworth said with a shrug. "You speak a dozen languages. And clearly, you're ill-suited for retirement. I'm asking if you'd like to go to the Continent and gather intelligence on the other Syndicate factions."

Something about the idea made Gabriel's mind riot. Flashes of Moscow rippled beneath the surface of his memories. And suddenly, abandoning Lydia again seemed like leaving behind a fundamental part of him. "I seem to recall the Home Office forcing me out of the operation because of my title."

"And your absence made them overlook that Medvedev was still alive." Wentworth made a soft noise and pushed his hands into his pockets. "If you wanted back in, I'd put in a word for you. Lord Montgomery will go on an extended holiday abroad."

The clamour in Gabriel's thoughts persisted, but he didn't immediately turn Wentworth down. The answer stuck in his throat. After all, what would he do if he said no? He would continue to put Lydia's life in danger. If she decided to leave him for New York, Gabriel would stay in London, resuming his role as Lord Montgomery. Finding the occasional fight as an outlet for his violence. Experiencing nightmares about Moscow every night without Lydia there to ease them.

What purpose would he serve in that life? *None.*

A dry laugh escaped him. "Forgive my hesitancy. This seems a strange request on what's supposed to be my honeymoon."

Wentworth's eyes met his. "I thought your marriage wasn't real. If you've changed your mind about it, you need only tell me, and I'll offer the position to Callahan."

Gabriel almost accepted. But, no, he couldn't do that again. Could he?

And yet...

He could not be the husband Lydia needed, either. Taking her to Moscow for one night wasn't the same as a lifetime of nightmares. That was a burden she had not asked for when she married him. She'd declared him to be a good husband – and all he could think of was that last night, he might not have heard her if she'd said *England*.

Perhaps one day in the future, she *would* say that word,

and he would ignore her pain in the confusion of his memories.

Unforgivable.

Gabriel preoccupied himself with rolling up the map. "I'll consider your offer. Please excuse me. I need to check on Lydia and Lady Derby."

The two women had just left the drawing room as he came down the hall, and Gabriel watched them embrace. When Lydia eased away from her aunt, Gabriel noticed the redness to her cheeks. Had she been crying? What had Lady Derby said to her?

Gabriel pushed aside his worry. "Lady Derby, have you decided whether you'd like to stay?"

To his relief, she said, "Not this evening. My friend Mrs Dunmore lives nearby and asked me to visit her. I shall leave you two on your honeymoon and prevail upon her for a room. Would you accompany me to my carriage, Montgomery? Lydia, if you could give us a moment?"

"Of course," Lydia replied. "I'll go see if Mr Wentworth requires anything."

Gabriel took Lady Derby's arm and led her outside. "I hope you've been well, Lady Derby," Gabriel said, forcing a polite smile. "And that you'll revisit us for an extended stay."

"I intend to. I worry about Lydia when she isn't with me." They strolled down the front steps, and Gabriel sensed her slow pace was deliberate. She was stalling for time. "I only want what's best for her."

"Of course," Gabriel murmured. "We're in agreement."

"Good." Lady Derby's hand tightened on his arm. "Then I only have to tell you this once: if you hurt my niece again,

I will hunt you down wherever you are and cheerfully murder you."

Gabriel let out a surprised laugh. "I admire your protective instincts, Lady Derby. I'm pleased that my wife has someone who cares for her so passionately." He smiled at her. "Other than me, of course."

But Lady Derby didn't seem pacified. If anything, her expression hardened. "I'm uninterested in your deceptions, Montgomery. When it comes to Lydia's happiness, my threats are not idle."

Gabriel abandoned his society role so seldom that it took a moment for the charming smile to fade. When it did, he saw a sort of acknowledgement cross the dowager countess's face. A silent message: *There you are.*

"I understand your concern, Lady Derby," he said. "And I share it."

She studied him as they approached her carriage. "You'll forgive me if I'm doubtful. I comforted my niece for years during your absence when every season was a reminder of the promise you broke. And I held her after your return when you pretended the woman to whom you had offered marriage was little more than a distant acquaintance."

A sliver of pain pierced Gabriel as he recalled Lydia standing on the doorstep of his London house, bravely trying to hide her tears. Lydia, sitting in the corners of ballrooms, as if she were trying to conceal her very existence. He had done that to her. Worse: he had recognised the pain it caused and did it anyway. Watching her despair had become his burden to carry.

"I deserve your censure," he told her.

"Yes, you do."

She waited, as if expecting him to summon some reassurance. But he could not promise Lady Derby that he wouldn't hurt Lydia again.

Instead, he grasped her hand and gave it a squeeze. "I can't offer the sort of reassurances you want. But one thing I can do is keep her safe. I always will."

"Now that, I do believe." Lady Derby signalled to the driver. "But I want you to know one thing, Gabriel St Clair: my niece deserves far more from you than that."

∽ 32 ∽

Over the next few days, Lydia occupied herself by exploring Langdon Manor. The old estate was not in the same condition as Meadowcroft, but its peeling wallpaper and old, dusty furnishings held charm. If nothing else, the ancient house distracted Lydia from her concerns and doubts.

Ever since their first night at Langdon, Gabriel had kept his side of their connecting door locked. When she did manage to locate him during the day, he treated her with polite cordiality. But his attention had a kind of fixed focus, as if he were weighing up some critical decision.

A choice that would impact their future.

With a sigh, Lydia roamed the long upstairs gallery, stopping to examine the immense portraits of the Earls of Montgomery and their families. Each shared Gabriel's austere, handsome features, auburn hair, and green eyes.

Then, finally, she came to the portrait of Gabriel. She supposed the late Earl of Montgomery had had it painted before Gabriel left for Vienna; she recalled that his hair was longer then, his shoulders less broad.

But what struck her most was his eyes: in this picture, they did not have that remote, cold stare that revealed both nothing and all too much. Now she'd learned more about his time in Moscow, Lydia marvelled at how he had managed to fool her after returning to England. She had observed him across the ballroom and resented his broken promises rather than ask herself why he had deserted her in the first place.

The sudden creak of the heavy gallery door startled her. A slow tread of boots crossed the gallery until the object of her anguish stopped beside her.

Somehow, Lydia could not bring herself to look at Gabriel – this man she loved but who had carried the weight of his burden in Moscow alone. Guilt flared hot, sinking inside her with shame as its companion.

"You didn't come down for dinner," Gabriel said quietly. "Are you unwell?"

Lydia tried not to think of how his voice stroked her like a loving caress. She wanted to shut her eyes and ask him to speak nonsense words, forget her remorse, bask in his attention. But she could not move. She could not accept that she merited those things.

"I wasn't hungry."

Gabriel was silent beside her. Out of the corner of her eye, she watched as he tipped his head back and examined the portrait of himself. "I remember when my father commissioned this," he said finally, his voice soft. "I had recently come down from Oxford, ready to use all those hours of studying languages. I wanted to be an—"

"Ambassador," she finished softly. "I remember."

"My father was proud that I wanted to go into the diplomatic service," Gabriel continued. In her periphery, she saw his head turn toward her. "And he was proud that I wanted to marry you."

A pain stabbed through her heart as she remembered the late Earl of Montgomery. Lydia recalled that he had a kind smile. Whenever he came home, it was with a bag of sweets for Gabriel to share with Lydia.

"You've mentioned them so little," she murmured. "Your father and brother."

He returned his attention to the painting. "They were good men," Gabriel said. "Father did the best he could after my mother died and left him responsible for two young sons. And Thomas…" A soft breath came from him. "I was relieved he was the heir instead of me."

"Why?" Lydia asked.

After all their years apart, she felt as if she was relearning everything about this man who had become her husband. He was not the optimistic youth in the painting. That youth had gone into the world, and the world had sought to crush him.

"Thomas was so responsible," Gabriel murmured. "He modelled his sense of duty on our father's example, and he planned to use his position to campaign for progressive laws."

"I remember. He wrote articles while you were away." A smile touched her face. "When I saw him at balls, he always asked me to dance."

His lips tightened – but just as quickly, the expression was gone. "When I was in Moscow and was able to read my letters securely, he spoke about you."

That surprised Lydia. Other than those infrequent dances, she barely knew his brother. At six years Gabriel's senior and eight Lydia's, he seemed so much older when they were children. By the time Lydia was introduced into society, she regarded Thomas St Clair as a welcome acquaintance – but she could never see him without a pang of pain. Thomas, after all, had so closely resembled Gabriel.

"He did?" she asked.

Gabriel dipped his head in a nod. "He demanded to know why I hadn't come home and done right by you. Shortly before the accident that killed him and Father, he'd threatened to propose to you himself if I didn't return to England."

Lydia's heart slammed against her ribcage. Perhaps she might have accepted him. She'd been so angry with Gabriel for leaving her, for ignoring her letters and breaking his promise. Five years ago, she might have been furious enough to marry Thomas.

"Did you reply?" she whispered.

"No." The word was curt. "His letters, too, went unanswered. To maintain my cover in Moscow, I could have no family, not even under my past identity. So I burned every letter, even yours."

"They were silly," she said, trying to speak around the stabbing pain in her heart. She thought he'd ignored her. "Nothing of substance."

"I said I burned them," he said softly. "I never said I didn't read them."

Lydia looked at Gabriel for the first time since he entered the gallery, but his gaze remained fixed on the painting. The square line of his jaw was taut with a muscle working beneath. His beautiful features were severe. As if he were encased in ice.

"You read them," she echoed, her words barely above a breath.

"Sometimes, I would nearly tear them in my haste to break the seal," he said. "I read each one three times. The first to hear your voice in my mind, because I worried I was forgetting it. The second, to imagine you writing it. To picture all the ways you had changed in my absence. And the third…"

"The third?" she prompted. She clasped her hands to still them, to stop herself from reaching out to touch him. She did not want to break the moment.

"The third was to memorise it." Though his voice was faint, its deep timbre slid across her skin like a brush of fingertips, a revelation. "So I could read your letters in the privacy of my mind in Moscow and remember what I left behind in England. And then you stopped writing."

Lydia's heart constricted. Her eyes clouded over with tears. For years, she wondered if those letters went out into the world only to fall into an abyss. Later, she wrote more out of routine than in anticipation of a response. She'd imagined each one became a joke at the Home Office: Poor, poor Lydia Cecil. Writing yet again, after years without an answer. A bit pathetic, isn't it?

"I never even knew you received them until the Duchess of Hastings' house party," she said.

His jaw tightened at the reminder of the disastrous game of croquet the year before. I have no letters to return to you. I threw them out with the rubbish.

"Each one spoke to me as if I were still this man," he

said, motioning to his portrait. "Sometimes, I thought of responding. But then I wondered if you would immediately be able to tell your childhood friend was gone, and the man in his place couldn't love you in the same way." Then, as Lydia tried to think of a reply, Gabriel abruptly asked, "Do you miss him?"

Her childhood friend. The one in the portrait.

Lydia did not look at the painting now. Instead, she focused on Gabriel, this man who had been a fundamental part of her life for so long. Her heart had been his for almost as long as she'd been alive. "I no longer think in terms of your past and your present," she told him. "You'll always be Gabriel St Clair to me. Just as you are."

And I love you.

But she did not say those words. Much as she longed to do so, they stuck in her throat like a barb. She worried that confessing her feelings might make him pull away from her until he retreated once more behind that icy wall she could not penetrate.

Gabriel's gaze dropped. "But I am not only Gabriel St Clair, am I? Alexei Borislov is the reason you're in this gallery, instead of enjoying the freedom to wander the gardens. And Alexei Borislov is why you'll never be safe with me." Before Lydia could reply, he gently grasped her hand, tugging it towards him. Then he lifted it and pressed a soft kiss to the back of her wrist. "Goodnight, Lydia."

As he walked away from her, Lydia found herself able to speak. "Will you take me to Moscow again?"

Gabriel paused. She noticed the tension in his shoulders. "Not tonight," he said, and then he walked out of the gallery.

Lydia stared at the door long after he'd shut it. She felt as if Gabriel were slipping through her grasp like fine sand. As each grain tumbled between her fingers, thoughts coalesced into a plan.

If he did not take her to Moscow, she would find a way to bring him back to England.

33

G abriel folded the telegram and tossed it onto the table in his bedchamber. The messenger had brought it earlier in the day while Gabriel was out patrolling the grounds with Callahan. By the time he finally sat down to read it, night had fallen, and Gabriel's nerves were frayed.

Raid last night in the East End, Wentworth wrote. *Accomplices captured. Bear on the run alone. Have you given more thought to my offer?*

Wentworth's proposal had plagued Gabriel for days. Several times, he had considered riding to the telegraph office to accept that offer, but some lingering doubt always stopped him. The previous evening, it was Lydia in the gallery, asking if he would take her to Moscow. He'd thought of her delicate features, pale and wan from lack of sleep, but she had looked at him with a burning hope that he wanted both to satisfy and violently reject. Those conflicting emotions had occupied his mind during his earlier ride with Callahan – a complication that was far too dangerous.

Lydia's soft laughter drifted through the connecting door as her maid prepared her for bed. Gabriel rose from his desk and lingered at the threshold, listening to her movements. The cadence of her voice and laughter was like sunlight. He shut his eyes and let the sonance roll across his skin like soothing water.

He wondered what she did in the privacy of her bedchamber. If she ever stood beside the wood panelling and heard him tossing restlessly at night. If she was ever tempted to knock.

But the locked door between them might as well have been an ocean. A reminder that intimacy with her could not be a distraction from the truth: his homeland now felt as foreign to Gabriel as the life he once had lived.

The way Lydia had gazed up at his old portrait in the gallery had tugged at something in his chest, chipping away again at the pieces of ice still lodged there. Bit by bit, she had melted nearly every part of him until his blood ran almost as red and warm as that of the man in the gallery portrait.

But Gabriel was not the same. Lydia was the only thing that tied him to this place; she was the rope that anchored him, saving him from being cast adrift. But therein lay her own danger. His heart might pump blood instead of ice now, but it held the memory of cold. Like a lake in winter, it could quickly freeze again.

With a sigh, Gabriel went to seek a distraction outside. He found Callahan in the stables, grooming his horse. If the other man was surprised to see Gabriel, he didn't show it.

"Monty," he said simply.

Gabriel watched Callahan run the brush smoothly across the horse's quarters. "You're putting my stable lads out of a job, I think."

Callahan's lips quirked up. "Gave them the night off. Said you ordered it."

A short laugh escaped Gabriel. "If you're looking for more work, all you had to do was ask."

"Not looking for more work," Callahan said. "Just seeking a distraction. Reckon you're out here doing the same."

Gabriel grunted. "And what makes you think I need distracting?"

Callahan shrugged. "You've got a pretty wife who looks at you as if she wants you to fuck her, and you're out here watching me groom a horse. Can't attest to a fancy education, but I'm not an idiot, either."

Gabriel looked away sharply, staring out at the dark beyond the stable doors, back toward the house. "Does Wentworth appreciate your impertinence?"

"I assume my honesty holds a bit of appeal, or he would have booted me out on my arse years ago." Finally, after a long moment of silence, Callahan asked, "You going to take his offer?"

Gabriel hadn't realised Wentworth had made his proposition known to Callahan. "Wentworth gossips too much. I thought he was supposed to be busy looking for Medvedev."

"Only a matter of time," Callahan said, dropping the brush in the bucket and giving the horse an ear scratch. "With his men in custody and Wentworth and Thorne on his tail, he won't last long unless he flees back to Russia."

Callahan glanced at Gabriel. "Surprised you haven't raced to London to aid the search."

Gabriel sought his old anger toward Medvedev but found it had cooled – what had once been molten was now solidified, cold, and practical. He cared less about hurting Medvedev than he did about protecting Lydia. After what happened on the road to Langdon Manor…

He could have lost her so easily.

"I won't leave my wife," he said simply. "Medvedev is resourceful, and he has more reason than ever to come after me. His entire operation here in England is compromised."

"For a man who cares about his wife so much, you do a great deal to avoid her."

Gabriel glared at Callahan. "For a man who seems to value his life, you talk too much."

Callahan laughed.

Later, Gabriel returned to his bedchamber. His attention settled on the connecting door. Was Lydia already asleep? Or did she lie awake, waiting for him to visit her?

He edged closer to the door, pressing his ear to the wood. He just wanted to hear her breathing. The rustle of her moving about. To know that she slept safely, and—

A sound stirred from within, one that ignited him.

A low, breathy moan. Then another. A soft gasp of pleasure had him curling his fingernails into the door panel.

She'd mentioned pleasuring herself back in the library at Meadowcroft, a small detail that had preoccupied him during the quiet of his afternoon rides. He had contemplated all the ways she might touch herself. Bring herself to climax. These became small details that he longed to learn about. He wanted her to educate him on the terrain of her body, every part that made her shudder with pleasure. He wanted to know what she pictured in the bedroom next to his own. Did she think of him at all? Or was she thinking of a new lover, perhaps one not so broken?

God, but it didn't matter. He wanted. He needed. Her breathing heaved as she unabashedly took her pleasure, and that set something off inside him. Gabriel flicked open his trousers and took out his cock. And as he listened to her, he imagined that it was his own hands on her pussy. His fingers plunging into her until she was wet enough. He gave himself a hard stroke at the thought of shoving inside her slick quim, timing his movements to the pace of her breaths, moving faster. He knew that she was close – and he increased his speed to match hers.

Then, with a moan he stifled by biting his tongue, he heard her muffled cry. And the answer to his earlier question came to him like a bludgeon.

"Gabriel," he heard her whisper. Perhaps she knew he was there, sensed his presence on the other side of the door. She seemed as connected to him as the tides to the moon. "I love you."

Gabriel pressed his forehead to the door and shut his eyes.

ɔ 34 ɔ

Lydia was writing a letter to Lady Derby when she heard a woman scream.

She jolted in her chair, nearly knocking the furniture over in her haste to yank open the curtains. While the source of the shouts wasn't visible from her window, Lydia noticed servants racing down the garden pathways.

Lydia threw open the door and dashed down the stairs. A maid sped past her in the hallway, sobbing and incoherent – not in any state to offer an explanation. Lydia hurried out the terrace doors to the garden.

The voices of staff were coming from just past the rosebushes, the uproar reaching Lydia's ears as she hastened down the footpath. More maids ran past her, their eyes filled with tears. Then, as Lydia entered the rose garden, she spotted Gabriel's broad form standing with Mr Callahan at the edge of the flower beds.

"Gabriel!"

He spun at her shout, his eyes filling with… was it *fear*?

In a few strides, he gripped her shoulders. "You can't be out here."

"What's happened?" Lydia's pulse raced as she looked past him. "What—" A strangled cry lodged in her throat.

There, just beneath the roses, lay the body of a maid. Lydia only identified the girl from the blood-covered uniform she wore. But her face was turned away, her hair entirely matted red, and her face and neck covered in scratches. Her torso was a map of violence, its geography crafted in rage.

Lydia pressed her hand to her mouth as bile rose in her throat. Gabriel made a soft sound and moved in front of her, blocking her view. "Don't look at it, love. All right? Don't look." Lydia leaned against Gabriel for support. "Callahan, take my wife back inside to my bedchamber. I'll be there directly."

The other man came and gently took her arm. "Come, my lady."

As Lydia let herself be led back toward the house, Mr Callahan supported nearly all her weight. "I'm sorry to have you nearly carry me," she said faintly. "I'm rather dizzy."

Mr Callahan gave her a grim smile. "Understandable."

He was silent as he helped her up the stairs. "Do you… do you know who it was?" she asked him.

"Scullery maid," Mr Callahan said, easing her up another flight of stairs. "Reckon she went into the garden for a bit of a rest."

Lydia pressed her lips together. She had seen so little of the kitchen staff. She'd regretted not even knowing the girl's name – the girl who had died in the garden below her window. "Shouldn't I have heard?" she whispered.

"Heard what?" Mr Callahan stopped at her door and nudged it open, urging her inside.

"Her die." A faint noise escaped Lydia as she crossed the room and settled in her window seat. "She was by the rosebushes just out of view of my window."

"Some men know how to kill quietly," Mr Callahan said, shutting the door. "Medvedev is evidently one of them." His eyes settled on her. "Are you all right now?"

"No." The answer was little more than a breath. "I'm not certain I am." At his silence, she said, "You've seen that kind of thing often, haven't you?"

Though his handsome features didn't change, she noticed a stillness come over him. "Often enough," he said.

A breath heaved through her, one that hurt to the very bones. "Why do you do this job, Mr Callahan," she murmured, "if that sight is so common? How do you bear seeing it?"

A muscle leaped in his jaw as he leaned against the wall. "Perhaps I figure it as a penance."

Lydia was surprised by that. "A penance for what?"

A bitter smile crossed his face. "You might have some idea, based on your husband's previous work. The difference between us is that I've done it for a lot longer, and I don't have a wife to go home to."

Lydia's fingers curled into the soft muslin of her day dress. "I'm sorry. I feel foolish for asking."

Mr Callahan made a noise that sounded almost like a dry laugh. "Don't be. Between you and your husband, he's the bloody fool."

Gabriel pushed through the bedchamber door before Lydia could ask what Callahan meant. Though his breathing was calm, his expression betrayed his agitation. Those beautiful features were bleak. "Your men go out in shifts tonight," Gabriel said to Callahan. "I don't want more than three sleeping simultaneously, and make sure everyone goes out in pairs."

Callahan gave a sharp nod. "The staff?"

Gabriel's lips compressed into a line. "I've instructed everyone to return to their families for the time being, with a bonus for their trouble. The constable was none too pleased once he got a cable from Wentworth instructing him to leave this to the Home Office." He motioned with a hand to the window. "You'll take care of the body?"

The other man gave a mirthless smile. "I'll make sure she gets a proper burial, and I'll update you if the others find anything." Mr Callahan left the room, shutting the door firmly behind him.

For the first time since entering the bedchamber, Gabriel's attention rested on Lydia. She watched as the hard angles of his face softened slightly. "I've secured this wing of the house, and the cook left us a basket before she went to visit her daughter. We will be staying here until Wentworth comes up from London with Thorne's men to assist in the search."

A dart of fear went through Lydia. "Do your guards know how Medvedev managed to get into the gardens?"

The grim look returned to Gabriel's features. "We found one of the guards with his throat slit." Lydia shivered. Gabriel must have noticed, because he came to sit beside her. "I'll do whatever I can to make it safe for you. Do you understand?"

Lydia grasped one of his hands and pressed her lips to his palm. "I trust you."

If anything, his expression only grew bleaker.

∽ 35 ∽

Gabriel had been looking out of the window for hours. Some time ago, Lydia had settled into the corner of their private sitting room and taken up her embroidery to pass the time.

Gabriel couldn't stop himself from glancing over to the corner of the room, watching as his wife delicately threaded her needle. A curl of hair rested softly on her forehead, and he longed to push it back. To soothe away the line of concern from her brow.

I trust you, she'd said.

She shouldn't. She should trust him with nothing, certainly not her heart.

The abrupt sound of her voice jolted Gabriel from his thoughts. "When do you expect Mr Wentworth to come?"

Gabriel stared out into the darkness. "Sometime tomorrow morning. He might want to stop at an inn on the way."

Lydia gingerly set aside her embroidery frame and leaned

back in her chair. "I'm eager to visit the gardens here when it's safe. I noticed an ivy-covered wall from my window. Do you know what it is?"

He caught his breath to see how the fire illuminated her skin and cast its shadows lovingly across her delicate features. Her eyes were dark pools of ink that watched him with the kind of hope he had forgotten in all his years away. A part of him wanted to say something that would disabuse her of that longing, set her on a different path, one that she could walk without him. But he could not find it in him to say harsh words to her.

"Langdon Castle," he said, letting his gaze linger on her. Once he accepted Wentworth's offer, he would see very little of her. She would be a wife in name only. "It burned down two centuries ago and was replaced by this house."

Lydia stood, approaching the window seat. She, too, looked out into the dark garden. "That's one of the things I love about these old estates," she murmured, putting her hand on the window frame. The air around Gabriel became redolent with the scent of her lavender soap. "Finding history in its gardens. Wondering about the people who lived there and built it." Her eyelashes lowered. "I have made no such mark on a place."

Gabriel wanted to argue with her. Tell her it wasn't true. She'd made marks all over him. When he was buried in the earth, they would find her written on his bones.

But he only leaned back against the wall and said, "Perhaps you ought to make a change, then. Something for history to remember you by."

She smiled softly at him. "Like what?"

Gabriel lifted a shoulder. "Whatever you like."

The smile remained on her face – such an uninhibited and trusting expression. The sight of it pricked him like sharp claws. "What if I longed for a little cottage, like something out of a storybook?" she murmured. "One to visit when I want to be alone, away from staff and the obligation of my position? What would you think of that?"

He wanted to tell her she was like a woman out of a fable. That she seemed as real to him as the cottage in her imagination and that it fitted her just perfectly. "What would you do in your little cottage, with no staff or obligations?"

"Work in the garden with my hands," she said. "Wear trousers everywhere. Come in at the end of each day exhausted and covered in mud." Her eyes met his. "Kiss you wherever I'd like."

Gabriel went still. He imagined himself in Lydia's fantasy, working the land and finding comfort in the movements of his body. Physicality without violence. And he envisaged himself kissing her in the garden, sitting her down on a bench, and making love to her as the sun warmed their skin. Then, months later, she would have to abandon her trousers for new ones to fit her expanding belly, full with his child.

That last unbidden image ripped him out of the fantasy. He was reminded of Wentworth's letter sitting on his table just across the room. The missive that decided his future must be without her because that garden was a fabrication.

Gabriel turned away from her. "It's late. You ought to sleep if you can."

She sighed, and the air grew cold as she moved away. Gabriel swallowed, listening to the rustle of fabric – Lydia removing her garments.

After a beat, she spoke again. "This dress has buttons up the back," she said. "And you've sent my maid home."

Gabriel shut his eyes briefly, cursing his decision to send her maid away. Cursing the sudden stiffening of his cock, which did *not* help matters.

Lydia turned to offer her back, sweeping aside the tendril of hair that had escaped her coiffure. Gabriel was left with a view of her graceful nape, the tidy row of buttons like a gift to be unwrapped. He wanted to press his lips *right there*, to the small expanse of exposed skin bared like a taunt.

It was as if their bodies suddenly became mirror images of one another: same heart, same set of lungs, same need. Gabriel flicked open the top button, and Lydia's entire body responded to his touch, a shiver passing through her.

Gabriel unfastened another button. And another. The triangle of exposed pale skin expanded until he bared the top of her combinations, then the stays of her corset. Frustration paused his hands as he contemplated these obstructions – both of them denying him this moment. This opportunity. This *excuse* to see all of her. An excuse he would not have, once he answered that goddamn letter on his desk.

He set his jaw and tackled the remaining buttons with a determination to get it over with and find some way to collect himself while she slumbered. He would relearn to breathe if he had to.

But Gabriel had overestimated his ability to resist her; when he had finished, he could not bring himself to move. Lydia pushed her dress down her shoulders. The gown slithered to the floor, where it landed in a whisper of fabric. Gabriel watched as her long, graceful fingers unpicked the tapes of her petticoats. Those, too, joined the heap of material on the floor.

Gabriel closed his fingers into fists and fought the urge to put his hands on her. Her undergarments represented another sort of intimacy: no other man but he would glimpse the dainty lace lining the drawers of her combinations, nor the ribbons and tiny rosebuds adorning her pink corset. Garments made so beautifully, just to be hidden away. A blessing for him alone.

Lydia turned her face slightly until he had a partial view of her profile. Of the faint dusting of freckles across the bridge of her nose. "My corset," she whispered.

Gabriel held his breath as he reached for Lydia again, plucking at the laces of the garment. It yielded beneath his ministrations, the silk encased boning parting to reveal the delicate muslin combinations beneath – such a tiny scrap of fabric to hide her from his view. When the corset landed on the floor, her remaining undergarment did little to conceal her body. Her pale skin was visible beneath the white fabric, the outline of her shape illuminated by the firelight. All he had to do was remove one more layer, and she would be entirely naked. Her nudity was a gift he had not fully enjoyed back at Meadowcroft.

Gabriel heard Lydia swallow. "My combinations."

He was aware that removal of the delicate undergarment didn't require his help. Yet he could not bring himself to remind her, nor could he refuse her request. It was as if she had stirred a compulsion within him, a strange hunger that could only be sated by touch – and only hers would satisfy.

Unable to stop, Gabriel slid his arms around her gently

to untie the ribbons at her breasts. She stilled, a soft moan escaping her as his hand grazed the nipple that hardened through the flimsy fabric. Something about that sound caught fire in his lungs, spread heat through his bloodstream. He dropped his mouth to the nape of her neck and pressed his lips to the bared skin there.

"What are you doing to me?" Gabriel whispered. She was a fire melting every part of him, right down to his very foundations.

As if she read his mind, Lydia shoved the combinations off her shoulders. The fabric dropped to the floor with the rest of her clothes, that final impediment absent. All that remained was hot bare skin against his hands.

His teeth gently scraped her neck, a wordless request for an answer.

He ought to have known she would not cower away from such a demand. Instead, Lydia turned in his arms, those dark eyes meeting his own. "I want to keep you," she said firmly. "Understand?"

That voice might as well have been steel. It ought to have battered against his better instincts – reminded him of the letter on the table not ten feet away – but Gabriel no longer had defences against her. Everything he'd built crumbled beneath her touch. Perhaps it had been formed of flawed foundations to begin with. She had known every vulnerable part of his anatomy.

Gabriel's gaze dropped to her body, proudly bared before him. The jut of her small breasts, the dip of her waist – both features he traced with his palm to feel their shape. Her skin was lined and marked from the corset, marks that only his eyes would see.

His desire ignited when she grasped his chin and forced his gaze up. "I am yours. You are mine," she said. "Yes?"

Because those words were true – because he could no longer deny them – Gabriel answered with a single word, spoken in a rough growl: "Yes."

And then he claimed her lips with his own.

Gabriel ought to have remembered what her kiss did. When their lips touched, he lost the capacity to think and reason. All that mattered was having more of her.

Frantically, he flicked open the buttons of his clothes. His movements were inelegant, concerned only with removing those obstructions that separated them. Her fingers were cleverer – she had his garments off in seconds. Her desperation gratified him, reminded him that he was not the only victim of their shared passion. She had declared herself his, and he had always been hers. They were equal in their need.

Gabriel gently bit her lower lip, his hands moving down her hips to find her quim wet beneath his fingers. "Is this what you've wanted for days?" he asked her, sliding his fingers inside her.

Lydia grasped his shoulders as if for balance. "Yes. *Yes.*"

A satisfied noise escaped Gabriel's throat as he picked her up and carried her to the bed. "Tell me you want me to fuck you."

Her hot lips tracked down the line of his jaw. "I want you to fuck me."

Gabriel shoved her down onto the bed. "Tell me you're mine again."

Lydia's teeth pressed to the skin above his shoulder, then he felt the wet edge of her tongue. "I'm yours."

Gabriel settled on top of her, pushing her thighs open. He wanted her exposed to him like his soul was to her. Retribution for her breaking him wide open, fracturing the walls that he would have to construct all over again.

Gabriel pressed his hands to the mattress on either side of her. He looked into Lydia's eyes and whispered, "Tell me you love me."

Gabriel wanted her to say the words she had whispered in the darkness, thinking he wouldn't hear. Words she'd never spoken to him ten years before. He didn't deserve the answer to this demand – not when he was going to abandon her again. Gabriel had already made his decision.

But before he left, Gabriel wanted to hear her declaration just once. He knew he was a selfish bastard.

Lydia's breath caught in her throat. With their bodies pressed together so intimately, Gabriel felt her hesitation. But her eyes remained on his, as unerring as a blade finding its mark.

"I love you," she breathed, her voice like a curl of smoke in his ears. So soft, he might have imagined it, had he not seen her lips move.

Gabriel thrust inside her, gratified by the sound of pleasure she made. Lydia hitched her leg around his hip to urge him closer. He had never watched a woman in the middle of this intimate act, never so closely catalogued the little details that demonstrated her arousal: the way her lips parted, the broken staccato of her breath, the gradual softening of her features as she gazed back at him. These were things he would memorise. Things he would analyse after he left her safely in England. He would no longer be so careless with her memory; he would not leave it behind when life became too harsh. Instead, he would carry it with him, use it to eclipse his memories of Moscow and Kabul – he did not deserve this pleasure, but he took it like a villain.

Gabriel increased his pace, watching her face as climax grew closer. "Tell me again," he demanded.

He was insatiable. He wanted those words. He wanted them branded on his bones. She was the only thing in this world he wanted to carry with him, like the scar from a knife.

"I love you," she gasped, shutting her eyes as he slammed back into her.

Her fingernails found the skin of his back and scraped him roughly. But not deep enough to leave a mark – the ones he wore of her were private, written beneath his skin.

That feral, animal part of him demanded more. It would not be satisfied; he, after all, had many years and nights ahead of him where he would have to content himself with this. This short time with her that he'd stolen like a new identity.

"Open your eyes. Look at me," he said. She complied, those beautiful dark eyes like twin pools of ink in the low light. Like the space between stars. "Tell me again."

Nails dug deeper into his back. Gabriel pounded into her, holding off his climax. Needing those words again. Needing to hear them one last time.

Her eyes met his like an arrow striking true. "I love you, Gabriel St Clair."

Then her throat arched as she cried out her release. Gabriel let his control go, gathering her into his arms as he came. He pressed his lips to hers and said in that kiss everything he could not express in words.

↶ 36 ↷

When Lydia woke, it was still dark.
   Gabriel held her against his naked body. Hours
earlier, she had been roused by his uneven breathing – a
nightmare that left him hot and beaded with sweat.

Lydia had asked quietly, "Moscow or Kabul?"

His answer came in a whisper. "Moscow."

She'd leaned forward until her lips were at his ear. "Then
take me with you again, so you're not alone."

Lydia had sensed his indecision. But in the end, he had
turned to her. Pushed her down into the mattress and took
her roughly from behind. He had not said anything, had
not demanded anything from her. He replaced words with
ragged exhalations of breath as he thrust into her.

Afterwards, he had quietly gathered her into his arms
and nuzzled her neck as if in apology. But he never said
I love you back.

With a sigh, Lydia pulled out of his arms and lit the candle
at her bedside. She rose from the mattress, staring down at

her husband as he slumbered. The candlelight played on his beautiful features, but his countenance held a weariness. She had noticed it earlier when he stared out of the window. When Medvedev was caught, she hoped the lines would smooth from his brow, that tonight was an indication of a future where she could ease his nightmares. Where she could watch over him while he slept.

Lydia went to retrieve her needlepoint from the table. Her attention was caught on a paper that had been folded and refolded so often that the creases made it fragile. The label from the telegraph office peeked from underneath one of the folds.

Frowning, Lydia picked it up.

Raid last night in the East End. Accomplices captured. Bear on the run alone. Have you given more thought to my offer?

Offer? What offer?

"Lydia?" Gabriel's lovely, fatigued voice reached her. She heard the blankets rustle. "Can't sleep?"

Her eyes met his. He must have noticed something in her expression because his gaze fell on the paper in her hands – and his entire body froze.

And that was when Lydia knew.

She knew what the offer was, why those lines of exhaustion had settled so deeply into his features. Why he had made her say all those things while he made love to her? Why he demanded her love and said nothing in return?

He was still abandoning her.

"Lydia." This time, he spoke her name in a ragged whisper, almost like a plea.

"Where are you going?" Her voice was flat; she felt almost numb. "Moscow again? Or elsewhere?"

His gaze was searching. "I don't know yet. The Syndicate has expanded beyond Moscow, but I know its hierarchy better than anyone. Wentworth will send me where he believes I'm needed."

Lydia crumpled the note in her fist. "When are you leaving? Immediately after Medvedev's capture?"

Gabriel's expression was bleak. "Lydia."

"You can't use the same script as ten years ago," she continued. "You've fulfilled your promise, after all. Came back, married me. I suppose you made no vows to stay." She gave a dry laugh. "I said I wanted to keep you. I was a fool not to notice that you never said you wanted to keep *me*."

She heard his soft sigh as he rose from the bed. Lydia flinched at his nudity, at the beauty of his form – a temptation even now. She was glad when he spared her by pulling on his dressing gown.

"It's not about my wishes," he said simply.

"Then what is it about?" Lydia snapped. "It's certainly not about *mine*. If it were, we wouldn't be discussing your departure. We would—" She broke off with a bitter noise. "These last few days, while I thought you might have changed your mind about our marriage, you were making plans with Mr Wentworth. Earlier, when you asked about my little cottage, you were so careful in your responses. I imagined kissing you in those gardens, and you knew you wouldn't even be there." Her shoulders bowed. "When you told me to say I loved you, you knew you wouldn't say it back. So what future did you imagine when I foolishly told you of my little cottage, thinking you'd be with me?"

Lydia watched the emotions play across his face – he seemed so open now. So vulnerable. But this was no victory for her; those sentiments came with shards of glass that cut her open.

"One where you were safe," he said gently. "Where you could enjoy your little cottage without fearing a corpse beneath the roses, a sharpshooter in its trees, or an assassin in the dark. Do you need reminding of the last time we kissed in a garden?"

Lydia's fingers tightened around the letter, feeling the softened edges of the paper. A future declared in so few words. She felt like a pebble being rolled inexorably with the tide, forever moving but never by choice. Decisions made for her. A life at the whims of others: Gabriel, her aunt, society. What about her needs?

"And my choice in the matter?" she asked him, her voice faint. She was so tired. "Did you consider it at all?"

A soft breath left him. "Perhaps I was otherwise occupied with your life."

Lydia set the missive on the table, her fingers tracing its lettering, now faded from its harsh treatment in her hands, from the folds that had marred it before she'd ever set eyes on it. She wondered how many times he had read it and puzzled over the words. How long it took for him to decide their fates.

"I could die tomorrow," she said, very softly.

Gabriel looked up sharply. "What did you say?"

She lifted her eyes to his. "I could die tomorrow." Her voice seemed to fill the expanse of the room; it pounded in her ears. But she did not relent. She came around the desk, her movements deliberate as she donned her own dressing gown, slowly pulling it around her shoulders. "Perhaps you're the one who needs reminding, Gabriel St Clair," she said, belting the garment with a swift jerk. "All this time, you think of death and imagine your world of violence in Moscow and Kabul. You picture corpses in gardens or my life ended by a bullet in the forest. Not once have you bothered to consider that tomorrow, or a fortnight from now, or months into the future – maybe when you're off on your next mission, attempting to spare me the danger of your presence – that the thing that kills me won't be a sharpshooter's bullet, but a derailed train." He flinched at the reminder of his father and brother, two men killed so tragically. Lydia took that moment of vulnerability to continue. "Or the same swift illness that killed my parents. Maybe what we just did in that bed results in a pregnancy, and nine months from now, I'll die in childbirth."

Gabriel took an abrupt step back, as if she'd shoved him. "*Lydia*."

"You can't stop me from dying any more than you can stop me from loving you," she told him. How she longed to touch him, but she couldn't let herself. Not now. "But you can choose to waste your years apart from me, living someone else's life while you disavow your own. You've done it before, and I let you go." Her gaze lowered to that scrap of paper on the desk. "But if you accept that offer, I won't take you back next time. And I won't waste my years grieving over a future you rejected twice." When he didn't say anything, Lydia's hand fell on the knob of the bedroom door. "Give me some time to myself before you seek me out. I can't look at you right now."

Lydia jerked the door open and shut it firmly behind her.

As she crossed the hall, she could not shake from her mind the desolate look on his face. She had finally succeeded in shattering his icy shields – but that victory was meaningless. It came with no sense of achievement. All she'd found behind the ice was the empty landscape of their future.

Tears burned Lydia's eyes, falling freely down her cheeks. Her breath scorched through her chest as she attempted to inhale, but her lungs wouldn't fill. She panted against the pain in her chest – as if an arrow had struck her right through the heart.

She needed air.

Lydia pushed open the library door and slammed it shut behind her. The large windows ahead seemed like a refuge, a place to gather herself, find her composure again. She lurched toward it, fumbled with the lock, and shoved it open.

Lydia heaved. The rain and mist battered at the windowsill, but she didn't care. That weather suited her. The brisk air filled her lungs and made it past the burning in her heart. She pressed her palms to the window frame and leaned out, shutting her eyes as she gathered herself. Rain pelted her skin. None of it mattered.

Gabriel, she thought, as her chest painfully constricted. *Gabriel*.

She had never before considered how painful it was to love someone. She had loved him before he left for Vienna, but not like this. This time, she had known his kiss. Had felt the hardness of his body against hers. Had made declarations that were inscribed deep down in her soul because she believed he'd finally felt the same.

But he didn't. She was just another obligation. Another

mission, another life to be saved, like the others he'd protected against Medvedev. She was his duty.

You will get through this, she told herself. *You will. Just like before.*

She turned away from the window and focused on calming her emotions. When Gabriel came to find her, she did not want him to see her weeping. Like him, she would have to build barriers to protect her heart.

Just as she had finally caught her breath, someone grabbed Lydia from behind. A hand pressed hard to her mouth, and a thickly accented voice whispered in her ear, "You should not have opened that window, Lady Montgomery."

37

Gabriel leaned over the table, his mind repeating Lydia's words. Everything she had said was held up and examined, filtering through the ache in his heart.

You can't stop me from dying any more than you can stop me from loving you.

He had to restrain himself from telling her that he loved her back. He had left so many words unspoken that he now wished he had said.

I won't waste my years grieving over a future you rejected twice.

I could die tomorrow.

His head rose as he imagined her on the same train that had killed his father and brother. A fate he could not save her from. He imagined himself in a city across the continent, living under a different name, pretending to be another man.

And one day, he would open a missive informing him of her passing. If he considered the speed of the post and the safety of his identity, that message would take time to reach him. The death of his father and brother had taken two months.

Gabriel stared down at Wentworth's letter, imagining the future it offered him. He'd already lived without Lydia once, and it had been the biggest mistake of his life. If he did it again, and something happened to her...

He would never recover. Lydia was right; he had already wasted years. Ten that he could have spent in her arms every night. How many more would he squander? Two years? Five? A lifetime? He longed to kiss her everywhere in the garden of that little cottage, just as she desired.

He wanted to keep her, too.

"Lydia," he breathed, pushing away from the desk. If enough time had passed for her to collect herself, perhaps she would let him beg her forgiveness. Tell her that he was an idiot. A fool. A bloody bastard.

He needed to tell her he loved her.

Gabriel threw open his bedchamber door and checked the room next to his, only to find it empty. "Lydia," he called, crossing the hall.

Where had she spent her days? Where would she go to think, if not her bedchamber? The library.

Gabriel quickened his pace. "Lydia," he called as he reached the door. "Lyd—"

The room was empty. The only indication of previous occupation was the wide-open window. A cold, rainy breeze swept through the room, chilling Gabriel's skin. The carpet beneath the windowsill was soaked through from the downpour. Was that open window his wife's error, or—

Terror swept over him.

"Lydia." His voice echoed through the empty house as he left the library. "Lydia!"

Gabriel rushed down the hall, throwing open every door he saw, closet, bedchamber, sitting room, and servants' quarters. Each empty room only seized his heart further in an icy grip of dread.

"Lydia!"

Footsteps pounded down the hall. Gabriel whirled, but his relief was short-lived. Callahan came to an abrupt stop, panting hard. Rain plastered his hair to his forehead. "Jones is dead," he said briskly. "Hart and Grant spotted a rider a short while ago and left in pursuit but lost sight of him in the rainstorm."

Gabriel started down the hall. "Did the rider have anyone with him on the horse?" he asked as Callahan followed him up the stairs. "She might be gagged or otherwise unable to alert them."

Callahan looked at him sharply. "They didn't say. Lady Montgomery?"

Gabriel gave a grim nod as he entered his room and threw off his dressing gown. He pulled on the same clothes he'd worn earlier. "She sought solitude about an hour ago and isn't anywhere to be found."

Callahan gave a frustrated breath. "I thought you were supposed to—"

"Keep her with me?" Gabriel clenched his jaw as he fastened the buttons of his jacket. "We had a row. She found out about Wentworth's offer."

"So she found out you're being an absolute idiot."

Gabriel pulled on his greatcoat, flashing Callahan a glare. "Save your lecture for another time. We need the horses saddled, and I want to know where Grant and Hart last saw Medvedev. Wake up every one of your men. This ends tonight."

His hands shook with fear as he realised that his wife might be dead. But, no. His mind would not let him consider that option. For now, Medvedev would keep Lydia alive. She was a tool with which to taunt Gabriel, nothing more.

But that didn't mean Medvedev wouldn't hurt her.

☙ 38 ☙

Lydia stirred, the scents of stone, rain, and smoke overwhelming her.

She opened her eyes, blinking against the warmth of a small fire nearby – trying to remember where she was. *Medvedev. The library. She was grabbed from behind and knocked unconscious.*

The reminder jolted her senses from their daze, exacerbated by the dull ache at the back of her skull. She ignored it, concentrating on her surroundings: the rope securing her hands behind her back, the cold stone floor under her, the arch of rock above the fire pit. She was in a cave – and she did not know if this cavern was anywhere near Langdon Manor or if Gabriel would locate it. He had to know she was missing by now. But the downpour outside dimmed her hope of discovery – riding in such conditions would put Gabriel and his men in peril.

Footsteps sounded near her, and a man emerged from the cavern's shadows. Medvedev. He was an older man with dark hair, powerfully built and broad-shouldered. His physique matched his codename: *Bear*. He wore a patch over one eye that partly concealed the narrow scar over his cheekbone. But that only added to his impact – even Lydia knew to fear this man just by looking at him.

He stepped over to the firepit and settled on the pallet near the blaze. Then he reached into his coat and took out a gleaming knife. Dread seized Lydia, but he only lifted a fragment of wood and began to whittle it, flicking the blade with deft precision.

"You're finally awake," he said calmly, his Russian accent adding a lilt to his words. "I'd worried that I had hit you too hard. I've heard the English have hard heads, but yours is very small."

With a bit of a struggle, Lydia pulled herself into a sitting position. Her arms ached from being tied behind her back, and the ropes numbed her hands. "Do you care for my welfare, sir?" she asked, keeping her voice calm.

"No." His answer was honest as he concentrated on his task. Chips of wood scattered to the ground as the carving took shape. "I care to keep you alive because it suits me."

Concentrate on finding a way out, Lydia told herself.

She felt for some yield in the rope that secured her hands, but he had fastened them in a knot that permitted no movement. Lydia tried to focus on him as she felt around behind her. "And what do you intend to do with me?" she asked.

Medvedev shrugged. "I haven't decided yet. I will have to see how I feel about your husband in the next hour." His gaze flicked to her. "He has made me very angry, *kotik*."

Lydia slid her hands across the stone behind her, seeking

something sharp to cut through the rope. "Because he took your eye?"

There. The sharp edge of a rock pricked the tip of her finger. Lydia carefully placed the rope against it and began the painstaking process of sawing at the binding. She tried not to let anything show on her face as she gently pressed and pulled. Pressed and pulled.

The criminal raised a hand to his face and tapped the side of his missing eye. "This is no great sin, *kotik*. In my world, we expect to sacrifice a bit of flesh to the brotherhood; it's in our nature. No, what Alyosha did was far worse: he betrayed his oath. *That* is the sin I cannot forgive."

Lydia felt the edges of the rope as it frayed, fighting the impulse to saw faster. "Because he came home?" she asked quietly. "Because he married me?"

Press. Pull. Press. Pull. The effort was slow and agonising. The sharp rocks began to abrade her hands.

Medvedev set aside the piece of wood and rose to his feet, his dark stare intent on her. Lydia went still as he approached, his craggy features shaded in the firelight. When he crouched before her, Lydia began to understand why Gabriel had so many nightmares of Moscow – why this man had become his nemesis. His coldness scraped beneath Lydia's skin like fingernails, and his expression as he studied her was the equivalent of a pistol to her temple.

Except that he still held the wicked blade in his hand, so close to her leg.

"Did Alyosha tell you the code among the *vory*?"

Press. Pull. Press. Pull. Lydia kept her motions slower now, so he would not see the movements in her shoulders.

"The *ponyatiya*?" She forced herself to keep her gaze steady on his. "He said it does not allow family."

Medvedev gave a nod. "No wives, no children." Lydia held her breath as his blade lifted, touching the edge of her cheek. "Maybe you understand, *kotik*. Women like you leave a *vor* vulnerable. Alyosha fled from place to place, sent me all over this country, all for you. And now here you are." His blade slid across her skin, not yet drawing blood, but close enough to give Lydia a feel of its sharpened edge. "And I may as well be holding a blade to his heart, yes?"

The rope began to give. Rock lacerated Lydia's hands, painful pricks that made her bleed, but she didn't care. She kept rubbing: *Press, pull. Press, pull.* She was so close now.

"But it's not just you, *kotik*," Medvedev continued. "Beautiful women are a temptation I can almost understand, and you are lovelier than most." His lips pressed into a firm line, and his blade nicked her cheek. Lydia froze. "That Alyosha was a spy in my organisation, working for this English queen, is something I cannot forgive. Understand?"

Lydia was close. So close. Blood slicked her hands and wept from her cheek, but she kept rubbing. Already, she could sense that his polite façade was beginning to change into something violent and deadly.

"What do you intend to do with me?" she asked Medvedev again. She didn't care if her shoulders moved as she worked the rope – the quickness of her breath disguised her efforts. Her entire body was trembling now.

Medvedev watched his blade track down her cheekbone. "An eye for an eye first, *kotik*," he said. Then his black gaze met hers. "And I'll start with yours."

He raised the blade once more...

And Lydia's hands were finally free.

She didn't hesitate – she slammed her fist into his throat. He choked and staggered back. Lydia scrambled to her feet and fled into the night. Rain battered her as she escaped the cave, soaking straight through her nightdress. She could barely see. Mist and rain saturated the atmosphere, but Lydia didn't give a damn. She stumbled around the rocks to locate a place to hide, not caring that the plants, sticks, and pebbles sliced her bare feet. Her only thought was to survive. *Live.*

See Gabriel again.

She clung to the rocks, edging into a tight space where she could conceal herself from view. But then she heard it – a horse in the darkness. If it were one of Medvedev's men, she'd be caught. And if it were Gabriel, she would have to sacrifice her hiding spot – and possibly her life. But it was her only chance; the mist was too thick, and Lydia's husband would never find her in the haze.

She took the risk. "*Gabriel!*"

She heard the horse pause. Then a voice came that made her entire body shake with relief. "*Lydia!*"

"Gabriel!" She pushed out of the spot between the rocks. "Gabriel, I'm here! I'm—"

Someone grabbed her from behind, shoving a hand over her mouth. "I'm going to take both of your eyes, *kotik*," Medvedev hissed in her ear. His blade pressed to her throat.

"*Lydia?*"

Gabriel again, searching for her. She needed to call to him, but Medvedev was dragging her back, his hand firm over her lips. Finally, she managed to yank it away and bite down hard on a finger.

Medvedev's abrupt, startled shout echoed through the night. Lydia used his surprise to her advantage: she struck her elbow into his stomach and smashed his knife hand into the rock behind her. His blade hit the ground, hidden by the shadows. He grabbed her again, ripping at her nightdress as she struggled.

She took her chances now that he was without his weapon. *Survive. Survive. Fight!* She clawed and hit and kicked. She twisted and slammed her knee between his legs. His sharp cry of pain was another signal sent through the mist.

Lydia yanked out of his grip and staggered forward – straight into Gabriel's arms. She hadn't even seen him through the brume.

His grip tightened. "Lydia? *Lydia*. Are you—" Gabriel looked over her shoulder. "Medvedev." His voice was cold as he gently moved Lydia behind him.

Medvedev was on his feet. Somehow, he had managed to locate his knife. The weapon glinted in the moonlight as his eyes met Gabriel's. "Alyosha."

Gabriel's hand found Lydia's. "My name," he said softly, "is Gabriel St Clair. And my business with you ends tonight."

A crack echoed through the darkness. Blood exploded across Medvedev's face as he staggered back and collapsed.

Callahan emerged from the mist with a pistol in his grip. He looked over at Gabriel. "Thought you might like to get your wife home without wasting time on a fight," he said, his voice almost flat. "It's damned cold out here."

"I might have appreciated some warning," Gabriel said, swiftly putting his greatcoat over Lydia's shoulders. It was wet, but at least it covered her soaked nightdress.

"Just doing what you hired me to do, boss," Callahan replied with a sardonic grin.

Gabriel gave him a look and then returned his attention to Lydia. "You're all right?" he whispered, his hands running down her body. "Are you hurt anywhere?"

Lydia shook her head, dazed. "No, I don't think so."

"Let me get you home," he said tenderly, pressing a kiss to her forehead. To Callahan: "You'll deal with Medvedev?"

"Yeah, I'll make sure he stays dead," Callahan said. "Now, take care of your wife. And try not to mess up this time."

〜 39 〜

Back at Langdon Manor, Gabriel made a fire and quietly peeled the wet clothes from Lydia's body, pushing her down into the chair beside the hearth.

There, he treated the lacerations on her hands and wrists. Rage burned through him as he examined the bruises where her hands had been bound with rope. Lydia winced as he pressed a warm cloth to the bleeding cuts and instructed her to hold it while he tended to her feet. She would not be walking much until she healed.

"Damn Callahan," he muttered, putting her feet in a bowl of water he'd warmed by the fire. "I ought to have murdered Medvedev myself after what he did to you."

Panic had nearly consumed him as he rode through the mist earlier. When he heard Lydia's scream and saw her struggling with Medvedev... he had never before known such fear. He could have lost her in an instant.

He'd never told her how he really felt.

Lydia wordlessly stared into the fire, holding the cloth to

her hands. "I suppose you have a reason to leave now," she said flatly. "With Medvedev gone."

Gabriel paused, staring at the bowl of water pink with her blood. "Medvedev could have killed you." The words stuck like a barb in his throat.

"Gabriel—"

"Medvedev could have killed you," he repeated, interrupting her. Then he raised his head and met her gaze. God, he loved her. He loved her so damn much he ached with it. "After what you went through, do you still want to keep me?"

Lydia's features softened. "Yes. I still want to keep you."

"Why?"

He had to know. Before Gabriel gave Lydia his answer for their future, he had to know.

She sighed and reached for him, her thumb brushing his lip. "Because I already lived for ten years without you. And I want to be wherever you are, whether it is Moscow, Kabul, England, or elsewhere. Do you understand me?"

Gabriel leaned forward, his lips touching hers. "Then keep me."

He heard her breath catch, but she didn't say anything. Instead, she pulled him close for a hard kiss.

"I love you, Lydia," Gabriel whispered against her lips. "I choose you, every day of my life."

Days later, back in London, Gabriel entered Wentworth's study. He found the other man at the window with a brandy in his hand. Wentworth seemed contemplative, more so than usual.

"How does Lady Montgomery fare after her ordeal?" Wentworth asked.

Gabriel discreetly shut the study door behind him. "Recovering. We leave town tomorrow morning. I'm eager to give her a proper honeymoon once Lady Derby is convinced I'm madly in love with my wife."

Wentworth's lip curled in a half-smile. "I assume she won't need much convincing this time." He gestured to Gabriel's face. "You actually look happy for once in your life."

Gabriel thought of the woman in the carriage outside Wentworth's house. Despite their hours of exhausting travel from Langdon Manor, these past few days with Lydia had been... a revelation. Gabriel had made love to her every evening and woken up in her arms every morning. When she smiled at him, her face no longer wore the wary expression of a woman uncertain of his affections. She touched him so easily. Even the slightest brush of her hand against his was a marvel that spoke of trust; she had chosen him. He would spend the rest of his life making damn certain he was worthy of her. He had ten years to account for.

"I am," he said softly.

Wentworth laughed. "I assume this is you formally turning down my offer?"

"If you require my expertise, send me a missive," Gabriel said. "But yes, I'm turning you down."

"Then allow me to give my congratulations on your marriage." Wentworth set down his brandy and went to his cabinet to retrieve another snifter. He poured a finger of the golden liquid and handed it to Gabriel. "I hope you and Lady Montgomery are happy together wherever you stay."

Gabriel took a sip and let the sweet taste linger on his

tongue. "Scotland," he said. His expression was tender as he glanced out the window towards his carriage. Towards his future and the woman who had given it to him. "I have an estate in the far north that I discreetly purchased after returning from Moscow. She'll be safe there with me."

Wentworth followed his gaze. "I'm happy for you, my friend. And I'm glad you finally came to your senses."

After polishing off his drink, Gabriel rejoined his wife in the carriage and tapped the roof. As the conveyance set off through the streets of London, Lydia smiled at him. "Did everything go well with Mr Wentworth?"

Gabriel watched Wentworth's house disappear around a bend. "I gave him our address in Scotland. He'll have a great deal of difficulty once the other Syndicate leaders hear Medvedev is gone."

Lydia made a sympathetic noise. "I assume Mr Callahan has taken your place?"

"Yes." Gabriel was quiet for a moment. "You understand that if they need me…"

"Of course." Her expression softened. "Of course I understand."

Gabriel stared at her, taking in the delicate features of the woman he loved. Since when had he become so lucky? She was more than he had ever dared hope.

Without a second thought, he reached for her, pulling her into his lap. Lydia gave a little squeal and then a laugh. His blood ran warm now; every part of him had thawed, only for her.

With her, he had finally come home.

EPILOGUE

Two years later

"Can I open my eyes now?" Laughter rumbled through Gabriel's voice as Lydia attempted to steer him down the uneven path. The late summer sun was high in the atmosphere and glinted off the dark auburn hair presently pushed back by the blindfold.

"Not yet," Lydia said. She clicked her tongue. "You're so impatient."

Gabriel raised her hand to his lips. "Impatient to get back to kissing you. Lady Derby's visit has me stealing time with you like a thief."

Lady Derby had come from London to stay with Lydia and Gabriel in Scotland. When Lydia bounded into her arms, the matriarch had smoothed a hand over her cheek and remarked, "You look happy." Then she'd glanced at Gabriel. "I'm pleased I haven't come all this way just to murder you."

Warmth filled Lydia as she directed him around a bend

on the path. They had spent two years at his estate in Sutherland, where the quiet, slow Highland life had taken getting used to. But in their years together, Gabriel had been an attentive husband. He stole kisses between meetings with his tenants. During his visits to London or his other estates, Lydia missed him, and he made love to her for days upon his return. Some nights were difficult – Kabul and Moscow still lingered in his mind – but Lydia did not leave him in those places alone. Never.

"She's threatening to stay another month," Lydia said.

"Another month? Good Lord. Do you have any idea how many hairs I'll have pulled out of my head by then?" Gabriel groaned. "Does she have any friends nearby we can convince her to visit?"

Lydia grinned. "No. But *I* have a solution for us." She pulled him to a stop and gently tugged down his blindfold. "Now, you may look."

To one side of the path, there was a small, charming stone cottage. The dwelling had been entirely Lydia's design, right down to the blue shutters and the flowers for the garden.

Gabriel gazed down at her tenderly. "So you've finished your mark on the world."

"Oh, I haven't finished." She grinned. "I'm only getting started."

"Mm." He dropped to his knees and pressed a kiss to her rounded belly, so close to delivering their first child. "I can see that, and I can't wait to meet her. She's going to be just like her mother, a force to be reckoned with."

"And how do you know this baby will be a she?"

Gabriel pressed more kisses to her belly. "Because when I

had my ear to your belly yesterday, she kicked me so hard I could feel her personality. I thought, 'ah, that's my girl.'"

Lydia smiled again, running her hands through his hair. He was going to make an exceptional father. "Would you like to see inside, or do you intend to remain on your knees in the dirt?"

Gabriel gave her a wicked look. "I'll look inside. But I don't think I'll be off my knees for long." He grabbed her hand. "Never tell your aunt or any of our future children about this cottage," he said firmly, dragging her toward the door. "I'm going to steal you away here every afternoon."

She laughed and let him lead her inside, where they enjoyed the solitude of their home away from home.

AUTHOR'S NOTE

For years now, I've been keenly interested in the Great Game, the political tension between the British Empire and the Russian Empire that spanned much of the 1800s, as well as organised crime groups in Moscow. There are many exciting spy stories from this period, though I fictionalised and dramatised a great deal for Gabriel's characterisation. This book was my effort to marry these two interests.

Once again, I have to thank readers for their patience with this book. Your kind messages kept me going, and I hope Gabriel and Lydia's story was worth the wait. I hadn't planned on this book being the next one I wrote, but I couldn't ignore the history of these two characters after their scenes in *His Scandalous Lessons*. Sometimes it's better not to fight characters and just let them talk, so I did!

Thank you again for your support, which means the world to me.

Kind regards,

Katrina Kendrick

ACKNOWLEDGEMENTS

As I sit at my desk, trying to tame the unruly characters, I can't help but think how grateful I am for the support and care of those around me. While writing may seem like a solitary endeavor, the truth is, it takes a village.

My husband, bless his heart, brings me coffee and surprise chocolates when I'm deep in the throes of character-wrangling. I couldn't do any of this without him, and I'm grateful for him every day.

And, of course, I couldn't have gotten to where I am without the guidance and support of my agent, Danny Baror. Danny, you are truly phenomenal.

Likewise, my editor, Rosie de Courcy, has been a dream to work with. Her sharp eye and insightful feedback have helped to shape this series into something even better than I ever could have imagined. Thank you, Rosie, for your dedication to making this story the best it can be.

I also want to express my gratitude to the amazing team at Head of Zeus/Aria who've been working tirelessly behind the scenes to bring this series to readers. From the stunning cover designs to the amazing marketing efforts, I'm in awe of your hard work.

Last but not least, I have to thank my incredible friends, Hannah Kaner and Tess Sharpe, as well as all the ladies in the Trifecta, for their unwavering support. You have lifted me up when I needed it most.

And, of course, a big thanks to my readers. Your enthusiasm for this series has been overwhelming and just simply fantastic. You make all of this worthwhile.

ABOUT THE AUTHOR

KATRINA KENDRICK is the romance pen name for *Sunday Times* bestselling science fiction and fantasy author Elizabeth May. She is Californian by birth and Scottish by choice, and holds a Ph.D. from the University of St Andrews. She currently resides on an eighteenth-century farm in the Scottish countryside with her husband, three cats, and a lively hive of honey bees that live in the wall of her old farmhouse.

www.katrinakendrick.com